Homicide in Hawaii

An Emily Swift Travel Mystery

by

Lorrie Holmgren

Copyright 2017 by Lorrie Holmgren

For information, email **Cozy Cat Press**, cozycatpress@aol.com or visit our website at: www.cozycatpress.com

COZY CAT
PRESS

ISBN: 978-1-946063-33-5

Printed in the United States of America

Cover design by Paula Ellenberger
www.paulaellenberger.com

1 2 3 4 5 6 7 8 9 10

Acknowledgements

Thank you to the Split Rock writers' group, who read many drafts of *Homicide in Hawaii* and gave extremely valuable suggestions: Abigail Davis, Linda Donaldson, Peg Wangensteen and Christopher Valen. I remember with gratitude Bart Baker, who brought us together on Madeline Island, and Archie Spencer.

I am also very grateful to my daughter, Katy Miketic, vice president of marketing and communications at Cogran Systems, who designed my beautiful website and offered excellent ideas for improving the novel.

Thank you to Patricia Rockwell at Cozy Cat Press for editing and publishing my novels.

And a special thanks to George Lohmer whose hair-raising adventure on Big Island inspired the climactic scene in *Homicide in Hawaii*.

CHAPTER 1

On a flight bound for Hawaii, Emily Swift sat wedged between Jack and a squirming toddler, who was beating a tattoo on her lap with his tiny sneakers and patting her hair with his sticky fingers. Twelve hours previously, the child had seemed adorable and she had made the mistake of encouraging his affection. If she could roll back time, she would not have smiled and cooed at him.

Leaning against the window, Jack was sound asleep with his long legs sprawled at an awkward angle. Emily brushed a strand of dark hair away from his forehead. She envied his ability to fall asleep anywhere, anytime, a skill he'd developed during his medical residency when he had to slip in a quick nap whenever possible.

As a travel writer, Emily didn't really mind the tedium and discomfort of the long flight from Minneapolis. She was excited about going to Hawaii where she and Jack would spend lazy afternoons lounging by the pool and romantic evenings walking hand-in-hand along the beach. She pushed away the memory of the last time she had looked forward to a romantic vacation. It had turned out to involve a murder. This time would be different. For one thing, she was going with the right guy.

The trip would not be "all fun and games," as her mother had reminded her. For much of the time, Emily would be writing travel articles while Jack attended a medical conference. Honolulu with its famed Waikiki Beach was hardly new ground for a travel writer, but

Emily was sure she could find a fresh slant. At least, she had managed to convince her editor, George, that such was the case.

Her former college classmate, Amanda Blake, would probably have excellent suggestions about little-known restaurants and activities. Emily had emailed her, saying she was coming to Hawaii and suggesting they meet. Amanda had written back a puzzling letter. She wanted advice of some sort. Emily found that odd since they hadn't spoken since their college reunion three years ago.

The flight attendant offered Emily a Honolulu newspaper, but she had a briefcase full of information on Hawaii beneath her seat, so she refused. If she had glanced at the paper, she would have seen the headline: "Prominent Philanthropist Slain," and would have recognized the name of Amanda Blake. Providence spared Emily this painful knowledge during her flight.

By the time the plane touched down in Honolulu, Emily felt drained of energy, and stuffed with food. She realized it was a mistake to have eaten a chicken-like substance, encased in moist breading, followed by thick pudding. She might have to wear a huge, shapeless muumuu to the beach instead of her new bikini.

Emily followed Jack down the aisle, behind other weary travelers into warm tropical air where palm trees rustled and taxis blared their horns. A woman in a flowered dress held a sign with their names on it: Emily Swift and Jack Flynn. Emily croaked out a greeting. The woman tossed a lei of creamy white Plumaria and lavender orchids over Emily's neck, arranging the flowers so they hung Hawaiian style like a wreath. Emily's spirits lifted as she breathed in the glorious aroma.

After a few minutes of conversation with her lei greeter, Emily mentally composed a Traveler's Trip for her article:

"Sprinkle your lei with water, put it in a plastic bag and store it in the refrigerator. It will keep beautifully and you can wear it the next day."

She turned to Jack. "We made it. This is Paradise."

"Aloha to good times." He grinned at her and pulled her close.

Although it was 11 p.m. in Minneapolis, it was rush hour in Honolulu, and traffic crept slowly as Jack drove the rental car to Waikiki. Emily gazed with delight at the flowers and palm trees. This morning there had been snowcapped pine trees outside her window. It would be easy to write articles about this beautiful island.

"I have the best job in the world," Emily said.

"Which you richly deserve after all you went through to get it," Jack said.

Recalling their adventures on Madeline Island and her near-death experience, Emily agreed. The articles she had written at that time had catapulted her from covering community news to writing travel features.

"Not to mention the amazing articles you've written since then," Jack added.

Emily smiled. A little appreciation was always nice.

In their hotel room, the telephone was flashing an insistent red message light. Emily stared at it with dismay. "I suppose we must answer it, but whoever it is will expect some sort of coherent response and I'm not sure I'm up to it."

"It's probably your mother, wanting to let us know the wind chill factor in Minneapolis. I can almost hear her sad, left-behind voice."

"Or George, wondering how I'm coming along on my article." Her editor was not a patient man.

"Whoever it is can wait," Jack said, herding her toward the door. Emily's curiosity was easily overwhelmed by his insistence that it was long past the cocktail hour.

Soon they found a Thai restaurant open to the warm night air, lit by flaming torches. A bronze Vishnu with toes turned up and a sweet smile on his face sat in a bower of flowers at the entrance. As they made their way to the back of the room, Emily noticed with approval the vases of cascading pink orchids on the tables and watercolor paintings of tropical flowers on the walls. They settled themselves at the bar and Emily asked the bartender, "What's best for jet lag? Something in the rum family perhaps?" She felt beyond making decisions.

"A Mai Tai definitely." The bartender, an earnest young man with spiked blonde hair, created a concoction of healthful fruit juices with dark Meyer's rum swimming on top, adding a slice of fresh pineapple as the festive finale.

"You can get a 95-cent Mai Tai on the beach," he said, leaning forward, lowering his voice to a conspiratorial whisper, "but it's not the same. Only one kind of rum splashed on top. You wouldn't want it."

"This calls for some scientific investigation," Jack murmured. "Perhaps an inferior Mai Tai on the beach tomorrow? Just to compare."

"My readers deserve it."

Emily basked in the pleasure of being on firm ground, a cool drink in hand, and humid tropical air enveloping her. She glanced back at the intricately carved wooden pillars supporting the thatched roof, the gently turning ceiling fan. It was an exotic and lovely place. They ordered an appetizer. When the shrimp triangles arrived, Emily wolfed one down.

"Delicious," she announced, licking flaky crumbs from the corners of her mouth. "A far cry from airplane food."

"You *would* eat the chicken-like substance," Jack said. "I warned you."

"And you were right." Emily drew in the lovely fragrance of her lei. "How thoughtful of Amanda to arrange a lei welcome."

"You seem to have a college chum in every port."

"A great advantage when I'm looking for someone to pump for local color to enliven my articles, but unfortunately it usually limits our meetings to five-year reunion intervals. Not nearly enough time to keep informed about the dramas of my friends' lives."

"You seem remarkably well informed. I usually follow your chums' ups and downs with interest, but I don't recall you ever mentioning Amanda Blake." Jack took a huge bite of shrimp triangle.

"Amanda's an interesting and thoroughly nice woman. I didn't know her very well at college, but I talked to her quite a bit at our reunion three years ago. She seemed much happier than I remember her being at college."

"Do you wonder? It's chilly in upstate New York. Poor soul was probably pining for sunny beaches."

"I suppose." Emily gazed with delight at the palms and bougainvillea outside the window and recalled how icy cold it had been this morning in Minnesota. "We're lucky to be here."

Jack put his hand over hers and agreed.

After a delicious curry dinner, Emily felt much revived.

"Back to the hotel?" Jack suggested, a hopeful glint in his eyes.

"It's only seven o'clock here. The only way to combat jet lag is to stay up until the local bed time."

Jack groaned.

"Let's find the Sheraton where you have your conference tomorrow. We can take a quick look at the ocean." Emily grinned at him. Just the thought of salt water made her happy.

Emily and Jack walked past motels, the Waikiki shopping mall, Chinese noodle shops, and tourist booths selling Hawaiian shirts and grass skirts. Emily had heard her well-traveled friends disparage Waikiki as too crowded and touristy, but she loved its bustle and energy, its cosmopolitan flavor. She wanted to share her enthusiasm with her readers.

When they reached the Sheraton, Emily and Jack walked through the lobby and stepped out onto the famous Waikiki beach, stretching from Diamond Head to the Ala Wai Harbor, which was lined by tall hotels much more elegant than their own budget lodging.

"Why didn't we stay here?" Jack asked, looking longingly at the pool and beachfront.

"Not everyone can afford to be right on the beach. I want to give my readers a range of options."

Emily pulled out her little red book.

Travelers Tip: You don't have to pay beachfront prices. There are perfectly fine hotels a few blocks from the beach and the walk will do you good.

Emily and Jack walked hand in hand along the raised boardwalk curving in front of the hotel, then stepped off into sand. Rejoicing in the smell of salt air, and soft white sand lit by moonlight, Emily ran barefoot into the frothy waves. Jack rolled up his white slacks and splashed in beside her. Emily turned and flung her arms around his neck. This was definitely going to be a romantic vacation.

On the way back to the hotel, they passed an open air bar with a thatched roof, twinkle lights strung on the tropical plants, and a young man playing a ukulele, singing an island song. A bulletin board advertised cheap Mai Tais during happy hour, which apparently extended until past 9 p.m.

"Scientific curiosity makes its demands on the weary traveler," Jack said, heading up the steps to the bar.

"Do you think these are the inferior Mai Tais we've been warned about?"

"I fear they are."

In a few moments they reached consensus and Emily jotted down a hint for her readers: *Traveler's Tip: "The cheap Mai Tai has a charm all its own."*

Emily and Jack were determined to stay up until ten o'clock to combat jet lag. The assignment had seemed impossible when the lei greeter welcomed them to Hawaii. Now, Emily found it easy. Jack was beginning to yawn.

When they returned, wet and sandy, to their hotel room, Emily hit the message button.

"Hello, Emily. It's Sarah Gardner. Please call me right away." Sarah's voice quavered. There was a pause, a sharp intake of breath, then she left a phone number and clicked off.

It took a moment for Emily to recognize the name. Then she remembered. Sarah had been a senior when Emily and Amanda were college freshmen. An image came to mind of a tall, hearty girl loping down the lacrosse field, her stick held menacingly. Emily recalled information she had gleaned at the reunion. When Sarah had moved to Hawaii, she and Amanda had become close friends, partly because the two of them comprised the entire Wells College Alumnae Club and partly because there was some sort of business connection. No doubt Sarah wanted to reminisce about happy college days. That would be fine, but first Emily wanted to experience Hawaii on her own. She glanced at her watch. Ten o'clock. Too late to call back, she realized with relief.

Resolving to call Sarah after breakfast, Emily fell into a deep and happy sleep enjoying the soft tropical breeze wafting through the open window. She awoke too early, at 5 a.m., but felt as alert and tingling with joy as if it were Christmas morning. Outside, the moon shone on whispering palm trees. Beside her, Jack slept peacefully, his long lashes fluttering, as if he were reveling in some delightful dream. Emily dressed quietly and hurried downstairs.

The lobby was empty. The staff was just opening the ceiling-high folding door panels, opening the lobby to the street, letting in the morning breeze and the rustle of palm trees. Emily sat in the lobby, drinking Kona coffee until the sky lightened. Jack had slept long enough, she felt. It was time for the free breakfast that came with the room.

Traveler's Tip: *Skip the free breakfast that comes with your room.*

Emily had expected to enjoy a quick complimentary meal in the hotel coffee shop, but that was not to be.

"Just a short ride to breakfast," the young man at the desk told her with a reassuring smile. Glancing at each other with misgiving, Emily and Jack boarded a festive red tram that wound through streets whose names were short on consonants, such as Liliuokalani, and Kapahulu, stopping to pick up vacationers at several hotels. Finally they arrived at a large hotel in a remote part of town where they were herded into a room that resembled a church basement. The curtains were firmly drawn and only a faint silhouette of waving palms was visible.

"Why is it so dim in here?" Jack bellowed.

"They know if we could see the outside world, we would bolt for freedom," Emily said.

A bald man in a wrinkled suit began to explain the benefits of package tours. "Polynesian Village! Scuba Diving Adventure! And they could sign up right now! Special rates apply today only!"

"We've fallen for a promotional breakfast," Jack said in his voice of doom.

A young woman began to pluck her ukulele and wail plaintive Hawaiian tunes while the wrinkled-suit man passed out brochures.

Jack nudged Emily, "We're making a break for it."

"How far did the tram take us? Where are we?" Emily asked.

"We'll find out."

They slipped out the back way to find a soft mist falling and gray clouds scudding across the sky. Tall skyscrapers rose above them and cars honked. Jack whipped out his phone and consulted his GPS.

As soon as Emily and Jack reached the beach, they saw the sun come out in glorious splendor. A rainbow arched over the sparkling turquoise sea. They hiked along a stretch of beach where high rise hotels soared to the sky, past happy vacationers on beach towels. Small children splashed close to shore, shrieking with joy.

"What high-pitched little voices they have," Jack commented.

To Emily a day at the beach seemed perfect. She remembered the happy hours spent on the sand when she was about twelve, old enough to be on her own, but not old enough to be expected to have a summer job more rigorous than an occasional babysitting stint. Every day she and her friends walked to the beach at Lake Harriet, and lay in the hot sun, slathering on lotion, listening to rock and roll on the radio, whispering gossip. Who was stuck up or conceited? Who liked a certain boy? Secrets and speculations. Whole summers slid by in lovely idleness. Home from the beach, she would lie on the glider on the back porch, drinking iced tea or real, homemade lemonade. With one foot hooked over the back of the creaking glider, she would rock slowly and read novels that transported her to far-off shores and exciting adventures. No wonder a day on the beach remained her idea of perfect relaxation.

Emily later learned how wise they were to flee to the beach. The next morning one of the women from the promotional breakfast told her that the tour bus inmates had spent the whole day shopping, which they could have done in the Mega Mall on a cold day in Minneapolis. They were driven to the Pearl Palace to stock up on cheap coral trinkets, then herded onto the tram and driven off to Hula Hattie's to buy souvenirs.

"I did get some rather nice coral earrings though," the woman told Emily. "And chocolate-covered macadamia nuts."

Emily sighed.

"Some people have trouble realizing when they have attained paradise and just keep on striving, buying, trying to find a better, more perfect deal," she commented to Jack later.

"We can only pity them."

Emily suggested to her readers a better choice.

Traveler's Tip: On your first day, go to the beach at Waikiki. Trust me, it's the very best one on the island. Yes, of course, it's crowded, but there's a good reason why. Lie in the sun, watch the catamaran with its bright pink sails cut through the turquoise water, swim, ride the waves, admire the surfers, read a mystery, bake in the sand. At 2 p.m. a tortoise is supposed to swim up to the beach for a handout.

When Emily and Jack returned to their hotel to change into their bathing suits, the phone was ringing and Emily reached for it.

"Emily, where have you been? It's Sarah." Unaccountably, she sounded frantic.

"I just got here. We'll have lots of time to get together."

"The funeral's on Wednesday," Sarah said.

Emily's heart skipped a beat. "A funeral? Whose funeral?"

There was a long pause. "Emily, I'm sorry. I thought you knew. It was on the front page of the paper. I thought you must have seen it."

"No, no. Seen what?"

She heard Sarah draw in a deep breath. "Amanda Blake was murdered.

I knew you'd want to be at her funeral," Sarah's voice broke. "That's why I've been trying to reach you."

"How horrible! Amanda's dead? What happened?" Stunned, Emily tumbled out questions, without waiting for answers.

"Just the other day, Amanda and I were making plans to get together and show you the island and now…" Sarah's voice trailed off.

"Sarah, can we meet? I know this is horrible for you, so tell me if you're not up to it, but…"

"Yes, yes. Come over right away. I want to see you."

Jack had offered to go with her, but Emily knew he had arranged to meet his colleagues and prepare for the conference. She urged him not to change his plans, but she was glad he put her welfare first.

After following Sarah's directions, Emily turned the car into a long driveway, shaded with palm trees, past tennis courts, up to a Spanish-style home draped with bougainvillea.

Sarah flung open the door. "I'm so glad you're here," she cried.

Sarah was only a few years older than Emily, but the sun had aged her, etching wrinkles around her eyes and mouth.

Traveler's tip: Don't forget to splash on 30 sunscreen. You won't be sorry!

Sarah pushed her short frosted hair behind her ears. Her fingernails were polished bright pink.

"Poor Amanda," Emily said. "How terrible!"

Sarah glanced away, holding her elbows as if she felt a cold wind. "I thought it would be the three of us, a real reunion. Just like old times."

Emily didn't mention that she didn't recall the three of them being together often, if at all. She could see Sarah had been rearranging old memories.

"I'll miss her terribly," Sarah said, taking a deep breath.

Emily noticed her puffy eye lids, the pouches under her eyes. Maybe it was grief that made Sarah seem older. Emily felt guilty for noticing her wrinkles at such a time.

Where's Jack?" Sarah asked.

"He's preparing for his medical conference, conscientious soul that he is. But he'll be at the funeral tomorrow."

"Good. I'm looking forward to meeting him. Amanda told me you had met someone." Walking forward with the long strides of an athlete, Sarah led Emily into a sunny room with cream-colored walls and vases of white orchids, then through French doors toward a pool ringed by palm trees, where they settled into pale yellow armchairs.

Sarah slumped in her chair, her broad shoulders sagging and closed her eyes for a moment. "It's all so hard to believe."

"How did it happen?" Emily asked. "Do the police have any idea?"

"No. It must have been a stranger. Nobody who knew Amanda would have hurt her."

"A robbery I suppose," Emily offered.

"The police don't think so," Sarah straightened up and her gaze sharpened. "Amanda was wearing rather spectacular jewelry when she died but nothing was taken—although I suppose a common criminal might be forgiven for thinking that her necklace was fake. Those huge diamonds and emeralds! She didn't have a purse with her. It was found in the ballroom after the party. Maybe the robber was angry because Amanda had no money and only wore what he imagined was a cheap, dime-store necklace. Or maybe he panicked. But I don't really think this was meant to be a robbery. The circumstances were too peculiar."

"How so?"

Sarah reached toward the coffee table, picked up the clipping of a newspaper article and held it out, her hand trembling. Emily looked closely at a grainy, pixilated photograph of a body heaped with flowers beneath an altar of some sort. "Prominent Philanthropist Slain." She looked questioningly at Sarah.

"Amanda disappeared from a fundraising ball in Waikiki but her body was found miles away in a sacred grove on a mountain. It was used as a holy place by ancient Polynesians, an outdoor place of worship."

"Why on earth?"

"I don't know. Maybe it has some sort of symbolic meaning to the killer. The old religion is being revived. People bring pineapples, bananas and flowers up to the altar and leave them to the god Lono. I've always thought it was very innocent and back to nature."

"It doesn't make sense. Amanda was such a gentle soul. Who would do something like that?"

"It was probably a maniac of some sort." Sarah's mouth twisted in bitterness.

I hope not a serial killer, beginning his spree, Emily thought. "Who found her?"

"A family of tourists trooped up the hill and found Amanda heaped with flowers. At first they thought it was some sort of pageant, Hawaii's living history, but of course, it wasn't." Sarah was clearly trying for a light tone, but tears stood in her eyes. "It was a macabre touch in a senseless murder."

"Amanda was a quiet, gentle soul. I can't imagine her provoking fierce passion or hostility," Emily said.

"No, not at all. And in recent years, she had become almost saintly. Constantly doing good deeds, giving to the poor, arranging fundraisers for charity." Sarah pulled a tissue from her pocket and wiped under her eyes in a quick impatient sweep of her hand. Emily noticed that her pink nail polish was chipped, not the festive touch she had supposed.

Sarah's husband Brent padded in wearing a beach robe, carrying two cups of coffee. His dark hair was wet, his brown eyes troubled. "Emily, what a terrible welcome for you. Just last week, we were talking with Amanda about your visit, making plans to get together. This seems unbelievable." He shook his head. Emily remembered seeing Brent long ago at fraternity parties, a tall, courteous boy who always said the right thing.

Brent held out a cup of coffee. "I was afraid Sarah would forget to offer you anything." He smiled at his wife and gave her the other cup. "This must be a shock for you," he said, turning back to Emily, patting her shoulder.

"Yes, but much worse for you," she said, taking a sip of the strong brew.

"We were good friends," Sarah said. "When I first came here and didn't know a soul, our having been at college together seemed like such a strong bond. Amanda was welcoming and kind." Sarah was struggling to keep control.

Emily reached over and lightly touched her arm.

"It's a terrible loss for Brent too," Sarah said, looking at her husband. "They worked together at the trust."

"I had heard that," Emily said.

Brent nodded. "Amanda set up a trust to preserve the old Hawaiian culture. It's a grim irony that the people she wanted to help turned on her," he said.

"Brent, you don't know that," Sarah said.

"Why else would she be laid out on an altar on a mountain top? There's no real Hawaiian religion here anymore. Just a phony revival of old superstitions. Amanda's murder must be a political statement of some sort. God knows what. Someone protesting what the Trust does, I suppose."

"What are you talking about?" Emily turned to see a young woman with straight black hair and wide hazel eyes standing in the doorway. She was looking at Brent with deep and terrible contempt.

He slowly walked forward, his hands outstretched. "Come on, honey, I'm not going to pretend I have any sympathy for Amanda's killer."

"What makes you think she was killed?" The girl shifted her weight, and looked up at him, her small body radiating a challenge.

"I know it's hard to believe." Brent tried to put his arm around her, but the girl flinched away. "It was in the newspaper," he said quietly, decisively, as if all was settled.

"Newspapers aren't exactly infallible," the girl snapped. "The police have no idea what happened. They're just guessing."

"Honey, we have to accept what happened to Amanda."

"Brent, let it go," Sarah said. "Everyone's upset." She cleared her throat and stood up. "Emily, I'd like you to meet our daughter, Kari."

Introductions smoothed over the tension. Kari said a few polite words to Emily, then slipped away.

"Kari loved Amanda," Sarah said after the girl had left the room. "This is a terrible shock for her. If we hadn't adopted Kari after her mother died, I think Amanda would have. She is....*was* ...her godmother."

"No wonder the poor girl's upset."

Brent changed the subject, "You're here on business, Sarah told me." Suddenly, he sounded formal. Emily supposed he must be upset by her hearing Kari's reaction to him.

"Yes, I'm writing a series of travel articles. But, of course, I'll go to the funeral and support you in any way I can."

"Attending the funeral is all you can do. Then you can concentrate on your writing. I'll tell you where to go," he said. "Hanauma Bay. It's a perfect place for snorkeling. Sarah and I were there last week and the water was crystal clear. Next you should drive up the coast...."

Emily had sketched out a plan that was remarkably similar to Brent's so she didn't mind his officious helpfulness.

A cell phone trilled and Brent pulled it out of his pocket. "Hey, buddy, how are you holding up? Yeah, yeah, it's a rough deal. Don't let the bastards wear you down." He walked toward the corner of the room, talking more softly now, concern evident in his voice.

"Sarah glanced back at Brent, then lowered her voice, "That must be Todd."

"How is he?" Emily asked, realizing it was a dumb question since his wife had just been murdered. Amanda's husband had been at Cornell, a nearby college. Emily remembered him as a good-looking, outgoing boy.

"He's devastated," Sarah said. "You can imagine. He adored her."

Emily dimly recalled that it was Amanda who had done the adoring.

"We're going to see him this afternoon. Would you like to come? I know he'd love to see you."

Emily declined. She felt she would be intruding. It had been too many years since she had seen Todd for her to show up on his doorstep at such a terrible time. Tomorrow at the funeral would be soon enough.

Brent tucked the phone in his pocket and walked toward them. "If you plan to go to Hanauma Bay today, you don't want to wait too much longer. The water gets cloudy."

Emily wanted to ask more questions about Amanda's murder but she could take a hint. No wonder Brent was ready for her to be on her way so he and Sarah could to be alone at this sad time.

She began to gather up her handbag.

Sarah walked her out the door, down to her car. "I do want to see Todd, and offer whatever comfort I can, but let's meet later today. Maybe tea at the Moana Hotel?" Her wide green eyes looked anxious.

"I'd like that."

CHAPTER 2

Riding shotgun as Jack drove to Haunama Bay, Emily watched gray clouds scudding across a misty sky. Not an ideal day for the beach, she realized, but Sarah had told her not to pay any attention to the weather. Change comes quickly on the islands, a rain in the morning brightens to sunshine in the afternoon.

Fortunately Jack didn't have a meeting this afternoon and could join her on a scenic drive up the coast. Emily didn't want to be alone when she read the newspaper account of Amanda's murder.

"It feels heartless to be working on my travel article so soon after Amanda's murder, but my deadline for the first article is in just a few days."

"You've already tried to comfort Sarah and Brent," Jack said, "whoever they may be."

"I told you about them. Sarah was at college with me and Amanda. Her husband Brent was in the same fraternity as Amanda's husband Todd and, coincidentally, with my old boyfriend Drew. I don't know Sarah and Brent well, but I remember them from my youth, which is always a bond."

"I'd need a scorecard to keep all your old college friends and acquaintances straight." Jack turned into the parking lot and Emily gazed with wonder at the glittering turquoise water of Haunama Bay, encircled by black cliffs. It was a breathtaking sight. Huge waves slammed against the cliffs, shooting spray up fifteen feet.

Gathering up towels and beach bags, Emily and Jack climbed out of the car and headed for the beach. Emily stopped to take a few wide-angle photographs before she and Jack made their way down steep steps. Wind was whipping the stinging sand into a maelstrom. They broke into a run and sought shelter against the brick wall along the back of the beach.

"Why are all these people subjecting themselves to something that seems like a natural disaster?" Jack asked, dashing sand out of his dark hair with both hands. "Lawrence of Arabia would feel right at home here."

"It won't be bad if we lie flat," Emily said. Setting a good example, she flopped down on the beach towel and shut her eyes tightly.

"Are you sure this is a good idea?" Jack bellowed over the howling wind. He was trying with no success to unfurl his beach towel with a smooth neat snap of his wrist. It kept recoiling, writhing into a tangle around his knees.

"Brent said it was perfect last week. Maybe the wind will die down in a few minutes."

"Hah." Jack wrapped his beach towel around his head and burrowed down in the sand.

Emily pulled the newspaper out of her bag and tried to straighten it. The wind whipped it in her hand, threatening to blow it away altogether. She would have to wait or risk shredding it. Torn between curiosity and dread of reading about her classmate' murder, Emily was glad of an excuse to put the news aside.

The wind did not abate. Conversation as well as newspaper reading was clearly out of the question. Emily began to wonder how she could present this tourist attraction in an upbeat way to her readers.

"I think I'll be happier in the water," she yelled. Grabbing her snorkel and face mask from her beach bag, she made a dash for the shore, pounding along as fast as she could, trying to ignore the flying needles of sand. When she reached the shore, she put on her gear and belly flopped into the shallow water. High winds and the fluttering flippers of the tourists had stirred up the sand, making the water thick and murky. Still Emily found snorkeling a marvelous experience.

Travelers tip: For $6 you can rent snorkeling gear at Haunama Beach. Or if you shrink from putting something in your mouth that has only been rinsed lightly in a communal vat of water, bring your own. For $3, you can take a shower, which is very refreshing, especially if the winds have blasted sand onto your sun screened body.

Emily floated motionless, rising and falling on the waves, blown by currents, hurried and scurried over coral reefs. Emily let go of all thoughts of Amanda. She drifted along, watching graceful, striped Angel Fish, listening to the rhythmic sound of her own breathing. Suddenly her foot was grabbed and held firmly. Octopus attack? Surely they don't ooze about in such shallow water. Emily dropped onto one knee.

Her foot was yanked up sharply. "I caught a fish, Daddy!" the child's cry of triumph rang out.

Lifting her dripping face out of the water, Emily turned to face her captor. The small boy stared in dismay at her toes, released his grip, then ran away, splashing and wailing.

Ideal snorkeling was eluding her.

Emily stood up, removed her snorkel and mask, pulled off her fins and ran back to Jack, who was huddled under a towel.

"I've been mistaken for a fish."

"I have never regarded you in such a finny light," Jack said, peering out from under his towel. "Perhaps it's time to go," he added hopefully.

"Let's check out the park building before we go," Emily said. "We could take a shower."

Later, clean and refreshed, Emily and Jack started up the steps.

At the next stop on their itinerary, the Blow Hole, Emily and Jack climbed out of the car and walked to the edge of a precipice. For a moment they watched tremendous waves crashing and foaming over rocky cliffs. Suddenly, a plume of white water shot straight up fifty feet in the air. Emily gasped.

Traveler's Tip: Don't miss the Halona Blow Hole. Waves have carved out a cave under the thin layers of lava that form this coastline and when waves rush into the cave, they are forced out in a tremendous geyser.

Emily took a few photographs before she settled down on a large black rock by the side of the road and unfolded her newspaper.

Jack sat beside her and she leaned against his shoulder as she read aloud. "Heiress Amanda Blake's body was discovered early Monday morning at an ancient site of human sacrifices."

"Human sacrifice! Good lord." Jack put his arm around her, and peered over her shoulder at the paper. She was glad for his comforting presence.

"I know. Isn't that grisly? A maniac must have killed her." Emily read on, "Questions about a possible connection between the apparent homicide and the worshippers, who bring fruit and flowers to the altar, brought a strong denial from spokesperson Mau Koolani. 'This was a desecration of our sacred temple where we worship Lono as our ancestors once did. We don't condone violence.'"

"It sounds like some sort of hideous ritual murder," Jack said. "A religious fanatic perhaps. I hope the police are keeping a sharp eye on these worshippers."

"Sarah said they've always seemed harmless."

"So does a viper lying in the sun...until it strikes."

"Listen to this. 'Blake was known for her generous support of the Island Trust, which supports Hawaiian cultural events. She was last seen Saturday night at a fundraiser for the trust at the Sheraton Waikiki. Her husband, Todd Blake, reported her missing Sunday night.'"

"Why would he wait twenty-four hours to report her disappearance?" Jack asked.

"A minute ago you suspected Lono's followers. Are you switching to poor Todd?"

"I'm keeping an open mind, suspecting all and sundry. You must admit that Todd seems strangely oblivious to Amanda's comings and goings. I would certainly notice if you were missing for twenty-four hours."

"I'm sure there's an explanation. Perhaps Sarah knows. I'm having tea with her this afternoon. When I saw her this morning, she and Brent were just rushing off to comfort Todd so I didn't have a chance to find out many details. Besides I don't like to pry."

Jack hooted.

Later that afternoon, Emily met Sarah at the Moana Hotel, a white colonial building, recalling the grace and splendor of the Victorian British Empire. On the verandah, they sat in white wicker chairs and looked out at Waikiki beach. Ceiling fans stirred a gentle breeze. A waitress brought tea with thin slices of lemon, thick cream, cucumber sandwiches, scones with marmalade. It was quite unlike Emily's idea of Hawaii.

"Tell me about Jack." Sarah said. Her frosted hair was neatly brushed. She wore sun glasses and a lavender sundress. Signs of grief were no longer emblazoned on her face. "Amanda told me you had posted photos of the two of you on Facebook."

"Jack's a physician. I met him a couple of years ago when I was working on an article about Madeline Island." She didn't mention the murder that had brought them together.

"Is it serious?"

"Well…sort of. We just moved in together."

"We can expect a wedding soon then." Sarah smiled.

"You sound just like my mother." Emily hadn't meant to sound irritated but her tone was definitely snappish. Ever since she had moved into Jack's arts and crafts bungalow near Lake Harriet, Emily had been sure it was the right move. They were happy and comfortable together. But her mother was eager for them to take the next step. To her horror, Emily had discovered a stack of bride magazines at her mother's apartment. She pretended not to notice.

Sarah backed off. "This place is beautiful, isn't it?"

Emily nodded. "Gorgeous."

"Amanda and I used to come here. She thought of it as a guilty pleasure," Sarah said. She took off her dark glasses and laid them on the table.

"Why guilty?" Emily asked, her mouth full of scone. Sea and sun had given her an enormous appetite; she had to muster all her restraint to eat daintily rather than falling upon her meal like a starving sailor.

"I don't know." Sarah took a sip of tea. "It sounds silly to me but Amanda was embarrassed about being a descendant of the old aristocracy of the island, who used to come here when the hotel was new. Her ancestors were among the missionaries who came to these islands with not much more than a Bible to their name, but then her grandfather made a fortune in sugarcane. He was one of the wealthy people who came to parties at the Moana Hotel to mingle with movie stars and the Prince of Wales. This was a very fashionable place. In the lobby you can see some of the old photographs."

"I didn't realize the hotel was so old."

"It was built at the turn of the century, but you'd never guess it. It's been completely restored, an incredibly expensive project."

Emily longed to pull out her little red notebook and start jotting down notes, but she thought it might seem rude.

"Why did Amanda feel guilty about her family?" Emily knew enough about Hawaii's history to have a pretty good idea, but she was curious to hear what Sarah would say.

"You should hear Kari on the subject. She would tell you this land was stolen from the native people who had no concept of property."

"Did Amanda agree?"

"She never said. Not outright. But she wanted to give something back to the native people. That's why she started the Trust. When we came out to the islands, Amanda's father had just died, leaving her a great deal of money. She knew what she wanted to do, but had no idea how to go about it. Fortunately, Brent was able to help."

"He set up the Trust?"

Sarah nodded. "Right. As a way to fund a cultural revival. Amanda enjoyed being generous. She said she had more money than she really needed."

Emily heard a shade of envy in Sarah's tone.

"Of course, we benefited too. Amanda paid her staff well and she relied on Brent. He's a good businessman and Amanda wasn't interested in the business aspect. She just wanted to do the right thing. Todd, on the other hand, thought the Trust was a crazy idea that would be forgotten if no one encouraged Amanda. There was some tension between Brent and Todd at the time."

"You saw Todd this morning. How is he?"

"Terribly broken up. You know how madly in love they've been ever since college."

"Yes." Emily sipped her tea. She remembered how Amanda had doted on Todd and was trying to conjure up exactly how he had treated her. Of course, it was a long time ago.

Emily remembered Todd coming up to her at a long-ago fraternity party, his tie flopping over his shoulder, a plastic tumbler of some purple concoction combining grape juice, orange sherbet and vodka. His face was flushed.

"Where's Amanda?" Emily had asked this question quickly because she fancied she saw a look of inebriated lust and meant to forestall any unwelcome overtures by reminding him of his girlfriend. Her own date had wandered off somewhere, probably in search of a beer.

Todd had taken a long swig of the nasty purple beverage. "Gone to visit her parents for the weekend." He bent down to whisper, "She thinks I'm going to marry her."

"Oh."

"I'm not ready for that. Not by a long shot." He winked at her. "Not a word, remember. I'm heading off to L.A. She'll be surprised, but she'll get over me."

He reeled off in the general direction of the garbage can that held the purple beverage. "Want a drink?" he called over his shoulder.

"No thanks."

Despite his air of secrecy, Emily was not Todd's only confidante as she discovered that night in the dorm. She and her roommate Mindy were closing off the evening by eating cheddar crackers held together by peanut butter. Emily shuddered as she remembered the dorm food she had once wolfed down. Mindy told her about a strangely similar conversation with Todd.

"Poor Amanda. How will she cope?" Emily asked.

"She'll manage. Todd's not the prize she thinks he is."

"It will be a horrible surprise."

The surprise was theirs. A few weeks later, Amanda came rushing down the path from Macmillan Hall, her scarf flying, her eyes ablaze with joy. She grabbed Emily by the sleeve of her navy blue pea coat and held out her left hand to display a lovely little diamond ring.

"We'll be married right after graduation. You'll be there, won't you?"

Emily knew she looked stunned rather than delighted.

Later, Amanda said rather crisply, "My roommate is the only person who has congratulated me with complete happiness. Everyone else looked so odd. What is it?"

Emily did not explain that her roommate had missed the party where Todd was sharing confidences right and left. She let Amanda assume it was jealousy that had taken the enthusiasm out of her voice.

Whatever doubts Emily had about a lasting marriage between scholarly, quiet Amanda and Todd faded with the years. Letters and issues of the *Alumnae News* detailed a life of pleasure and plenty. Hawaii. A beautiful home.

"You'll come back to the house for the reception after the funeral, won't you?" Sarah asked, bringing Emily back to the present. "Todd really wants to see you."

"Yes, of course, I'll come. But I won't know what to say to him."

"Just your presence will mean a lot."

Tea time seemed to be coming to an end. Sarah was gathering up her purse.

"The newspaper said that Amanda disappeared Saturday night," Emily blurted out.

"Yes." Sarah slumped back in her seat. She looked around, lowered her voice, "We were all at the fundraiser together. One minute Amanda was there, and the next minute she was gone."

"Todd must have been terribly worried."

"Not at first. He'd had a little spat with Amanda. No big deal. But when he couldn't find her at the end of the evening, Todd supposed Amanda had gone to a motel to cool off. When she didn't call by Sunday night, he began to worry. It wasn't like Amanda to go off like that."

"Poor Todd. He must feel horrible."

"He does, but I don't think the full impact has hit him yet. He's busy planning the funeral and that takes his mind off it a bit. Kari is bringing her little pupils to be in the ceremony, which I think is sweet. She teaches third grade. Adorable children."

"Kari seems to be a lovely girl," Emily said, hoping Sarah would tell her more.

Sarah brightened. "Yes, she is. Of course, the poor girl is heartbroken."

"No wonder," Emily sympathized.

Sarah looked down at her hands. "I suppose you noticed the tension between Kari and Brent yesterday. I'm sorry you had to see that. They've always been close, but now Kari wants to find her roots." Sarah pursed her lips as if the word had left a nasty aftertaste, then took a sip of tea.

"That's not unusual," Emily said.

"She wants to find out more about her birth mother."
Sarah set her cup rattling back into its saucer. "There's
no point, of course. The woman's been dead for years."
Sarah twisted her ring, an emerald set in a circle of
diamonds. "Her mother was killed in an automobile
accident when Kari was just a little girl. Tragic. Such a
young woman. We adopted Kari. We never knew who
her father was. Ever since she was three years old,
we've thought of Kari as our own daughter."

"Of course." Emily murmured encouragement. Sarah
clearly needed to talk with someone and apparently had
chosen Emily as her new best friend. It promised to be
an arduous job.

"It all started a few years ago when Kari began to get
interested in cultural history, the hula and songs of the
Polynesian people. More and more, she began to
wonder about her own family." Sarah leaned forward,
lowered her voice. "Then a few weeks ago, Kari
contacted her aunt, her only blood relative. It upset
Brent terribly."

"Most adopted kids are curious about their heritage."

"I know. Brent knows that too. He just loves Kari so
much." Sarah sighed and leaned back. She folded her
napkin and placed it neatly on the table. "Ready?" she
asked brightly.

Emily nodded. She followed Sarah out into the
lobby, hurrying to keep up. Sarah still moved with the
long strides of the athlete she'd been in college.

Emily stopped in the lobby to admire the historical
display. Roped off by a red velvet rope, mannequins in
white Victorian dresses trimmed in lace posed beside an
antique baby carriage.

"Amanda didn't like to look," Sarah said. "We had
to hurry past. And yet I think she was secretly
fascinated by her family's history."

CHAPTER 3

That evening at a restaurant patio under blazing bamboo Tiki torches, Emily asked Jack to tell her all about his medical conference. The topic was covered quickly, leaving the murder the sole subject of dinner conversation.

"So tell me about Amanda," Jack encouraged Emily, falling upon his shrimp curry with gusto.

"Amanda was serious, active in student government, a nice woman. When I wrote to her, letting her know we'd be in Hawaii, she wrote back and said she needed my advice."

"What sort of advice?"

"I don't know. Amanda was sketchy on details, but she said she valued my good sense. I don't recall much about the letter but a compliment is always memorable."

"Do you still have the letter?"

"Not with me. At the time, it didn't seem important. I knew I would be seeing her in a few days." Emily still found it hard to believe that this letter held Amanda's last words to her. She wanted very much to read it again, to hear Amanda's voice in her mind.

"So tell me more about Amanda. You must have known her pretty well if she considers you a fountainhead of good advice."

"I really didn't. That's why I was surprised by her letter. But we were in a few classes together. Perhaps she noticed my keen mind."

"No doubt."

Emily cast him a sharp look, checking for an ironic glint in his eye but Jack looked innocent. "I think Amanda missed Hawaii," she said, thinking back to her college days. "Once her parents sent her a huge box of orchids and leis. I remember the day the gorgeous flowers from Hawaii arrived in the college mail room. Amanda was ecstatic." Emily remembered how joy had lit up Amanda's face, transforming her.

"New York State must have been very different for Amanda. She'd never seen snow and sometimes we had blizzards so severe the roads in and out of the college would be closed for days. When huge, heavy flakes fell, we would run outside, hold out a coffee cup, let it fill with snow and then pour chocolate sauce on it. So far out in the country, the air and snow were pure enough to do that. Amanda said it reminded her of shaved ice at home.

"Amanda tried to like college. She joined us when we went sliding downhill on huge, round trays from the cafeteria and, on weekends, she went skiing a few times. Her mother, who was originally from New England, had told her about the joys of winter, but I don't think Amanda ever really thawed out. She was cold the whole four years."

Emily scooped curry sauce onto her sticky rice and paused to savor it. She recalled that Amanda had worn a heavy sweater even on mild days and hunched her shoulders against the chill. Emily, on the other hand, had loved the snap in the air on snowy days when she headed off for class, walking over the wooden bridge that spanned the creek, up the hill, past tall snow-frosted pines. The college was set on the shores of Lake Cayuga, amid rolling hills, farms and apple orchards. Some of the college dorms were graceful Victorian homes with spiral staircases and widows' walks. Emily had loved Wells College; her fingers had to be pried off the ivy on graduation day. But she knew that some girls felt lost and pined for home or sometimes just a city. After all, the nearest town of any size, Ithaca, was twenty-six miles away. Wells was in the tiny village of Aurora which featured an old fashioned inn on the lake that served fabulous ice cream pie, a small musty general store, and a gas station.

Had Amanda ever been happy at Wells? Emily had never paid much attention to her former classmate. Now she tried to recall her smile and could only conjure up the day the box of leis arrived. She did remember Amanda's earnestness in class discussions, the way her brow would furrow, her cheeks flush.

"And her husband. Is he from Hawaii?" Jack's question jerked her out of her reverie and sent her plunging eagerly into another story.

"No. Todd grew up in the Midwest. Kansas, I think. But he was born for the tropical life. The minute he saw Hawaii he was a happy man. He loved surfing. Amanda begged him to give it up. She thought it was too dangerous."

"You have an amazing fund of information about a woman you barely know," Jack said, polishing his plate with his fork, scraping up the last remaining bits of sauce

"Amanda told me all this at reunion three years ago, but I knew Todd from our college days. He went to Cornell, which was only a half-hour drive from college. Amanda met him at a mixer, one of those ghastly events where girls start out huddled on one side of the room and boys on another and gradually they drift together and try to find a compatible soul. Todd and Amanda seemed a mismatched couple in some ways. He was a typical fraternity guy, very outgoing and popular. Amanda was quiet and studious."

"Attractive?" Jack raised his eyebrow, a trick Emily had struggled in vain to master.

"She was attractive enough, but she didn't care about appearances. No make-up, not much interest in how she was dressed."

"And he fell for her?"

"Yes. Looks are not everything." Emily spoke sharply and fixed him with a steely eye.

"Of course not. I am simply spoiled because I have the good fortune to be with a beautiful as well as a highly intelligent woman."

Emily smiled her approval.

"Were they happy together?" Jack asked.

"If you can believe Amanda's own accounts in the *Alumnae News*, they were enthralled with one another."

"Do I detect a note of skepticism?"

"It seemed like a one-sided relationship. She doted on him and he seemed...." Emily struggled to find the right word.

"What? Was it her money that attracted him?" Jack leaned forward, his elbows on the table, his wayward lock of hair falling over his forehead.

"Maybe. Who knows? It was all a long time ago. People change. Anyway, we'll see him at the funeral tomorrow."

"Is he a suspect?"

"Todd? Nobody has said so. According to Sarah, the police are not very forthcoming. They have, however, made an appointment to talk to her and Brent tomorrow."

"I wouldn't care to be questioned in connection with a murder."

"It's only because they're friends of Amanda's and because Brent worked for the Trust. The bizarre placement of the body on the altar makes it pretty clear the killer must be a lunatic of some sort, as you yourself have pointed out."

"Maybe. When was Amanda last seen?"

"You sound just like a police officer."

"I'm gathering data before making a diagnosis." Jack grinned at her.

The next day at the funeral, Emily and Jack sat in the middle of the crowded church. Plain pine beams supported the pitched ceiling. Yellow hibiscus, the state flower of Hawaii, bloomed beside the altar. Emily recognized Todd, a little heavier now, his sun-blonde hair sleeked down. He was sitting next to Sarah and Brent. Emily wondered where Kari was. Then drumming began.

A procession of small girls in red silk blouses and rustling skirts made from Ti leaves walked slowly down the aisle chanting, "*Aloha he.*" Kari, wearing a simple gray dress and a white flower lei, followed them. She moved her bare feet slowly in tune to the drums, hands undulating, hips barely swaying. The children filed into a pew and sat down. Kari sat in the row behind them.

A priest with fiery red hair faced the congregation. He lifted his hands and said, "*Aloha he Ahua.*" His piercingly sharp Adam's apple moved when he spoke. "God is *Aloha*. A person who has the true spirit of *aloha* loves even when love is not returned. Amanda Blake loved this island, her neighbors, her family."

He did not say that someone had not loved her in return, that, in fact, someone had hated her enough to kill her. Emily looked around the church and wondered if the murderer was present, bowing his or her head in prayer.

"Our grief in losing her…" the priest's voice droned on, but Emily could not attend. It seemed unlikely that anyone who knew Amanda was guilty. The sobbing she heard throughout the church attested to the good will and affection Amanda's friends seemed to feel for her. She could see Sara's shoulders shaking. Brent offered her a handkerchief and took her hand. Across the aisle, Kari was whispering to a dark-haired woman.

By the end of the service, Emily too was on the verge of tears. Only now did the reality of Amanda's death strike home.

"I thought you didn't know Amanda that well," Jack said, handing her a handkerchief.

"I didn't, but we were girls together," Emily sniffed. "And now she's dead."

Jack took her hand.

The door to the home where Todd and Amanda Blake had lived during their married life was ajar. Emily and Jack walked into a room already crowded, but quiet and subdued. The cathedral ceiling was pierced by skylights, and white walls displayed huge watercolors of tropical flowers. Emily stepped up from the sunken living room to the dining room where a buffet was arrayed on a long glass table. Stress had suppressed her usual hearty appetite, but Jack made a beeline for the buffet.

Emily looked around the room for Todd. Fortunately, the bereaved husband's height made him easy to find. She grabbed Jack by the elbow and reminded him sharply that Miss Manners would advise him to greet his host before falling on the snacks, especially if his host were bereaved. He laid aside his plate with some reluctance and followed her.

Todd caught sight of Emily before she reached him. His once striking good looks had faded, but he was still a fine looking man. Emily noticed how his firm jaw was beginning to sink into jowls and tiny broken veins showed through his tan. His eyes were bloodshot, but perhaps he'd been weeping, poor man.

"Emily, I'm so glad you're here. And this must be Jack." Todd stuck out his hand, instinctively reverting to his hail-fellow-well-met style and clapped Jack on the shoulder, "Amanda told me you were coming. I hoped we could get together." His hand dropped to his side. His own words seemed to surprise him, the realization of bereavement hitting once again.

Emily and Jack expressed their condolences. Then Todd drifted away, calling out to Emily over his shoulder, "Call me, Emily. I have something to show you."

"He really does look shaken," Emily said.

"As well he might. The poor guy's lost his wife." Jack put his hand in the small of her back. "Would Miss Manners allow me a small bite of something now?" Jack asked.

"I suppose so." Emily started toward the buffet. Kari was standing by the table, talking to a burly young man. Like Kari, he seemed to be of Polynesian ancestry. Kari dipped her finger into a bowl of poi, a paste made from taro roots, then lifted it to lick in the traditional manner. Todd came up beside her. Putting his arm around Kari, he bent down, his mouth open wide as if to bite her finger. She giggled. He grinned at the girl and pulled her closer to him.

"Irrepressible, isn't he?" Jack commented dryly. "A minute ago he looked heartbroken."

Emily noticed Brent standing in the corner, arms folded, glaring at Todd.

Kari smiled, then turned away, looking embarrassed. She caught Emily's eye, pulled away from Todd and walked toward Emily.

"Aloha," she said holding out her hand. "We met at my parents' house the other day. I'm Kari Gardner."

She gestured toward the young man who had trailed after her. "And this is Matt."

Matt lowered his eyes, and muttered a greeting. He twitched his broad shoulders inside his suit.

Emily murmured her sympathy. "Did you know Amanda well?"

"Well enough. She was *aikane,*" Matt said. He tugged at his collar. His eyes darted away to the far corner of the room.

Kari hung on Matt's arm. Her eyes were red rimmed, her face pale. "Amanda was kind to him," Kari explained. "As she was to everyone."

"Amanda was an idealistic, generous woman even when she was in college," Emily said.

"That can be dangerous," Kari said. She stared into Emily's eyes as if willing her to read some hidden message.

"How so?" Emily asked quickly.

Matt put his arm around Kari and said, "We've got to get going."

She shook him off. "Amanda thought you could help her."

"How?" Emily asked.

Matt grabbed Kari's elbow. "Come on. We have to talk to a few more people, then we're out of here."

Kari seemed about to speak when her gaze shifted away from Emily. Across the room, a woman in a plain black dress was standing in the doorway, scanning the crowd. It was the woman Emily had seen sitting next to Kari in church.

"Excuse me, my aunt is here." Kari touched Emily's arm and started toward the door with a clearly relieved Matt following behind.

"How strange that Kari thinks I could have helped Amanda," Emily said to Jack.

Todd hove into view again. He was holding a Bloody Mary sprouting an enormous stalk of celery. "You met Matt. He's a hell of a surfer. Wins a lot of competitions out on North Beach. I used to do that before Amanda clamped down." His tone had been close to resentful, then he caught himself. "She took good care of me," he added and patted Emily on the shoulder.

Emily heard the sound of quiet quarreling and turned to see Sara and Brent approaching. Sara had apparently repaired her makeup. No sign of tears now except the redness of her eyes. She hugged Emily, held out her hand to Jack. "Jack, I'm so glad to meet you."

Brent shook hands with Jack, not quite meeting his gaze. He seemed preoccupied. Emily followed Brent's gaze and realized he was staring at Kari and her aunt, who were sitting on a sofa at the other side of the room, apparently deep in conversation. Matt lurked beside them, shifting from foot to foot.

"What's Lillian doing here?" Brent asked.

"Kari probably invited her," Sarah said. "To comfort her."

"You're her mother. She should turn to you. Not to some stranger."

"She's not a stranger. Lillian's her aunt."

Todd cut their argument short. "Speaking of strangers, I suppose you've noticed our guests from the criminal justice department." He nodded toward two men standing with their backs against the wall. One was tall, bald, wearing a khaki shirt, the other stocky, medium build, with dark hair.

"Awfully tacky of them to show up here," Sarah said. "Couldn't you have kept them out?"

"I suppose so. They did ask if they could come, but I didn't feel I could say, 'Hell no, this is my wife's funeral and I don't want you butting in.' I have to seem cooperative. And I am cooperative, damn it. I spent four hours explaining my every move to those guys."

"Why do you suppose they wanted to be here?" Emily asked.

"The husband is always the number one suspect," Jack said helpfully. Emily wanted to kick him. "It's nothing personal. Just statistics."

"In this case, the killer's obviously a maniac of some sort," Emily said quickly.

"They've grilled us too," Brent said. "The hell of it is nobody knows exactly how Amanda ended up fifty miles away from the hotel on a mountain top."

"We were all together at the fundraising party the night Amanda was murdered," Sarah explained.

"Then you all have alibis," Emily said.

"We don't know whether we do or not," Todd said. "I have no idea when Amanda was murdered and if the police know, they aren't saying." He took a long pull on his Bloody Mary, peering at the police officers over the top of his celery frond. "Of course, I want the police to find Amanda's killer, but I seriously doubt he's in this room."

CHAPTER 4

When they arrived at their hotel room, Emily flopped onto the bed. "I wish I'd paid more attention to Amanda's letter. I don't know why she didn't just email me."

"Why not call your mother and ask her to read the letter over the phone? Just don't tantalize her with reports of our balmy weather. No doubt it's snowing in Minnesota."

"I will definitely soft pedal the tropical paradise aspect of this trip." Emily's mother was staying in their house so she could take care of Stanley, their golden retriever. Neither of them wanted to put Stanley in a kennel. He'd made them suffer his revenge after his last abandonment, morosely chewing and shredding shoes, gloves, handbags, whatever was within reach.

Her mother answered on the third ring. She sounded wary, a woman who had been harassed too often by computer voices urging her to make urgent changes to her credit card account.

"It's me, Mom. Emily."

"Thank God you're all right. I've been worrying. I didn't hear from you."

"It's only been a day."

"Well, a lot can happen in a day, believe you me."

"How's Stanley?"

"Crushed. What would you expect? He's lying on the sofa with a very sad expression on his face. I can read him like a book."

"He's not supposed to be on the furniture."

"Don't expect me to tell him that. He's suffering like a dog from loneliness."

"He *is* a dog."

Emily heard a skeptical sniff. "How are you, mother?"

"As well as can he expected with this hip of mine. Cold weather is pure torture on my arthritis. But we can't all be wallowing in tropical paradises. Some of us have to stay home. It's snowing, you'll be glad to know."

"You're very kind to watch the house, mother."

"I don't mind. It's a darned sight nicer than that little hovel of an apartment I live in. I'm so cramped in that …"

Emily knew this would be a long sad story, which she had heard many time before, so she broke in ruthlessly. "Mom, listen, I want to ask you a favor."

"That doesn't surprise me. What else am I here for?"

"I left a letter at home, an important letter as it turns out, from Amanda Blake." Emily gave a quick account of the murder, for once capturing her mother's full attention.

"I had a feeling something horrible was going to happen. That nice girl. It could have been you, Emily. Just watch your step."

"Mom, you can see why I really need to know what Amanda wrote to me. Could you please find the letter for me and call back and read it to me over the phone? It's on the very top of a pile of mail in the den."

"Oh, there's no need for me to call back. I'll just get it now."

The phone clanked down. Emily could hear Stanley barking wildly in the background. She hoped he wouldn't barge into her mother. Emily and Jack had adopted their rescue dog, after she'd seen a heartbreaking Facebook post about a Golden mix, abandoned by the highway. He was scrawny and his fur was matted but when Emily saw his sweet, sad face, her heart melted. Fortunately, when she showed the photo to Jack, he responded the same way. "Poor guy. You can see he's a good dog. Let's go get him."

After a time, her mother came on the phone again. "Okay, I found it. You'll be interested to know it was not on the top at all. It was a ways down."

"Thank you for finding it. Could you read it to me?"

"That's just what I'm going to do, but I have to put my glasses on first so just hold your horses." She cleared her throat and began to read.

"Dear Emily,

How delightful that you're coming to Oahu. I am so looking forward to meeting Jack. I'm particularly glad you are coming because I'm faced with a dilemma and need to talk to someone who can give good, clear advice or, at least, act as a sounding board. I remember you in class, so forceful and sure of yourself, impatient with silly arguments and furious at any sort of injustice.

You may find it surprising that I turn to you when I have a husband and close friends here in Hawaii, but in this case, those closest to me have a stake in my decision. Even our pastor, a reliable spiritual adviser and friend, would be hard pressed to be impartial. I want to show you some documents that will shed some light on the situation. I know I'm rambling. Please forgive me.

How I wish you could stay with us, but I understand you must be near Jack's conference. Come for dinner on Wednesday. Sarah and Brent will be there too. Best wishes,"

Amanda"

"So what was this decision?" Emily's mother asked.

"I was hoping her letter would give me a clue."

Stanley was barking in the background.

"I have to let him out. He wants to chase a squirrel. Be careful, Emily."

The phone banged down, severing the connection.

"So what did you find out?" Jack lowered his *New Yorker* to look at her.

"Amanda wanted my advice in making some important decision, one that would have affected her husband and closest friends. That's why she wanted to talk to someone impartial. I wish I knew what she wanted to ask me. Maybe I should ask her priest. She says he was an adviser and friend. He must have some idea. I'll pay him a visit."

"It's a moot point, don't you think? She can't make decisions now."

"Curiosity makes its demands on an inquiring mind."

"Remember the cat in the adage, my dear."

That evening Emily and Jack met Brent and Sarah for dinner. In a patio garden, lit only by bamboo Tiki torches and candlelight, they dined under a huge parasol. Two girls in gold and red traditional gowns flashed six-inch-long fingernails as they wove a spell with stylized, intricate gestures. The tinkling music, the murmur of voices, a glass of white wine soothed Emily so that for the first time all day she relaxed.

"What a good idea to come here," she said.

"It's one of our favorite places," Sarah said, looking pleased.

Brent wanted to order for them and Emily was glad of the offer. The candlelight cast a soft glow, making everyone look lovely and romantic, but it was too dim to shed much light on the menu.

Emily ate huge coconut-encrusted shrimp, garnished with orchids and Ti leaves. "Delicious," she murmured.

Conversation inevitably turned to Todd and Amanda Blake.

"Do you have any idea what major decision Amanda had to make?" Emily asked.

"No," Sarah said, pausing with her fork halfway to her lips. "What makes you think she had to make a decision?"

"Amanda wrote to me. She wanted my advice."

"How odd. She never said a word to me." Sarah placed her fork down and stared at Emily.

"That doesn't sound like Amanda," Brent said. "Her life was set on a fairly even course."

Jack leaned forward. Since he tended to blurt out the first question on his mind without fear of how it might upset his dinner companions, Emily had her kicking foot ready to fly. She estimated its range so she would not inadvertently rap the wrong person.

"Emily said you were all at a party together when Amanda just disappeared," Jack said. "Would she go off on her own like that without telling anyone?"

"We've wondered," Brent said. "The ballroom was packed. We were all together earlier in the evening, but Sarah and I hadn't seen Amanda for the last hour or so of the party. Not surprising in such a large gathering. When we were starting to leave, Todd grabbed my arm and asked if I'd seen Amanda. He looked really worried."

"She may have stepped outside to get a breath of air," Sarah said. "That would be very much Amanda's style. She didn't care for huge noisy parties. Although she did a wonderful job of organizing them."

Brent pointed his fork at her. "Right. That's how it must have been. Amanda stepped outside. Then someone grabbed her, forced her into his car, drove her to Pu'u O Mahuka Heiau and killed her. Then he piled on all that fruit and other rubbish. Someone with a political agenda of some kind."

Everyone stared at him for a silent moment.

"That's certainly one possibility," Jack said.

"I'm just surprised the police haven't figured it out yet." Brent drained his glass of wine.

Emily decided to shift the subject slightly. "Sarah, you said Todd didn't report Amanda's disappearance because he'd quarreled with her. What was that all about?"

Brent interrupted. "That's the kind of thing the police could blow all out of proportion. The less said the better."

Sarah ignored his hint. "Todd adored Amanda, but he simply couldn't resist other women. It's his fatal flaw. The night of the party, his current young crumpet turned up. She was flicking imaginary bits of dust from his tuxedo and fluffing up his boutonnière, the sort of territorial marking that is so unmistakable."

"And such a mistake when it occurs in public, in full view of a wife and friends," Brent added.

"This is not his first girlfriend, not by any means, but Amanda never suspected," Sarah said.

"Poor kid. Gullible as they come," Brent said, shaking his head. "I felt sorry for Amanda, finding out about Todd's philandering like that. She was a lot happier not knowing."

Sarah gave him a sharp glance.

"To tell the truth, I always thought Todd and Amanda were an odd couple," Emily said. "Even in college. Do you remember, Sarah?"

"I remember being surprised when I heard they were engaged. And yet they've been happy together," Sarah said. "Todd fell in love with Amanda when he came to Hawaii. It was spring break. He and Brent and several other guys from the fraternity came here together."

Emily turned to Brent. "I always wondered how they got together. Tell us about it."

"Not much to tell." Brent speared up a shrimp.

"Tales of love and romance are always good," Emily coaxed.

"Well, this was many years ago, you understand, so the details are sketchy. But, as I recall, Todd and I were up at Wells one weekend. I had come to see Sarah and she set up a date with Amanda for Todd. Apparently, they had met before at a mixer."

"That's right," Sarah interrupted. "Amanda really liked him, but Todd hadn't called her."

"Sarah, who is telling this story, you or me?" Irritation glittered in Brent's brown eyes.

"Sorry, go on." Sarah looked down at her nails, turning them over as if checking for imperfections.

"Okay," Brent said, looking from one to another, making sure he had everyone's attention. "That evening, we went down to the Inn for drinks. I could tell Amanda was struck by Todd's dashing good looks. Her eyes were glowing with unmaidenly lust, but she didn't have much to say for herself and I could see he was getting bored.

"Then in my tactful way I steered the conversation toward our upcoming spring break, knowing that Amanda was from Hawaii. I wanted to give the poor kid something to talk about. And it worked. Amanda went on and on about how terrific it was here, the beaches, the sun. In the end she invited us both to stay with her.

"Later Todd said to me, 'Right. I'm going to spend my spring break with one of the mousiest, dullest girls I've ever met.'

Sarah drew in her breath. Brent shot her a look and continued, "But when we got to Oahu, he found out about Amanda's family, how prominent they are. We were driving along and Todd yelled out, 'Hey, there's a street named Tarkington. Do you suppose it's Amanda's family? We have to check this out.'

"So we called her up. Amanda was thrilled to hear from us. She told us to come on over, gave elaborate instructions on how to get to her family's house. We figured, what the hell. Why not? We started driving along following her instructions, and finally we came to this walled estate with elaborate gardens and a magnificent home with servants. Holy crap. Hardly the way we'd imagined the nondescript Amanda living."

Brent forked a shrimp into his mouth. "Todd saw her in a whole new light."

"Was he after her money, do you think?" Jack asked. Emily's kicking foot twitched but she was curious too.

"No, no. It was just that it changed his perception of her. She was now someone powerful and important, a sugar plantation heiress. The aura of the Tarkington estate reflected on her."

"The way Elizabeth felt after she saw Darcy at Pemberley," Sarah added helpfully.

Emily was not quite convinced.

Later that night, lying in bed with a mystery novel on her lap, Emily roused Jack who seemed to be dropping off to sleep. "Do you think Amanda was thinking of divorcing Todd?"

"How could I possibly know? You ascribe to me an omniscience that is flattering, but wholly undeserved."

"Maybe that was the decision she had to make. If Amanda had found out Todd was deceiving her, she might have considered dumping him."

"Why keep it a secret from Sarah?"

"Maybe she didn't. After the murder, anything Sarah or Brent say about a rift between them sounds accusing.

You saw how Brent tried to silence Sarah. Typical male solidarity."

"The timing's wrong. It sounds as if Amanda found out about Todd's girlfriend for the first time the night she was killed."

"Maybe she already suspected. Then she saw them together and realized it was true."

Emily picked up her novel. Her eyes skimmed over a paragraph, then she let the book drop. "Todd asked me to call him. I think I will."

"Your dance card is filling up. You said you were going to pump that priest. What about your travel articles?"

"It won't take long to ask the priest a few questions, then I'll go see Todd. Amanda was counting on me to help her make a decision. I have to figure out what it was."

"You think it has some bearing on the murder, don't you?"

"Not necessarily."

"Hmmm." Jack's eyes closed. His eyelashes fluttered. "George isn't going to like this."

The next morning, Emily was leaning back in her rumpled bed, lounging amidst travel brochures and books, listening to the anxious voice of her editor George, who was rushing through his limited supply of small talk. He cut to the chase.

"So what's the angle? How far did you get?"

"George, there's no cause for concern," Emily's voice took on the soothing tone of a nursery school teacher calming a fractious toddler. "The article is practically writing itself."

"Show me the goods, Emily. Email me something."

"I won't miss my deadline. It's days away." *Three days to be exact*, Emily recalled with panic. Only a handful of traveler's tips were actually transcribed on her laptop.

"I know how distracted you get, Emily. Disasters seem to occur in your immediate vicinity and you get sucked in."

"Not this time." Emily was glad she had not told him about Amanda's murder. "I'm concentrating one-hundred percent on the job."

A few more calming words and Emily said, "Aloha." She hoped that George did not sense how necessary his call to duty really was. She would stay up late or, better yet, bring her laptop to the beach.

"I deduce from your reassuring tone that was George," Jack said, putting on his crisp, light blue shirt. "Was I correct in predicting he would be impatient?"

"He's overwrought as usual."

"His physician should prescribe something. A constant state of crisis can't be helping his high blood pressure."

"He would be a non-compliant patient. His wife would have to grind his prescription into a fine powder and mix it into his black coffee."

"So I suppose this changes your plans for today," Jack said, adjusting his red power tie before the mirror. "A good strong start on your article instead of asking intrusive questions?"

Emily ignored his hint. "First I'm going to visit Amanda's priest and try to find out what he knows about her dilemma. She must have let something slip, even if she didn't trust him to give disinterested advice."

"Your readers will not be enthralled by a visit to a rectory, trust me on this." He turned away from the mirror. "Do I look powerful and forceful? A physician whose word would be accepted without question."

"Of course, you do. I suppose you're giving your views on an important medical matter at the conference today."

"Indeed I am, as I explained in some detail last night while your eyes were glazed and your mind was running over clues to Amanda's murder."

"I was listening avidly." She kissed him and straightened the power tie. "You will do a splendid job as always. Meanwhile I will meet the priest and find out all he knows. After this very brief conversation, I will sketch out the scenic atmosphere I need for my articles. Sarah and I will drive along the coast and visit the Byodo-In Temple, a notable tourist attraction my readers won't want to miss."

"Chances for spiritual enlightenment await you at every turn."

"My readers cannot spend all their time at the beach."

CHAPTER 5

Emily found Father Welch tossing a basketball to a group of small boys on the playground of the parochial school. He wore khaki slacks, a short-sleeved shirt, and sneakers. Cassocks, Roman collars, and shiny black shoes had gone the way of the dodo bird even at Catholic schools, Emily reflected. The priest walked along the chicken-wire fence, watching the boys dribble toward the far hoop. He ran one hand over his red hair, flaming in the sunlight. Emily waited just outside the playground.

When Emily had called him that morning, Father Welch had been delighted to hear from a former classmate of Amanda's and readily agreed to meet her. Emily heard the school bell ring, sending the children scurrying toward the doors. Father Welch turned to her and smiled. "You must be Emily Swift," he said, gripping the chicken wire and squinting into the sun. "I was just about to have tea. Will you join me?"

A few minutes later, Emily sat across from him in a cozy, overstuffed chair. The teapot was on a table between them. A thin slice of lemon floated in her cup. Emily took a reviving sip of tea and felt ready to pry.

Father Welch leaned forward, cradling the cup in his freckled hands. His book-lined study seemed a perfect place to seek counseling and advice. Perhaps Amanda had unburdened herself of secrets in this very room.

"You were kind to agree to meet me."

"Talking about Amanda will be a comfort for us both." He smiled at her.

"She told me you were her friend, as well as her spiritual adviser." Emily stretched the truth a bit. She had only Amanda's letter to go on.

"Amanda was a wonderful woman. I'll miss her." He looked away.

"I will too." Emily faltered for a moment.

The red haired priest was staring out the window, flexing his thin fingers.

"We've kept in touch ever since college," Emily said, thinking that reading the *Alumnae News* counted for something. "I was surprised to hear several people describe her as saintly. I don't recall Amanda being very religious."

"She was truly a good woman." The priest turned and looked at Emily. "More and more, Amanda devoted her life to good works."

"I can see how her idealism would lead her to work for charities like the Trust. She never had to earn money or build a career and I'm sure she wanted to do something worthwhile."

"Yes, Amanda felt she was challenged to prove her worth in less traditional ways. And since she didn't have children....Well, her life wasn't as easy as you might suppose."

Emily wondered if he meant her relationship with Todd. Trying to prove her worth as a woman by winning and keeping his love seemed an oddly old fashioned concept. She wanted to nudge the priest into being more forthcoming. "She was fortunate in having a happy marriage. Todd adored her, or so I'm told," Emily said.

"I suppose that's true. Although they were very different."

"How so?" Emily contrived to sound mystified.

He smiled, "God's gifts are not distributed evenly, but all is according to His divine purpose. More tea?" He reached for the pot.

Emily found his answer incomprehensible. It must be priest-speak designed to deflect unwelcome questions. Fearing their conversation was coming to a close before she could accomplish her purpose, Amanda said, "Amanda told me she wanted my advice about a life-changing decision she had to make. I know I can't help her now, but I still want to know what was troubling her."

"I'll pray that you are comforted."

Oops. Apparently she'd hit the wrong button, activating an automatic priestly response. Emily tried again. "Father, did Amanda say anything to you about a difficult decision of some sort?"

"Not exactly." He paused and took a sip of tea. "But it doesn't come as a complete surprise. Lately, Amanda had begun to question her priorities. Even the Trust."

"I thought the Trust was her life's work."

"It was. Amanda valued the Hawaiian native culture and traditions; she wanted to see their rebirth. That was the whole idea behind the Trust. But lately she was becoming more interested in the physical well-being of the poor. She talked about making a substantial donation to the poor of our own parish."

Emily heard a wistful note in his voice. She wondered if this was why it would be hard for him to give disinterested advice. He must have been rooting for the poor.

Father Welch sighed. "It would have been a very fine thing to have some of the money that was pouring into the Trust. Not all of it, you understand."

Her theory was confirmed. "Is there no chance that Amanda left money to your parish in her will?"

"Possibly. I don't know anything about her will. Amanda did seem to be mulling over a decision, but she only dropped a few hints to me. I know she was extending her concern to people in other lands. She has a friend in Thailand who works in an orphanage for the children of HIV-positive parents. Amanda admired her tremendously, and believed she led a life far more serious and worthwhile than her own."

"It sounds to me as if Amanda was very serious indeed."

"She was. And she has always given generously. Amanda was a rich woman and felt a certain *noblesse oblige*, but recently she had started to think giving money wasn't nearly enough. She was embarrassed to be praised for her good works when they seemed increasingly insignificant in comparison with people who made real sacrifices."

"Because of her friend?"

"Partly that..." He lowered his pale blue eyes and turned the cup in his hands. "Recently something happened. Amanda apparently had a profound spiritual experience of some sort."

"How extraordinary." Emily hoped she didn't sound too flabbergasted at an event far outside her own experience.

"Perhaps it was the work of the Holy Spirit. Although such a sudden change is often triggered by a troubling discovery, the destruction of cherished beliefs."

"And in her case, you think this was true? Did Amanda discover something that troubled her?"

"I would be betraying a confidence to say more." He pursed his lips and picked up his cup of tea.

"The confessional seal?"

"No, but the intimate conversation of a friend and parishioner. Confidence imposes its own demands."

"Since she's dead perhaps…"

"It would do no good. Any speculation could cause misunderstanding. I don't want to cause suspicion to fall on the innocent by gossiping about my parishioners."

He stood up and held out his hand. "How kind of you to come."

Emily drove through Waikiki, heading for Sarah's house. It was time to buckle down to work. The first installment in her series of travel articles was due in just two days. Luckily, Sarah had offered to go along with her to the Byodo-In Temple and act as tour guide. "It's marvelous," Sarah had said. "So different. Your readers will love it."

Emily was glad that Sarah had offered to drive to the temple, leaving her free to observe the countryside and jot down notes for her article. On the windward side of the island, they drove past Hanauma Bay, the scene of Emily's recent snorkeling adventure. No doubt the water was perfectly clear today and happy vacationers would be able to see the 150 varieties of tropical fish that swam in those turquoise waters. Looking inland, Emily saw mist drifting across fluted mountains, creating a vision of an Asian painting. Gazing back and forth from misty mountains on one side and the roaring ocean on the other, Emily, the navigator, almost missed the small road sign marking the turn to Byodo-In Temple. She called out just in time and Sarah drove up a winding road into the Valley of the Temples Memorial Park where red-roofed white pagodas and formal gardens were set against the craggy backdrop of the Koolau mountain range. Emily felt she had arrived in another country. She made a mental note.

Traveler's Tip: Visit the Buddhist temple of Byodo-In and you'll feel transported to Asia. This replica of a

900-year-old Japanese temple nestles in a valley amidst velvet green cliffs draped in mist. Peacocks strut across your path then turn to dazzle you with a display of their magnificent tail feathers. Saffron-robed monks give a traditional greeting, bowing over hands joined in prayer.

Sarah and Emily strolled from the parking lot across an arched footbridge to the temple buildings. Silenced by beauty, Emily gazed at the crimson temples, their tile roofs turned up at the edges like Persian slippers. Beyond were the magnificent *pali*, sheer cliffs half hidden in mist. She hurried after Sarah who was striding down the gravel pathway, catching up only when Sarah stopped beside a small gazebo with dark red pillars. In the center was an enormous bronze bell. "Ring it to assure a long life and blessings of the Buddha," Sarah advised.

Emily took hold of the battering ram suspended from the ceiling and gave the three-ton bell a good whack, then stepped back, listening to its sound reverberating through the valley. "I need all the blessings I can get," she said. "Now you."

"No, I've done it before. With Amanda." Sarah turned away and continued down the path.

Emily felt a shadow and looked up to see a cloud drift overhead. It was hard to put Amanda out of mind even for a few hours.

They meandered along the path beside a pond that reflected the temple buildings on its still surface. Emily peered into green depths to see Koi, huge orange, gold, and mottled carp, weaving in and out, jostling one another in a watery traffic jam. *Odd to see what is basically a gold fish grown to humongous size*, Emily thought. *If Jack were here, he'd say they were big enough to make a hearty shore lunch.*

At the end of the path was a white pagoda trimmed in red, open on all four sides. Emily took a few photographs, then kicked off her sandals and walked into the dimly-lit shrine. A nine-foot-high gold and lacquer Buddha sat cross-legged on the altar. Emily stared up in awe at the calm, magnificent deity.

Emily found Sarah waiting for her outside the shrine. Wearing blue and green paisley Capri pants, a green polo shirt, and white sandals, she looked crisp and preppy, not at all as Emily remembered her at college. She recalled a rather untidy girl who looked out of place off the playing field. They walked to the edge of the pond and leaned on the railing, watching a swan float gracefully forward, its arching neck leading like the prow of a ship.

So far the tranquil atmosphere of the temple had exerted its influence, keeping Emily away from the topic that occupied her mind. Finally, she broke the spell. "This morning I went to visit Father Welch, the priest who said the funeral mass."

"Why on earth?" Sarah turned to her, removing her sunglasses to give her a sharp look.

"A long shot really. I wondered if he had any idea about the decision Amanda had to make."

"Did he?"

"No, but he talked about an orphanage in Thailand that Amanda had wanted to help. Apparently she has a friend there who is doing amazing good works. Do you suppose Amanda was thinking of leaving Todd and going off to work in an orphanage?"

Sarah gave a whoop of laughter. "Amanda? I can't picture her bolting. Especially to such a very unpleasant place. Sure, she talked about the orphanage, even showed me pictures of adorable Thai children. It's incredibly sad. Many of them are going to die of AIDS. Amanda admired her friend Lucy who works there but she always said that she couldn't imagine how Lucy could stand it. Not so much the Spartan conditions and hard work, but the heartbreak of watching babies die."

"Maybe she meant to give the orphanage heaps of money or change her will." Emily gazed into the depths of the pool, speculating.

"Amanda never mentioned her will." Sarah turned away.

Emily saw the swan swimming right beneath them now, drops of water glistening on its snowy white feathers. "How would Todd have felt if Amanda left her money to an orphanage?"

Sarah didn't answer for a moment. She started down the path. "Not happy," she said at last. "He has developed expensive tastes. The simple life would not appeal to him."

"Does he have money of his own?" Emily had to hurry to keep up with Sarah's long strides.

"He sells insurance. Todd didn't want to be seen as a kept man, but truth be told, he doesn't work too hard."

"I had a feeling this priest didn't like Todd very much. He seemed lukewarm when I gushed about the happiness of their marriage. I was hoping he'd either join in or say, 'Hell, no, you've got it all wrong.' Sadly, he took a circumspect, middle-of-the-road approach."

"You couldn't expect him to gossip without restraint about his parishioners."

"I suppose not. So tell me about the crumpet, the woman dusting bits of fluff from Todd's tuxedo at the Charity Ball."

"Oh *her*." Sarah stopped and looked at Emily with narrowed eyes. "Heather was batting her mascaraed eyes and flirting. But Amanda must have had another reason to suspect that Todd was seeing her because she charged right up to them on fairly flimsy evidence. She was furious. Not her usual reserved self. Her face was extremely pale and her hands were trembling. Amanda whispered, but I was standing right there and couldn't help but hear. 'Todd, you son of a bitch, couldn't you have the decency to keep your trollop away from me and our friends? Aren't there enough sleazy motels for you?' Then she rushed away. I never saw her again."

Sarah's eyes filled with tears. She turned away and started to walk rapidly down the path. Emily followed.

"It was a most unpleasant scene," Sarah said, her voice tight and controlled now.

"It must have been," Emily sympathized.

"Todd was absolutely amazed to be found out. He stood there stunned for a moment. Then he said, 'I have to find her,' and rushed after Amanda, pushing his way through the crowd. I don't know if he ever found her. He says he didn't."

"No wonder the police suspect him."

"Todd isn't serious about this girl. Flirting is an automatic reflex for him."

"I suppose others overheard them."

"Maybe. Amanda only said a few words, but she sounded very angry. From the police point of view, a couple quarrel, then the wife is found dead, so the husband's the obvious suspect. The police questioned Todd again today. They don't like to think the killer could be a stranger, some maniac who could start terrorizing tourists on the beach."

"Yet that is the most likely scenario," Emily said.

"Of course. It's the only reasonable explanation. Todd would never hurt Amanda." Sarah was walking so quickly now that Emily was forced into a quick trot.

"Todd really didn't have a motive," Emily said, noticing Sarah's distress. "I suppose the police will think of the money but even if they had divorced, Todd would have ended up with a good deal." Emily sighed. She knew that for many people "a good deal" was not nearly enough. She wondered if Todd were one of those people.

"Todd didn't want a divorce. Certainly not for Heather." Sarah frowned ferociously, a look that had cowed many an opposing team.

They walked for a few minutes in silence and then stopped by willow trees drooping over the pond and watched a mock battle of saffron-robed monks practicing Kung Fu. The monks' white stockinged feet jabbed out in sharp kicks, their elbows were raised to fend off blows. Emily snapped a few photographs to illustrate her article then tucked her camera back in her beach bag.

Emily could see why Amanda had been attracted to Todd...for a while. But would such a physical attraction last a lifetime? Maybe Amanda was ready to dump him even before she discovered his infidelity. The scene at the party could have been the final push she needed.

"When Todd flirted with her, the silly girl thought it meant something," Sarah said. "She didn't know him very well."

Emily was surprised at the sudden bitterness in her voice. "So the Crumpet encouraged him and one thing led to another?" Emily prompted.

"Exactly. Poor Todd. He would never hurt a soul. At least, not intentionally. And now he's the prime suspect."

Sarah sounded ready to defend Todd against all comers. Emily wondered if Sarah ever doubted his innocence. Maybe not. It would be difficult to believe a good friend was guilty of murder. After all, Sarah and Brent had known Todd ever since college. He'd been to their home for dinner countless times. They'd gone to the movies together, out for drinks.

"I think the killer is a robber who tried to cover his

tracks by dragging Amanda to a distant location," Sarah said as if overhearing her thoughts. "The simplest explanation is usually the correct one."

It did not sound simple to Emily, but she did not say so, nor did she remind Sarah there had been no robbery. They walked on in silence for a while, then stopped to watch a peacock display its magnificent royal blue fan, then march away, lifting its feet deliberately as if it were in a procession.

"How far away is Puu O Mahuka Heiau?" Emily asked. She meant the place where Amanda's body had been found.

"It's quite a way up the north shore," Sarah said, looking at her with apprehension. "You don't want to go there, do you?"

"Not today. Not if it's far. I really do have to finish my article."

"I want to see where she died, but not quite yet," Sarah said, taking a deep breath. "Maybe another day." She started down the footbridge to the parking lot.

CHAPTER 6

As Emily and Sarah walked across the arched footbridge back to the parking lot, Sarah seemed lost in thought. When they reached the van, she stood, jingling the keys in her hand, looking back toward the Byodo Inn Temple. "When I talked to Todd this morning, he sounded desperately unhappy," she said. "I'm worried about him." She turned to Emily. "Why don't we just pop in and say hello? We have to drive right by his house on the way back anyway." Without waiting for an answer, Sarah clicked the automatic opener and reached for the car door handle.

"Don't you think we should call first?" Emily asked, climbing up into the Jeep Cherokee.

"Not really. This morning when I offered to come by, Todd told me he's too depressed to have visitors, but if we just show up...." Sarah turned the key in the engine.

"Maybe," Emily said doubtfully. "Miss Manners would advise us not to drop in without an invitation though."

Sarah ignored Emily's advice. After driving for an hour along the coast, she turned into a driveway under a canopy of palm trees and continued for nearly a mile before she reached Amanda and Todd's house. She parked in the circular driveway, then headed toward the front door. Emily lagged behind, making it clear that this was not her idea.

Sarah pressed the doorbell. "No answer," she called to Emily.

"Well, we tried," Emily said.

"I wonder if he's in there, all alone, too depressed to answer the door."

"Maybe he wants to be alone," Emily suggested. She stood by the van, one hand on the door. Sarah might know him well enough to barge in, but Emily felt awkward.

Sarah pressed the bell more forcefully.

"Come on, let's go," Emily said. She walked over to Sarah. "It's getting late. I have to work on my article."

Then the lock turned. Todd opened the door a crack. His face was unshaven, glistening with sweat. He was wearing gray shorts and a towel slung over his bare shoulders.

Panting slightly, he attempted a smile. "What a nice surprise. I was working out."

"Wonderful," Sarah said brightly. "So good for you. We don't want to interrupt. We found ourselves in the neighborhood and wanted to see if there was anything we could do."

"How kind." Todd reached forward and took Sarah's hand and squeezed it. He beamed at Emily. "I haven't had a chance to shower yet," he said, gasping for breath. Sweat beaded the hair on his bare chest. "You'll have to forgive me for not inviting you in."

"Todd, who is it?" A woman's voice rang out. Emily heard pounding footsteps.

In a sudden reflex, Todd started to close the door, Sarah firmly pushed it open.

An extremely tall young woman in a shiny pink two-piece exercise outfit stood before them. She held huge metal bar bells in each hand. Emily saw that the weights were much heavier than the five-pound pink ones she had bought with the firm intention of using regularly. This woman had ventured into the realm of plain metal weights that men lift, very strong men.

"Hi, Sarah," the woman said, waving at her with one barbell. Dimples appeared in her lean angular face.

Todd flung the door open and stood aside. "Come in, come in. Emily, I'd like you to meet my business associate, Heather Fielding."

"Hello," Emily said, examining the buff young woman with keen interest. Her short blonde hair had been brushed up into a tall wavy crew cut. Her eyes were brilliant blue, her eyelashes long and black, her lips vibrant red. How on earth could she keep her makeup in such minty-fresh condition while working out?

"Heather was kind enough to drop by with some paperwork from the office. She had her workout clothes with her so we decided to use the exercise room." Todd's voice came in gasps.

Sarah was staring at the young woman with ill-concealed horror. She did not say a word.

Heather's cheery voice piped up. "When someone is depressed? Well, I think exercise can really help." She gazed fondly at Todd and set down her barbells. "I talked him into it."

"We won't keep you. We'll stop by another time," Emily said. "So nice to meet you..." She just stopped herself from adding, "Crumpet."

Outside the door, Sarah began to seethe. "You'd think he'd have the decency to wait...at least a week."

"You think he's pursuing more than physical fitness with this young woman?"

"Please." Sarah strode forward, her jaw set.

"I didn't realize the Crumpet was a business associate."

"Oh yes. Todd claims she's a computer whiz. He insisted that the Trust hire her. I believe he met her on a scuba diving expedition, not the place where most interviews are conducted. Poor Amanda. You see what she had to put up with."

Sarah climbed into the car and slammed the door. "Well, you were right, Emily. We should never have come."

"Alas, my wise advice was acknowledged too late," Emily said to Jack later that afternoon while they were lounging on the beach. She was sitting cross legged on her striped towel, typing her article about the Byodo Inn temple. She could hear the lap of waves, the cries of sea gulls. What a delightful place to work!

"Admit you wouldn't have missed meeting the Crumpet." Jack was stretched out beside her, leaning on one elbow, reading the *New England Journal of Medicine*.

"The encounter was as interesting as it was embarrassing. Perhaps Sarah is wrong about the Crumpet being just a quick fling for Todd. She seemed to be casting proprietorial glances and taking a keen interest in his health."

"He is insanely reckless to have this young woman in his house while he's under suspicion of murder," Jack said, glancing at Emily.

"Perhaps he had no choice. You should see how frighteningly fit she is."

"You imagine this woman just barged in and pressed her attentions on an unwilling Todd?"

"I suppose not," Emily admitted with a sigh. "Sarah was horrified," she added, remembering how Sarah had seethed in unapproachable silence all the way home.

"Not surprising when she's just found the husband of her best friend sporting with his mistress just days after her murder. Do you think Sarah suspects Todd did away with Amanda so he could be free to marry the Crumpet?"

"No, of course not. Sarah says his flirting doesn't mean a thing. When we were at the Byodo-In Temple she stoutly defended Todd and pitied him for being the number one suspect."

"And later?"

"She didn't say a word on the drive home."

"If she doesn't suspect him, why is she so upset? Jealous, do you suppose? Maybe she has a crush on Todd."

"No. No! You must be concealing *People Magazine* in your scholarly journal. It's filled your mind with suspicion."

"I saw Sarah casting Todd affectionate glances at dinner the other night. Didn't you notice?"

"Those were sympathetic glances," she said firmly.

Emily finished her notes. She set her laptop aside and rooted around in her beach bag for her books on the history of Hawaii. The historical perspective would interest her readers, or so she hoped, for it certainly interested her.

She read aloud to Jack, "Hawaii was discovered by Polynesians from the Marquesas Islands who sailed here in 80-foot-long canoes with sails, navigating only by the prevailing winds, ocean currents and stars. For hundreds of years, they lived in peace and harmony in *Havaiti,* which means "home in the sun" or "underworld." Take your pick*.*"

Looking out at coconut palms swaying beside the glittering turquoise sea, Emily reflected on how lucky the Polynesians were to find this beautiful place. She picked up a handful of warm sand and let the grains trickle between her fingers.

"So all was perfection? They were Rousseau's unspoiled natural man? And woman, of course."

"Not for long. Warlike people from Tahiti came, bringing fierce gods, human sacrifice and a rigid social hierarchy. They imposed a series of *kapus*, ranging from the *kapu* against murder to the *kapu* against allowing your shadow to fall on the chief's house, against women eating with men, eating the suggestively shaped banana, or even making a noise during religious ceremonies. Retribution for infractions was swift and terrible."

"Your readers don't want to hear such distressing history. Dwell on the beauty of the beach. Tell them to go to a luau."

"Not I. They are interested in the off-beat historical and human angle. It enriches their travel experience."

Emily heard her cell phone's muffled ring and delved into her beach bag. It was Sarah.

"I'm sorry I was rude. Hardly said a word all the way home. I don't know what I was thinking. Forgive me?"

"Heavens. No wonder you were upset," Emily sympathized.

"I overreacted. It wasn't Todd's fault. That pushy young woman insisted on coming in and doing her revolting exercises with him. He had no choice."

"So you've talked to Todd."

"He called me right away and explained everything. Heather has no sense of decency. She was terribly jealous of Amanda." Sarah sighed. "Anyway, I've called to make amends. Let's drive up the North Shore. We could stop at Puu O Mahuka Heiau."

"Are you sure? We don't have to do this."

"I want to see where Amanda was murdered." Sarah's voice trailed out. Emily could hear her ragged breathing.

Emily hung up the phone and turned to Jack. "Sarah's nerves are in tatters. She wants to go on an outing." She didn't want to distress him by mentioning that their destination was the murder site.

"Sarah has certainly latched onto you with a vengeance."

"It *is* a strain being her new best friend. Be prepared to fortify me with Mai Tais on my return."

"You can rely on me," Jack said.

Emily had to admit it was nice to have a driver. Sarah drove like the wind on their trip from Waikiki up the lush, green windward coast of the island. She stopped only once, veering into the parking lot of Onomalo Gardens.

"One simply cannot have too many orchids," Sarah said, jumping out of the van and striding eagerly toward the greenhouse. Emily followed. An incredible variety of orchids were displayed on long wooden benches.

"I love the ones with faces like pansies. So adorable." Sarah scooped up several plants.

Emily selected one for her mother and one for herself.

"Poor Todd," Sarah said, as she started the car. "The police are questioning him again today. Maybe because Heather pushed her way into his home yesterday. What if the police were watching the house?"

Emily felt sure they were. "You mentioned that she was jealous of Amanda," she said.

"Insanely. Amanda had Todd plus all the money in the world, plus that gorgeous home on the ocean. Now that Amanda's gone, the Crumpet can move in. Don't think she'll lose any time either!"

Sarah was grinding her teeth.

Emily realized that time had not calmed Sarah's anger, just shifted it from Todd to the Crumpet.

It was late afternoon before they came to the turnoff from the main road right by the fire station. Sarah drove uphill until they came to a sign pointing the way to Puu

O Mahuka Heiau. Turning sharply onto the unpaved red mud road, they continued to drive uphill. Sarah's powerful Jeep Cherokee struggled up steep hairpin turns, churning through slippery mud to the top of a high bluff.

Sarah parked in the deserted lot and then she and Emily climbed out onto the windswept summit. Emily had read that the ruins of three sacred rock terraces made up the Puu O Mahuka Heiau, a sacred site. Otherwise she would never have realized that the lava rocks arranged in a rectangle were the remains of a temple.

She and Sarah strolled along the outside edge of the black rocks.

"It doesn't look much like a temple, but people still leave offerings to the ancient gods," Sarah said.

"The old religion seems pretty grim. Why would anyone want to revive it?"

"They haven't revived the *kapus* and human sacrifices obviously. But the native people want to preserve their sense of identity and their old myths. Kari's boyfriend Matt has really gotten her interested in the old religion."

Emily resolved to talk to Kari. Her interest in Hawaii's history could provide a fund of useful information. Emily walked through tall grass to the edge of the bluff and looked down. Tawny mele grass was waving in the wind and down below, ocean waves beat on the rocks of Waimea Bay. Emily could see for miles. Lava cliffs, lush green growth, the blue expanse of ocean. Dark clouds moved across the sky, casting a pattern of shadows on the green hills.

Sarah had already turned away and was walking slowly toward a bamboo structure at the end of the heaiu that was cordoned off with yellow police tape.

Suddenly filled with dread, Emily followed her. Pineapples, bananas and shells were piled on a bamboo table and heaped on the ground beneath. Someone had disregarded the police tape.

"This must be where Amanda's body was found. Here under the altar." Sarah's voice quavered.

"Why would anyone bring her to this strange, wild place to kill her?" Emily asked.

"Maybe it has some symbolic meaning to the killer. Long ago this was the site of human sacrifices. Three English sailors were sacrificed here in the 1700s. It was called the "hill of escape" but not too many managed to escape."

Amanda certainly didn't, Emily thought. She shuddered.

"Let's get out of here," Sarah said.

Back at Sarah's house, Emily refused the offer of lemonade, insisting that she needed to start working on her article. As she drove away from the house, she saw Kari wearing loose gym shorts and a black sports bra jogging down the road toward the house. The girl stopped by the side of the road and flagged her down. Panting slightly, Kari leaned in the car window. Sweat beaded her forehead and upper lip. Her dark hair was wound in a knot at the back of her head.

"I'd like to talk to you sometime. If that's okay." Kari seemed considerably less aggressive than she had in their last encounter, almost diffident.

"Of course, I'd like that very much, Kari. Your mother and I were talking about going to Diamond Head. Would you like to join us?"

"No." She was slightly out of breath. "I could meet you somewhere. Alone."

"Sure. What about Senator Fong's Garden. I'm planning to go there to take notes for my article."

Emily set a time to meet on Thursday afternoon and continued on to the house. Why would Kari want to meet her alone? She remembered how the girl had stared at her after the funeral and how her boyfriend had dragged her away. Emily realized she was being sucked into the mystery of Amanda's death, fulfilling George's worst fears that she would be diverted from duty. But setting a date to meet Kari that was a few days in the future assuaged her guilt. By Thursday she would have practically finished her articles and be putting on the finishing touches. Besides, Sarah had said that Kari was passionately interested in the cultural history of the islands, including the ancient religion. Kari could tell her about Hawaiian traditions, the current revival of interest in native crafts and dance. Just what she needed for her article. What a relief when duty and inclination coincide!

CHAPTER 7

On the sandy beach before the Sheraton Hotel, Emily sat making notes for her article, feeling pleased with herself for hewing virtuously to a stern work ethic. She resolved not to let thoughts of Amanda disturb her concentration. Jack was lounging beside her, no doubt eager to be instructed further about the history of the Hawaiian Islands.

"Hawaii was a feudal society before the missionaries came," Emily informed him.

"Hmmm." Jack's eyes were closed.

"Hawaiians had no concept of owning property. They believed that the land belonged to the gods and was held in trust by the royalty. Common people grew crops and turned over part of their harvest to the chiefs."

"Traveling with you is an education in itself," Jack said. "How was your outing with Sarah yesterday?"

Jack had gone to a dinner meeting the previous night so Emily had not had a chance to tell him about her trip to the murder site. She decided to work up to it gradually. It was bound to distress him.

"Excellent. First we stopped at Onomalo Gardens and I bought an orchid for mother. All the flowers were glorious. One smelled exactly like chocolate but then I thought of the constant temptation it would arouse. Mother is always on some sort of diet. Finally I picked a pale blue Vanna orchid just beginning to bloom, one for me and one for Mom."

"Did the poor little plants shrink away from you in terror? I can hear them begging, 'No, no, don't choose me. Please don't take me to icy Minnesota."

"I will coddle them. They'll have a lovely sunny window and lots of special orchid fertilizer."

"At first," Jack said ominously.

"If you had seen them with your own eyes you would realize how I couldn't resist."

"Was this the end of your shopping adventures or are there more packages winging their way toward Minnesota?"

"That is the only one so far but, of course, one must have souvenirs. And my readers will want to know where to buy them. Maybe we should walk down the beach to the Royal Hawaiian gift shop."

"You're awfully ambitious." Jack closed his eyes. The sun was having a soporific effect.

Emily decided to startle him awake. "After we bought the orchids, Sarah and I visited the place where Amanda's body was found."

Jack sat bolt upright. "Why on earth?"

"Puu O Mahuka Heiau. It's only a half day drive up the coast but it's incredibly wild and primitive. It amazes me that on this island, filled with tourists and high-rises, you don't have to drive far to be in a remote tropical land. Luckily we were in Sarah's Jeep Cherokee. I can't imagine any vehicle that doesn't have four-wheel drive making it to the summit."

"Why would the murderer drag Amanda up there to kill her?" Jack asked.

"Maybe it has some symbolic meaning."

"If it does, the police will figure it out. Isn't the murder site blocked off?"

"Not now. Only the area around the altar itself is bound by yellow tape."

"You didn't go there expecting to notice a clue that

the police had overlooked, did you?"

"Of course not. That's a job for competent forensic experts."

"It certainly is."

"The police must know more than they're revealing to the public. It would have been very difficult for the killer to go there without leaving a trace. There must have been tire tracks and foot prints left in the red mud."

Emily heard the insistent ringing of her cell phone and grabbed for her beach bag.

It was Todd. "Emily, I'm so sorry I didn't invite you in yesterday. After working out, I badly needed a shower, but I felt terrible, turning you away."

"Oh we didn't mean to come in. We just wanted to stop by and see how you were." Emily wanted to add that it was all Sarah's idea.

"How kind. Look, Emily, the reason I called is that I have something to show you. Amanda had set aside some documents for you. Do you think you could stop by this afternoon?"

"Sure, I think so," Emily said slowly, thinking about all the writing she had to do, plus her scheduled meeting with Kari on Thursday. Still, these documents might be the ones Amanda mentioned in her letter. Emily set a time to meet Todd and dropped the phone on the towel beside her.

"That was Todd. He wants me to stop over."

"I thought you were planning to write your article this morning."

"I am. There'll be plenty of time. Todd has the documents that Amanda wanted to show me. After I see him, I'll set my shoulder to the wheel."

"Did I mention that George called again?" Jack asked with a hint of reproof in his voice.

"I saw his message and guilt began to gnaw. But Todd is bereaved so it's a work of mercy to visit him."

"Not too bereaved to exercise with scantily clad young women."

"It won't take long. Besides these documents could very well shed light on the decision Amanda had to make. I can't help thinking her dilemma might have some bearing on this investigation."

"Then tell the police."

"Therein lies the difficulty. I have nothing to tell them. Only a feeling that if I can figure out what Amanda wanted to ask me, I would have a real clue."

"Humph."

Jack slumped back on the sand.

"It's a friend's last request. I can't ignore it. Amanda was relying on me."

"You are easily flattered, even by a voice from beyond the grave."

After making a good start on her article, Emily showered and changed, ready for a much needed break.

Todd's housekeeper opened the door and showed her onto the lanai where Todd was basking in the sun. He jumped to his feet and crushed Emily in a hug, enveloping her in the scent of his manly aftershave.

"Todd, I'm so sorry about Amanda," Emily said, drawing back, looking into his eyes.

"Amanda was looking forward to your visit. She thought the world of you."

Emily knew he was exaggerating, but she was touched all the same. Todd led her into the house.

Sun flooded though the window, backlighting his hair, bleached blonde by the sun. Or did he dye it? Somehow this seemed vain in a man, although very few women would leave their hair to Mother Nature's mercy.

Emily recalled how Todd had looked at Spring Prom their senior year. He had been spectacularly handsome in his tux, confident and smiling. Amanda had clung to his arm, her eyes glowing with happiness.

Why had serious, studious Amanda been so attracted to a boy whose favorite pastime was drinking beer with his buddies? Was it because she had been flattered by his attention? Amanda's low-key manner hadn't attracted many admirers. Emily wondered if she had been seriously depressed so far away from home.

Todd slumped into a chair. He looked exhausted. "Can I get you something to drink? It's awfully hot in here."

"No, no I'm fine."

"The week before she died, Amanda talked about you a lot, Emily. She was remembering old college days. Surprising really. She didn't seem to enjoy college much at the time."

"No, she didn't but when Amanda came to the reunion we had a chance to talk more than we ever did in college. She regretted that she hadn't made more of an effort to be happy and to make friends. At the time, four years seemed endless to Amanda, but looking back, knowing she would return to Hawaii, she thought her time at Wells could have been an interesting, maybe even a delightful interlude in her life. Of course, it wasn't. But she met you at college. And she said that made it all worthwhile, casting a golden light on all the sad days that had gone before."

Todd grinned at her and Emily saw that he was still a charmer. "Amanda was a sweet woman and we were happy together, confounding our friends." He gave her a sly, amused look.

"Amanda was kind enough to write back quickly when I let her know I was coming to Hawaii on business," Emily said. "She was particularly eager to see me and talk about a decision she had to make, one that could affect everyone she loved."

"That sounds like Amanda. She took everything seriously. She was not a light or playful person. But of course that was one of her charms. You could always count on her good sense. I relied on her completely."

"Do you know what the decision was?"

"I have no idea," he said quickly, looking away.

Emily didn't believe him.

"It doesn't matter anymore," Todd said. "She's past making decisions." His lip trembled.

Emily didn't know how to comfort him. "This must be terrible for you."

Todd leaned toward Emily, his hands clasped on his knees, his blue eyes filled with tears. "I've gone over that night so many times. Is there anything I could have done differently? Anything that could have prevented her death?"

Keeping your pants zipped might have helped, Emily was tempted to say. If there had been no confrontation about the Crumpet, who was here lifting barbells with Todd only yesterday, Amanda would not have fled the party and become an easy mark for the killer. Emily charitably did not mention this. Todd seemed genuinely heartbroken.

"She just mysteriously disappeared from the party, didn't she?" Emily asked.

"Yes. She left pretty early in the evening. When I saw her go, I followed her and looked around the lobby. When I didn't see her, I went back to the ballroom, thinking she'd return in a few minutes." His voice trailed away, he bit his lower lip.

"You couldn't have known," Emily comforted him.

"No, I thought she'd turn up. Then at the end of the evening, I looked all over for her. I thought maybe she'd taken our car and gone home by herself."

"I wonder why she would do that," Emily said, hoping he would give his version of the quarrel.

"She might have felt ill, or maybe was just tired and couldn't find me in the crowd to tell me so."

"That doesn't sound like Amanda unless she's changed quite a bit."

"No, but it was the only explanation I could come up with."

"You must have started to worry when you saw your car still in the parking lot," Emily said.

"I figured she must have taken a cab."

"Sure, I suppose that makes sense," Emily lied. "Then when you found Amanda wasn't at home you must have been really concerned."

"I was. I didn't know what to make of it." Todd stood up.

"Look, Emily, the reason I asked you to come over is I have something to show you. I was sorting through Amanda's belongings and found some things she'd set out, thinking you two could talk about them."

Emily realized she'd been pushing too hard, letting her curiosity get the better of her. "Good, I'd like to see them."

Todd went to a desk in the corner and returned with a manila envelope. Emily was surprised that he was so quick to start clearing out Amanda's personal effects. Was the Crumpet waiting in the wings, ready to move in, as Sarah had suggested?

"Amanda had set out these old family documents to show you when you came. I suppose they have some historic value. They should probably go to a museum. We never had children to give our family documents. We kept putting it off. I thought we had all the time in the world." Todd passed a hand over his face and turned away.

"I'll be glad to look at them, although I'm no historian," she said, opening the envelope. Perhaps the decision Amanda faced had been how to dispose of family memorabilia. It was a curiously deflating thought.

"You are kind to lend them to me. Do you have any idea why Amanda wanted to show them to me?"

"She wanted you to understand why she started the Trust and how much it meant to her. Amanda's ancestors came to Hawaii as missionaries, then made some shrewd land investments and planted sugar cane. 'They came to do good, and ended up doing very well indeed,' as some clever man said. Good for them, I say, but Amanda was an overly scrupulous person. For some reason, she felt guilty about her family's prosperity. That's why she set up the Trust."

"You didn't like the idea of the Trust, did you?"

"Why do you say that?"

Emily did not want to admit that Sarah had told her that Todd had tried to talk Amanda out of setting it up. "Your tone of voice," she said.

"That's very insightful of you."

"So why did you disapprove of the Trust?" Emily persisted.

"I didn't disapprove. It was Amanda's money. But I didn't see any reason to be ashamed of being wealthy. Then lately, the Trust has given her nothing but trouble. Amanda refused a grant request from people who she thought were a little too radical and they turned on her. Very rude. Especially considering how generous she's always been."

Emily wondered if the rejected fund seekers could have been resentful enough to kill. "Who were they? Do you know?"

"I'm sure their names are in the files somewhere. I don't remember them."

"Did you tell the police?"

"No, it didn't seem important. Hardly a motive for murder if that's what you're thinking. People are turned down for grants all the time. Come to think of it though, one of those guys was quoted in the newspapers as a spokesperson for the crackpots who practice the old religion. He was indignant about having Amanda's body placed at their so-called temple." Todd's voice faltered and he turned away. "Maybe I should tell the police about it. It would give them someone besides me to focus on."

Emily picked up the envelope. Printed on top was the word, "Pro." Emily used this same technique. When faced with a decision, she made two lists, one labelled "pro" and the other "con." Where was the list of cons? Emily wondered.

CHAPTER 8

Emily burst into the hotel room. "Look what Todd gave me. Old letters from Amanda's family."

A slightly damp and sandy Jack looked up from rummaging in his suitcase. He wore swim trunks and had a towel slung over his shoulders.

"We have boxes of letters from your own family in our attic. Why do you want more?"

"If Amanda set these letters aside to show me, they must be significant."

"Isn't it odd that Todd would give you important family documents?"

"He knew Amanda wanted to show them to me and now her wishes have all the force of a deathbed request. He was kind to lend them all the same."

"So you had a pleasant visit and your suspicions of Todd have been put to rest?"

"I never suspected him. You did."

"Why not? He has a motive. His rich wife was furious and possibly thinking of divorcing him. He may well have reasoned: best to kill her now before the rift becomes common knowledge. It would be unwise to wait until divorce lawyers were at work and the inevitable 'Enraged Husband Slays Estranged Wife' headline was likely to appear."

"I can't see him as a killer. I know what you're thinking. I never knew Todd well and haven't seen him for years. But you should see how sad and broken he is now."

"If Todd wanted an easy ride through life, he certainly got it by marrying Amanda. He dabbles in selling insurance, doesn't he? But just working hard enough to say he has a job. Not desperately scrambling like so many of his colleagues."

"Lack of ambition and an eye to the main chance don't a murderer make."

"No, but I wouldn't rule him out."

"Poor Todd. Did you notice how eager Brent was to discredit his alleged best friend the other night?"

"I did. A kinder man would have allowed the memory of his friend's youthful remarks to be forgotten."

"Yet Brent, despite the clear disapproval of his wife, was ready to dredge up this discreditable college tale. Why?"

"Police questioning may have made him nervous," Jack suggested.

"Or maybe the rift between Brent and Todd that Sarah mentioned hasn't healed. Brent helped Amanda set up the Trust and Todd was an unwilling partner. Sarah says that Todd was completely won over once it got going, but I wonder. He didn't seem madly enthusiastic. Perhaps there's been tension between them for years and now Amanda's murder has brought it into the open."

"Anything is possible. I'm going to take a quick shower and then we can go to dinner."

"I'll wait for you by the pool."

Emily settled into a lounge chair by the shimmering turquoise pool. She shook the letters out of the envelope marked "Pro." The missing "Con" still troubled her. Where was the other side of the story?

Emily untied the ribbon binding together a stack of letters. The first one had a note in Amanda's handwriting clipped to it: My great great great grandmother Hannah Goodhue who came to Hawaii with her husband Hiram. With growing excitement Emily began to read a letter dated 1820, Sandwich Islands. It was difficult to decipher the tiny, florid script but she bent eagerly to the task.

Dear Mother,

You can't imagine how different Hawaii is from Boston. The sun shines every day, and flowers bloom in great abundance. Truly God has smiled on these lovely islands.

When our ship arrived, natives, bedecked with flowers, came out to greet us, paddling outrigger canoes and singing. After they clambered on board our ship, one woman smiled at me and tossed a garland over my head.

You will be shocked to hear, dear mother, how often these innocent children of God, who have never heard His Word, sport in the sea without benefit of more than a few scraps of cloth made from Tapa, a pounded bark. I regret to say it dissolves in water and since they spend much of their time splashing in the waves, you can imagine the results. Modesty is unknown.

Truly we are needed here to do God's work. But I am often homesick for you and my own familiar life. Hiram tells me this is a woman's weakness and I should pray for strength. Of course, he is right and I know how much we are needed.

We are living in a thatched hut with just one room, no real furniture. Grass and mats cover the dirt floor and we are using trunks and chests as our tables and chairs. Hiram says not to fret

for we will build a real house. Hoping you and my dear little sister Anne are well,
I am your loving daughter, Hannah.

Emily glanced out at the pool, darkening now to twilight. Poor Hannah. Maybe she should have just dug in her heels and said no to Hiram. Hannah's voice sounded a bit like Amanda's. Emily could imagine Amanda acting the same way in the same situation, doing her duty as she saw it. The sun was beginning its rosy descent into the ocean. She reached for another letter, then jumped when she felt Jack's hand on her shoulder.

"Jack, this is perfectly fascinating."

"You can tell me all about it at dinner. It won't do to let hunger and thirst dull your mind. Let's go to the harbor and eat delicious seafood."

After dinner, Emily and Jack stood on the pier, admiring the Falls of Clyde, a ship whose four tall masts were silhouetted against the starry sky. Its figurehead was a woman with flowing hair, wearing a long nineteenth century style dress. Her expression looked grimly determined as she leaned straight out from the ship's bow over the ocean.

Traveler's Tip: Step back in time and discover Hawaii's nautical history. For one admission ticket, you can tour the Falls of Clyde and the ancient Polynesian craft, the Hokulea. While you're on the Pier, stop by the Hawaii Maritime Center and check out the exhibit on surfboarding.

"When Hannah wrote her letters home to Boston, sailing ships like this were carrying sugar across the Pacific to San Francisco," Emily said.

"An afternoon sailing on Lake Superior is enough of a nautical adventure for me," Jack said. "Imagine being confined for months, eating foul food, braving monstrous waves."

"But after their long voyage, the travelers arrived in Paradise," Emily said.

"Do you suppose the missionaries recognized their good fortune?"

"Maybe not. They bundled up in dresses suitable for a cool day in Boston. They must have been very uncomfortable."

"They soon had the Hawaiians bundled up as well, teaching them to be ashamed of their bodies and to wear shapeless muumuus that reached their toes."

"A lesson that has been unlearned through the ages. Did you notice the skimpy bikinis on the beach?"

"No, I didn't."

"Liar. Your eyes were starting from your head like those of a man amazed."

Jack grinned, took her hand and they walked the length of the pier. Emily drew in the smell of salt sea, listened to the clanking sounds of the yacht's rigging. The warm humid breeze felt soothing and caressing.

Under the lights of the pier, a double-hulled canoe rocked gently in the murky water of the harbor. Emily recognized the craft as the Hokulea, a replica of the kind of boat that had carried the Polynesian people here.

Back in the hotel room, Emily sat cross-legged on the bed and pulled out another letter. It was difficult to decipher, the writing in brown ink was small and cramped; people made use of every inch of paper in those days.

"Jack, listen to this."

"My closed eyes indicate rapt attention."

> *Dear Mother, God's hand is clearly visible in the timing of our arrival. Had we landed a year earlier I fear we would have been turned away*

for the people were in the grip of pagan superstition. You will wonder how this could have changed so rapidly and so much to the advantage of God's ministers.

It was all because Queen Dowager Kaahumanu wanted to end the tapus such as the one that forbade women from eating with men. She saw her chance when her husband died and left the kingdom to his son Liholiho, a dissolute youth who has five wives, two of them his sisters. Shocking indeed! The dowager waited until he was quite drunk–I'm sorry to say it was not a rare occurrence–and then talked him into sitting by her and some other women and eating the same food out of the same vessels. Such panic! Everyone was sure the pagan gods would strike him down but, of course, nothing happened.

The tapu was broken! The people saw their pagan beliefs revealed as a sham. The chiefs went on a rampage and smashed all the heathen idols. This left an emptiness of heart among these people that made way for our good work.

I can hear Hiram at the door and must conclude this letter for now.

All my love, Hannah.

"I wonder how Amanda felt about the missionaries," Emily said. Did she think they brought God's word, or that they imposed their own beliefs on people whose way of looking at the world was just different?" Emily let the letter fall to her lap. "Todd thinks that the very religion that was brought down in a clatter of smashed idols so long ago is being resurrected. He suspects a group he called "radical" of giving Amanda a native burial. These people were refused a funding grant and their leaders were extremely rude to Amanda. Todd suspects them of killing her."

"If everyone who was denied funding committed murder, the streets would be littered with slaughtered victims."

He reached out to her. "Tell me more about the sexual practices of the ancient Hawaiians."

CHAPTER 9

The next morning Emily and Jack ate breakfast in a small diner that offered an early-bird special of eggs, pancakes and bacon.

"George called bright and early this morning," Emily said as she poured coconut syrup onto her pineapple pancakes. "He demands action and adventure. 'Nobody wants to lie on the beach all day,' he told me. Well, George is sadly mistaken. Lots of people are perfectly content on the beach. Nevertheless, I shall seek out adventure and put aside the rest of Amanda's letters until later."

"What do you have in mind?" Jack asked. He leaned back in the booth and let his fork rest on his plate, his sunny-side-up eggs still untasted.

"Surf board. The ancient sport of Hawaiian kings. Skim down the waves."

"Just don't drown." Jack resumed eating.

"I have no intention of drowning," Emily answered quickly. But the grim picture that his words suggested lingered unpleasantly in her mind. Despite her love of the water, Emily was not a powerful, long-distance swimmer.

"Maybe I'll try wind sailing instead," Emily said. "At least there's something to hang onto, and if you go down, the life guard can find you because your lifeless hands are clinging to a brightly colored sail."

"There you go."

"Sarah suggested I take a lesson at that place where Matt teaches."

"Matt?"

"He's Kari's boyfriend. I think I'll wander over there." She took a bite of pancake and savored the lovely combination of pineapple and coconut.

After breakfast, Emily changed into her swimsuit, threw on a beach robe, and drove to the sailboard rental shop near Canoes' Surf, an easy break where the ancient Hawaiians' heavy old *koa* canoes once rode the gentle waves.

A lanky boy with beige dreadlocks lounged in a canvas chair in front of the thatched roofed hut. He was wearing cut-off blue jeans and an orange tank top, drinking Coke.

"Hey what's up?" He looked up at her, squinting into the sun. His green eyes seemed pale in his tan face roughened with blonde stubble.

"I'd like to learn how to wind sail." Emily looked around at the boards racked on the wall of the hut, the colorful sails leaning in the corner. She hoped to see a more reliable looking teacher emerge from somewhere but she feared she was out of luck.

"Have you ever tried windsailing?" The boy's skeptical grin was not flattering. He stood up and tossed his Coke can in the bin.

Emily straightened herself up to her full height of five feet, five inches. "Not exactly."

"How long are you going to be in Waikiki?" The boy unwrapped a stick of gum and popped it in his mouth.

"Another week."

"Plan to get in a fair amount of wind sailing, do you?"

"No, no. I only have time to do it today."

He snorted. "What! Man, you're a hoot. You can't learn that fast." He was chewing his gum rapidly.

"I believe I might be able to pick it up. The basics anyway." Emily looked out to sea where brightly colored wind sails soared among the waves. It looked easy enough. Perhaps he had mistaken her for a wimp. He did not realize that her body had been tuned up by Pilates and tennis.

"It's hard to learn in just one day on your vacation," the boy explained kindly. "Lots of tourists think they can do it. Then they're disappointed. You have to practice. A lot." He shifted his gum to the other side.

"Let's just give it a whirl," Emily said firmly, even though her confidence was oozing away by the minute. "I suppose you're the instructor? You're not just minding the store for someone else?"

"Yup. I'm your man. I'm Greg."

"Doesn't Matt work here?"

"Yeah, sure, just not today. You know Matt, huh?"

"Sort of."

Greg went over to the cash register and grabbed a clip board that was hanging on a hook beside it. "Now you'll need to pay first and sign the disclaimer. You have to understand that if you're blown out to sea it's totally not my fault." He handed her the clip board with a document in triplicate with a series of single spaced, bulleted warnings of everything that could conceivably go wrong, followed by a place for her signature.

Emily signed her name quickly, not wanting to read the fine print and find out what a bad idea this really was.

"That's just a formality, right?"

"In a way. The only danger is if the wind were to shift to offshore and you got carried off to sea. But don't worry, we've got a nice steady onshore wind going for us right now." He wet his finger and lifted it. "See, you can check it out for yourself; the wind's blowing straight toward the beach."

As if winds didn't switch around all the time! Emily gave Greg her credit card. Of course he wanted to be paid in advance; you can't present a bill to a waterlogged corpse.

"This board should be about right for you. Tuck it under your arm. Follow me."

When they had hauled their gear to the shore, Greg launched his board into the water and leapt up on it, rocking back and forth. "Just get up and get the feel of your board. Like this."

Emily shoved her board into the water, grabbed it, put one foot up and tried to hoist herself to her feet. The board shot forward and she splashed into the water on the other side. "I don't quite have the feel of it yet."

"Up you go again." Greg stood straight and tall, rocking just slightly as if it were easy.

On her fifth try, Emily managed to wobble to her feet and crouch for a minute wobbling on her board.

"Okay now grab the rope, bend your knees, and lean back," Greg yelled. "Use your weight to get the sail up out of the water."

For the first time, Emily wished she had more weight for leverage. She hauled on the rope. Finally to her astonishment, the sail rose rapidly toward her, her board shot forward and Emily slid off. The sail came crashing down on top of her. Emily dived down and swam out from under it. She held onto her board, resting. *Perhaps I'm not going to skim gracefully up and down the waves in the manner of the ancient Hawaiian kings,* Emily thought. She composed a traveler's trip.

Don't wait until you come to Hawaii to learn how to wind sail. Start lifting hand weights right now. Build up those muscles! Eat a raspberry chocolate chip ice cream cone at Sebastian Joe's to give you more leverage. Then go down to Lake Harriet and take lessons. Lots of lessons. On a quiet lake where you will not be blown out to sea and end up in a watery grave.

Emily looked out to sea where a man and a woman were swooping on their surfboards, joyously riding the waves. The woman in a tiny black bikini leapt in the air and did a flip, soaring down in the spray of the wave. Emily could hear her yell, "Wahooo!" The man was laughing. He was right behind her.

It did look easy. But even with a sail to hold onto Emily knew it wasn't.

She didn't give up until her hour had mercifully come to an end. But her dream of soaring off, riding the waves would have to be deferred until another trip.

Emily hauled her board back up the beach to the hut. She looked back and saw the two surfers she had so admired wading to shore. They seemed strangely familiar. Emily wiped the water out of her eyes and looked again. It was Todd and the Crumpet.

Todd was staring away from Emily, as if he were planning to walk on by pretending he hadn't seen her. But the Crumpet called out in a cheery voice, "Hi, Emily. I noticed you trying to get up on your board."

Grrrr, Emily thought. She walked toward them. "Hi, Todd. Hi…Heather." It had taken a moment to remember the Crumpet's real name.

"Emily, what a nice surprise," Todd said, his blue eyes crinkling as he grinned. "Wind surfing's not as easy as it looks, is it?"

"No," Emily said. "You both looked terrific out there."

She noticed the Crumpet's rippling muscles, gleaming with sunscreen. No wonder she could flip around like that. The girl was clearly as strong as an ox. She was wearing a skimpy black bikini revealing her abs of steel. And a navel ring! Good lord. Fascinated, Emily found herself staring at the woman's midriff.

Heather began to speak in her peculiar interrogative style. "Todd didn't feel up to it? But then I told him that surf boarding was the best thing for him. It clears away the cobwebs, helps you cope." She looked at Todd with sympathy. "It's so important for friends to be there for him right now, don't you think?" Her warm gaze included Emily as one of those who should rally round.

"She talked me into it." Todd shrugged and flashed his boyish grin. "We've got to get going. Look at the time." He took the Crumpet by one arm and headed for the parking lot.

"Don't give up, Emily. You were making real progress," the Crumpet called back, turning to waggle her red fingernails in a friendly wave. "You'll be in deep water in no time."

Emily sighed.

"At least you kept at it," Greg said. "Not everyone does, you know." He was putting away their rig.

Emily handed him a good tip even though his attitude had not always been tip top. Then she fed quarters into the Coke machine. She definitely needed a cold drink.

Emily sat down cross legged in the sand and took a long swig of Coke. "I'm exhausted. I'm just going to sit here for a few minutes and recover. Do you mind?" Emily didn't really care if he minded. She wanted to lie flat and moan.

"Naw, go ahead." Greg grabbed a PowerAde from a cooler.

Emily wondered if she should be stoking herself with similar strengthening beverages.

"So what days does Matt work?" she asked.

"Think you could do better with a different teacher, is that it?" The boy gave a derisive laugh that made Emily want to snatch back the tip.

"No, no. I was just curious."

"He's here Mondays and Saturdays. So, you know Matt. Weird. No offense, but Matt doesn't seem like the type of guy you'd hang out with."

"Oh, why is that? He seems nice."

"He is, he is. But he's into some weird shit. Some kind of native rituals. His friends are....well they're not the sort I see you hanging out with. They're angry, man. Now I'm not saying the native folks here didn't get a raw deal cause they did...but, man, it was a long time ago. They should just hang loose, get on their boards and let it go. Know what I'm saying?" Greg's brow furrowed, looking puzzled, trying to fit a nice tourist lady like herself into a group of radicals.

"Yeah, well I don't know Matt all that well. He's dating a friend's daughter."

"Oh, well then." Greg's frown faded. "That explains it. I wondered. It's not like you're the same age. Sometimes you see older women going after surfer dudes, but you didn't strike me as that type."

Older women! She was just thirty! Of course, this boy couldn't be more than eighteen. *Must keep it in perspective,* she advised herself.

CHAPTER 10

After taking a soothing shower, letting the hot water pound on muscles, which were sore from trying to haul up the wind sail, Emily sat down on the bed where Jack was napping and took out the next two letters from the envelope. She noted that the date, January, 1893, was forty-five years after Hannah had written to her mother in Boston. Why such a long gap in time? Amanda must have selected these particular letters for a reason.

Jack rolled over and opened one eye.

"Oh good. You're awake," Emily said.

"Hmmmm." Jack's eye closed. "Awake is an exaggeration. How was your windsailing lesson?" he mumbled. "Did you skim over the waves?"

"Not exactly." Emily changed the subject. "Shall I read aloud?"

"Mmm."

"All right then. This letter is from Eliza Tarkington, Amanda's great-great-great-grandmother. It was written to her cousin back in Boston."

"How is Eliza related to Hannah, our last heroine? There are altogether too many 'greats' to keep track of all this."

"Eliza was the daughter of Hannah and Hiram who came as missionaries. It says so right here in Amanda's note."

"All right then. Go ahead."

Dear Cousin Sophie,

Queen Liliuokalani is in prison! We are in such turmoil that I hardly know what to think.

There was a revolution and my son Benjamin was involved. Long ago, the former king turned over his power to an assembly of property owners, most of them children of missionaries and Benjamin's friends. When the new queen decided to rule as sovereign herself, they rebelled. With the support of American troops they have formed a provisional government and locked the Queen in her palace.

I cannot help sympathizing with the Queen. Surely, the Hawaiians have the right to rule themselves. Benjamin says it's ridiculous to think they could govern themselves without American help and, if they failed, Hawaii would fall into the hands of the British.

How can Benjamin be so sure they will fail? A mother's opinion is not allowed to count for much. Benjamin tells me these are matters for men to decide for they will affect business. Benjamin has bought a great deal of land at bargain prices and has built sugar plantations. Apparently, it will be bad for the sugar industry if Hawaii becomes British. There are no tariffs on sugar between the United States and the Kingdom of Hawaii but that could change. It troubles me that my son judges these events solely by their effect on his profits.

My dear Mother believed missionaries should devote themselves to God's work without hoping for rewards in this life. Benjamin thinks his success is proof of God's approval.

All my love, Eliza

"Jack, I don't care for this Benjamin at all. No wonder Amanda felt guilty having such a very disagreeable great-great grandfather, for that is who he must be."

"She did not pick him, he was thrust upon her."

"Still, you can see how she felt she had to make amends. Such a greedy, officious man and one who ignored his mother. I shall never forgive him for that."

"Amanda would have been gratified to find her ancestors are so real to you."

Emily delved into the envelope. "There's one more letter from Eliza, a short one dated 1895. It's to her cousin in Boston, apparently scribbled in haste."

Dear Cousin Sophie,

The monarchy has ended and Hawaii is now an American territory. At first the queen refused to sign the letter of abdication, but she was told that if she didn't, two hundred of her supporters would be executed.

Throughout the streets, I hear the song the queen wrote while she was in prison, "Aloha Oe," or "Farewell to Thee, a sad, mournful chant."

"Jack, that's the song we heard at Amanda's funeral. When the little girls were coming up the aisle. Poor Eliza. Listen to this.

"How strange it is to encounter resentment from the Hawaiian people. I was born in Hawaii. This is my home. Now my Hawaiian friends turn away from me on the street. I begin to feel like an interloper in my own land.

My son Benjamin has no qualms. He expects business to flourish. I am glad that Mother was not here to see this day.

My health has been poor these last few months. I fear I may never make the trip to Boston I have planned for so long.

All my love, Eliza Tarkington

"I wish Amanda were here to explain why she wanted to show me these letters. Well-meaning as her ancestors were, it is clear they had little regard for the native Hawaiians' rights and traditions. And then their descendants bought up land from native people who didn't understand the concept of owning property and they became extremely rich. So I can see why Amanda would want to establish the Trust and revive a culture that her family helped crush."

"But you said she was having second thoughts."

"Yes, and that's what's so mystifying. Amanda had every reason to keep the Trust going. And yet her pastor said she was considering other ways to use her money. Why?"

"Did this priest give any clues about what she had in mind?"

"Father Welch told me she had become interested in an orphanage in Thailand."

"It seems perfectly reasonable that she would expand her ideas of charity, but it does seem odd that she would shift her focus to Thailand."

"Amanda was very organized. These letters are all meant to represent the pro side of the argument. Does that mean pro continuing funding for the Trust? Or pro something else entirely? Maybe she was considering support for efforts to make amends that went beyond funding dance and cultural events. Something much more radical."

"Didn't Todd say she had rebuffed the so-called radicals? That suggests she was still thinking along fairly traditional lines. But can we believe him? Or did Todd just wish she had?"

"I don't think he'd lie about something when I could so easily find out the truth," Emily said.

"Perhaps he underestimates your tenacity. I'm curious about what those so-called radicals wanted."

"Todd did not explain and his look of distaste discouraged me from pursuing the matter. He said they were quite rude to Amanda."

"Perhaps their rudeness was the reason they were refused funding not the nature of their request."

"Perhaps. I would like to talk to them and find out."

"Unfortunately, you cannot know who they are."

"If they are involved with the revival of the ancient religion, I have some idea. Kari and Matt, her boyfriend, seem to be involved. Sarah told me the revival is all very innocent. But my windsailing instructor made it sound sinister. He said Matt is in it up to his eyeballs."

"Don't tell me you're going to interview Matt."

"No, I think the official spokesperson for the group would be a better bet than Matt. Todd pointed out that he was quoted in the newspaper."

"In the dangerous-characters-to-avoid section? You sound as if you're the investigating officer, when, in fact, you have a quite different job."

"Jack, you are not being helpful. Amanda had labeled these papers, 'pro,' so I must assume that there is somewhere either an envelope marked 'con' or she meant to tell me the arguments against continuing her present level of funding for the Trust"

"You think that her dilemma is directly linked to her murder, don't you?"

"I consider it a possibility."

"The bad thing about trying to track down murderers is it's likely to annoy them," Jack said. "An irritable killer may strike again."

Emily found the newspaper article quoting the spokesperson for practitioners of the traditional religion and skimmed it quickly to find the relevant section.

"Mau Koolani, who is interested in all aspects of Hawaii's history is a member of the Polynesian Voyaging Society and has sailed on voyages of the

Hokuluea, retracing the route of the Polynesians who settled in the Hawaiian Islands," she read.

Following this lead, Emily headed down to the wharf where she and Jack had admired the Falls of Clyde and the Hokulea, which was moored beside it. She stopped at the Maritime Museum to ask if Mau Koolani was around and was directed to the pier.

A young man wearing pink sunglasses, navy blue shorts decorated with white flowers and birds, and a T shirt, emblazoned with: "Hawaiians an Endangered Species," was standing on the Hokuluea, polishing the hull.

"Mau Koolani?"

He looked up at Emily, his eyes inscrutable behind his pink shades. His hair was a cloud of black curls.

"Yup."

"I'm Emily Swift, a reporter. I wonder if you have a few minutes to talk."

His smile faded and he looked at her with suspicion. "I've told the police and the press all I know. There's nothing to add." He turned his attention to the boat.

"Not a reporter for the Hawaiian papers. I'm from Minneapolis."

He rocked back on his heels and squinted up at her, one hand shielding his eyes against the sun. "So, even in your land of ice and snow, so far away from our islands, people are interested in a murder if it's sensational enough. Is that it? They sent you all this way?"

"Murder? No, no, let me back up and explain. I'm not here to ask you about a murder," Emily said. "I'm writing travel articles about Hawaii and I wanted to interview you about the Polynesian Voyaging Society and its reenactment of ancient voyages."

He relaxed. "Sorry. It's been a tough week. How did you find me?" he asked as if he were undercover instead of on a public pier.

"The Hokulea is mentioned in all the tour guides. I figured you'd be around the dock."

"Sorry to be so mistrustful. Not the Aloha spirit. I've become suspicious of reporters lately. Maybe you haven't read the articles and don't know anything about the murder."

"I did read about it. The poor woman was found on an altar."

He scowled. "The paper made it sound as if practitioners of the old religion were the logical suspects. Ridiculous. We would never kill someone and put her on our sacred altar. It's a sacrilege. We honor Lono, the peaceful god of harvest."

"You belong to the old religion? The newspaper made it sound as if your group was under suspicion."

"Whoever put Amanda Blake on that altar was trying to frame us. Most likely someone who hates the whole idea of our ancient religion. We're not violent, we keep the old ways of our people."

"I'd love to know more about it."

"Thinking of converting, are you?"

"No but my readers would find it interesting."

"There's no human sacrifice involved if that's what you were expecting to hear. We're not a lunatic sect. You'd find us boring."

"I haven't come to talk about religion. I really do want to know about the Hokulea. Do you mind if I just sit down on the pier? You could talk to me while you work."

"Here, you can help." He reached into the boat and tossed her a sponge.

"Then do you mind if I use a recorder? I can't take notes if I'm swabbing the deck." She pulled her small tape recorder from her beach bag and set it on the dock.

"Whatever."

"So tell me how this boat came to be built."

"Take the tour. Pick up some brochures in the Maritime Center."

"Sure, I will, but I wanted a more personal account. Have you ever sailed on a reenactment voyage?" She knew he had, just as she knew he was a spokesman for the old religion because she'd read it in the paper, but she was trying to keep the interview going.

His face lit up and he turned to her. "I was on the voyage to Easter Island. It was amazing. Voyages like ours proved that the ancient Polynesians colonized the South Pacific on purpose. They weren't blown off course and just happened to find their ignorant selves in this corner of the world. They used considerable skill to get here."

"Sure," Emily agreed. "They must have."

"Just think about it. They brought seeds, and pigs and chickens. You don't set out to sea with all your belongings, hoping to be blown onto a friendly shore. And now after the Hokulea has successfully sailed around the world, there's much more interest in traditional wayfinding."

"I agree. Absolutely," Emily assured him. "It sounds like the sort of project the Blake Trust would have supported," she added.

"I don't know anything about that." Mau shot her a suspicious look.

"The newspaper article said that the Blake Trust gave grants to organizations that were trying to preserve the native culture."

"You're certainly a close reader of random newspaper accounts.

"I'm a reporter. It's a professional interest. I just wondered if you had talked to someone at the Trust about a grant to support the revival of the old religion."

"You ask a hell of a lot of questions." Mau stood up and squeezed out his sponge. "We're done."

CHAPTER 11

Later that afternoon, Emily found Kari waiting for her at Senator Fong's Garden. She was wearing a tank top, black running shorts and tennis shoes. As she turned toward Emily, Kari tossed back her long dark hair, sunlit with glints of gold and red.

She's a beautiful girl, Emily realized, noticing Kari's slightly slanted hazel eyes and lips so full they seemed in a perpetual pout. At the funeral her face had been ravaged by grief, her eyes swollen with tears. Now with the resilience of youth she seemed to have recovered, at least physically.

"I know Senator Fong's Garden isn't the tourist attraction it used to be when the Senator was alive," Emily said, but a group is going on a tour today and I arranged for us to join it. I wanted to experience a rain forest."

Fortunately, the tram was not crowded so they were able to leave several seats between themselves and the other tourists. The tram crept downhill through the lush vegetation of the rain forest. Humidity made Emily's hair curl and her skin glow. No wonder everyone looks their best in Hawaii, no red frozen noses, pale pinched faces, dry lifeless hair here.

Their tour guide explained that a rain forest was defined by a complete canopy of trees and at least a hundred inches of rain a year. Emily made a note of it in her small red book. Previously she had imagined a rain forest was required to have parrots, shrieking monkeys, trailing vines, and so forth, but apparently this was not the case.

Kari seemed in no rush to say why she wanted to meet. She sat quietly, listening to the patter of the tour guide, a tan, muscular young woman who spoke with enthusiasm and knowledge. That was okay. Emily had questions of her own to ask.

At the bottom of the incline, the guide stopped the tram to point out the various trees—an African tulip tree with bright orange flowers, rubber trees, banyans rising on twisting roots, banana trees with miniature green fruit. Emily leaned out and snapped pictures.

"I like being in the rain forest," Kari said. Her dark eyes looked wistful for a moment then her gaze sharpened and she turned to Emily. "It reminds me of what Hawaii must have been like before it was spoiled by missionaries and tourists." She put special emphasis on "tourists."

Emily pretended not to notice her attitude. "Your mother told me you're interested in reviving the culture of the islands. How did you get into it?"

"When I was in college Amanda offered me a summer job with the Trust, teaching the hula to little kids. It started me thinking about my own heritage. Until that summer I hadn't really thought of myself as a *kanaka maoli*, a native Hawaiian. Living with my mother and father I felt like a *haole*. But I'm not."

"You were close to Amanda."

"She was a family friend, almost like an aunt. I saw her all the time when I was growing up. Then when I started to teach the traditional dances, Amanda began to confide in me. I think it was because we shared an interest in the old Hawaiian culture. She knew the hula is an important part of our heritage. Not the version for tourists with silver foil skirts, colored lights and sexy bumps and grinds. The hula was once a way of telling heroic stories to the people. It was banned by the missionaries and died out for a long time."

Emily heard the bitterness in Kari's voice and thought of Hannah's letter and how shocked the missionaries had been by a culture so different from their own. Too bad they had been so zealous in stamping out a beautiful tradition.

"The hula you and the little girls performed at Amanda's funeral was lovely," Emily said.

"Amanda would have wanted it to be part of her funeral. I suggested it to Father Welch. He was all for it, but I had a hard time persuading Todd. He didn't think it was appropriate, especially in a religious ceremony."

"Todd didn't share Amanda's interest in Hawaiian traditions?"

"No. Fortunately, Amanda was the one who made the funding decisions for the Trust. Todd always went along with whatever she wanted. After all, it was her money. The Trust has helped keep the revival of the hula going. Now everyone learns. There are even competitions for men and women. Matt is a good dancer."

Emily tried and failed to picture the sturdy Matt doing the hula.

The guide stopped the tram near a bog where broad leafed plants resembling rhubarb grew. "This is the taro plant, a popular food in Hawaii," the guide said. "*Poi*, a paste eaten with the fingers, is made from taro. It's definitely an acquired taste." The tram moved on.

"In our religion, the taro was one of the first children of the Sky Father and Earth Mother," Kari said. "The child was born deformed so he was buried in the ground. He sprouted up as the taro plant, a source of food for our people. Our gods take on many different forms, even that of plants."

"Your mom told me that you were interested in the old religion."

"I am. And not just in the myths. We're reviving ancient values, living in harmony with the land and sea, the spirits of our ancestors." Kari's eyes glowed with enthusiasm.

"Some people see the revival of the old religion as sinister," Emily said. "I took a windsailing lesson from a guy down at the beach, someone who knew Matt. He sounded pretty critical."

"That's because he doesn't know a damn thing about it. You mean Greg, right? He and Matt don't get along that well. He hasn't a clue."

"I suppose he was influenced by the way Amanda's body was found."

Kari winced, but Emily hardened her heart and pressed on. "Some people think Amanda was killed by a practitioner of the old religion. Is there someone you know in your group who…"

"No, no, of course not." Kari was so agitated she seemed ready to jump off the tram and run into the woods. "It's impossible."

Emily realized she had gone too far. "Of course, it might have been someone who wanted to make it look that way," she said quickly, trying to appease Kari. "How did Amanda become interested in Hawaii's cultural revival?"

Kari's answer was one she had heard before.

"Amanda was ashamed of her family's part in taking over Hawaii. This land was stolen. In our tradition the land or *aina* is our mother. It doesn't belong to us. We belong to it. The *haole* never understood this. There was an invasion by the United States marines, the rightful ruler was deposed, the Hawaiian culture stamped out."

"But Amanda was certainly nothing like her acquisitive ancestors."

"She enjoyed the money they piled up. Amanda tossed a crumb or two to the Hawaiian people, but it wasn't nearly enough. She would have done more."

"You mean by giving more to the Trust, keeping less for herself and Todd?"

Kari shrugged. "Maybe." She glared out at the green forest. "After she was deposed and imprisoned, Queen Liliukalani said, 'Do not covet the vineyards of Naboth's so far from your shores lest the punishment of Ahab fall on you, if not in your day, in that of your children for, be not deceived, God is not mocked...He will keep the promise and will listen to the voices of his Hawaiian children lamenting for their homes.'"

Emily was startled by the intensity in Kari's voice, also by the fact that she had committed this grim prediction to memory. Maybe someone blamed Amanda for the sins of her forefathers and meant this to be a symbolic killing. It might explain the body on the altar. Todd had mentioned a radical group that was denied funding and hinted that it was connected with practitioners of the old religion. Mau had hinted that Kari had helped them try to get the grant. Emily had to find out more.

Before she could ask Kari another question, their guide stopped the tram and stepped out to pick a glossy Ti leaf growing on a low plant beside the road. "This leaf, a relative of the lily, was used—and still is—to make an authentic hula skirt. But you can also use it to barbecue. Split it lengthwise, put in your fish. Fold the leaf over and tie it. Put it on the grill. After a few minutes, grab the stem and flip it over, cook the other side. You can use the leaf as a plate, eat the fish with your fingers, then throw the leaf away. It's biodegradable."

Maybe this would be a good traveler's tip, Emily thought, her pen hovering over her note pad. Would her readers want to barbecue? No, too much work, she decided. Much nicer to go out to dinner.

"Was the revival of the old religion the kind of project the Trust would fund?" Emily asked. She realized that she was peppering the girl with questions, but this was a rare opportunity, enclosed in a tram where the only escape was to bolt and run cross country through the trees.

Kari sighed. "I have no idea."

Relentless reporter that she was, Emily could not resist pressing on. "Todd told me that Amanda refused a request for funds and was very upset when the group she rejected became angry and abusive. Maybe it was practitioners of the old religion. Do you know why Amanda turned them down?"

Tears filled Kari's eyes and she turned away. "You're on the wrong track, Emily. The grant had absolutely nothing to do with the old religion. Neither did Amanda's murder." She turned away.

The tram was struggling uphill, sliding through red mud. When they reached the top of the mountain, a fine misty rain began to fall. Mele grass waved in the wind, rippling up and down the mountain like fur on a cat.

Their guide stopped the tram and stepped out to pick guavas from a tree and hand them around. Emily bit into the small orange fruit and ate it rind and all. Kari was mopping juice from her chin.

Emily leaned closer to her, "Kari…"

"No more questions, okay?"

"Fine. But, when we first met, you said Amanda thought I could help her. I've been turning that over in my mind, wondering what I could have done."

Kari didn't answer.

"Amanda was my friend too," Emily added gently.

Kari drew a deep breath. "Amanda told me she had found out something that really upset her. She wanted to talk to you because you're an outsider. She said you'd have the distance and judgment to look at everything impartially. Apparently this discovery changed everything and she had to make a decision."

"Did she tell you what kind of decision?"

"No. I wish she had."

Emily sighed. She kept coming up against a brick wall. Amanda had dropped exasperating hints to all and sundry but confided in no one. At least, not so far as Emily could discover.

"So that wasn't what you wanted to see me about."

"No. I have an idea for an article."

Inwardly, Emily groaned. So many people wanted to expound their ideas for an article and they were seldom of general interest. "Do you?" she asked brightly.

"About Hawaiians who want to track down their roots and find out about their Polynesian background."

"Few of my readers are Hawaiian."

"Everyone likes a story about finding your roots."

"Would this be your own story, Kari?"

"Sort of. I've been trying to find out more about my mother. There have to be pictures of her when she was a girl, letters from her family and friends. I started to ask questions. I dimly remembered an aunt Lillian and I wanted to know how to get in touch with her. My mother was evasive, but I think she would have told me if my Dad hadn't overheard us. He was seriously pissed off. He likes to pretend I'm not Hawaiian. Mom didn't say anything more. So I went to Amanda and she helped me out. Apparently, she had always kept in touch with my aunt Lillian. Amanda even told me her phone number and address."

"And your aunt was glad to hear from you?"

"I think she was. When I called, she told me she had a box of my mother's papers that she'd saved. Then when I got to her house, she said they were gone. She claimed she must have thrown them out when she moved."

"What a shame. Tidiness is easily carried too far." Emily thought with satisfaction of the boxes of memorabilia in her attic at home.

"I don't believe Lillian was telling the truth. I don't know why she changed her mind, but later, when I told Amanda about it, she reacted strangely. I couldn't exactly decode her expression. It could have been anger or fear."

Kari stopped talking and was looking at her expectantly.

"And..." Emily nudged her along.

"You're a reporter, right? You know how to go after information."

"This isn't about an article, is it? You want those papers."

"I think they may be important. If you tell my aunt you're writing an article about Hawaiians who want to track down their roots and find out about their Polynesian background, she'll be more likely to give them to you."

"That's absurd. If Lillian wouldn't give the information to you, her own niece, she won't give it to me."

"I think someone wants to keep the information from me specifically. Not necessarily from anyone else. There must be a secret connected with my birth."

"The secret Amanda discovered? Is that what you think?"

"I don't know. Maybe."

Emily took the card with Lillian's address and looked at it carefully, turning it in her hand. Maybe the troubling secret Amanda had discovered was the identity of Kari's father. Despite her claims to be a *kanaka maoli*, the girl did not look like a full-blooded Polynesian.

"You'll talk to my aunt?" Kari asked eagerly, touching her arm. Her house isn't far. You could just drop in, tell her I sent you."

Despite her misgivings, Emily agreed.

CHAPTER 12

Clutching Kari's scribbled directions to Lillian's house, Emily drove inland on twisting roads that led up and down steep hills until she came to a small stucco bungalow with a sagging roof and ramshackle porch, draped with bright pink bougainvillea. A woman wearing khaki shorts and a sleeveless white shirt, sat on the porch, reading a magazine. Emily recognized her as the woman who had been sitting beside Kari at the funeral.

"Hello," Emily called out as she walked toward her.

Lillian waited in silence. Her broad face was slightly pock marked and her dark hair was tied back.

Emily had no idea how she could persuade this perfect stranger to give her documents that had once belonged to her sister.

"How kind of you to let me come by! Kari thought we should meet," Emily said, bounding up the porch steps.

"Did she?"

"What gorgeous bougainvillea! I wish I could grow plants like that back home in Minnesota."

"Don't live in a cold climate if you want to grow tropical vines."

"You're right." Emily smiled. "I'm writing a series of travel articles on Hawaii and Kari has been very helpful. She told me a lot about Hawaiian customs and history, a subject that intrigues her." She heard her voice growing brighter and perkier every minute.

"Huh." Lillian folded her arms.

"Kari told me you two were recently reunited. She was thrilled to see you after so many years!" Emily gazed longingly at the canvas directors' chairs on the porch, hoping to be invited to sit and chat. Lillian didn't take the hint. This might be a short visit.

"I was glad to hear from her too," Lillian said. No joy was apparent in her flat monotone.

"It must seem odd to have me drop in on you like this, but when Kari told me how she had tracked down her birth family after so many years, it seemed like a great idea for my article. I mentioned the idea to Kari and she was really enthusiastic. She insisted I come to see you."

"You're a reporter?"

"That's right. From Minneapolis."

"Where it's cold all the time. How did you meet Kari?"

"I was visiting Sarah, her mother.....her adoptive mother, that is."

"You were at the funeral." Lillian jabbed her finger at her. "I knew you looked familiar."

"Yes. Amanda, Sarah and I were at college together."

"So, have you known Kari long?" Lillian seemed to thaw a bit now that she had placed her.

"No, I haven't. But she's a bright girl and eager to help with the article. She thinks the world of you. She insisted I call, but if you aren't willing to talk about something so personal, of course, I can understand it. Still, Kari made me promise..."

"That girl does have her own ideas." Lillian chuckled, a dry mirthless sound. "Always did. I suppose you should sit down." Lillian seemed resigned to complying with her niece's odd request.

Emily gratefully sank down in a chair, no longer fearing she would be thrown off the porch by this strangely unwelcoming aunt. "How did you lose touch with Kari?" Emily felt she was back on her old news beat. She longed to pull out her reporter's notebook and jot down Lillian's answers, but her welcome seemed too fragile to put to the test.

"It wasn't my idea," Lillian said quickly. "The Gardners didn't want me to contact Kari after my sister Julie died. They wanted Kari to be their very own child. At first I called a few times, went to the house with packages and toys, her own familiar things. Any child would want that, but it became clear I wasn't welcome."

Emily wondered why Lillian, her aunt, had given up all claim to the child.

Lillian answered her unspoken words. People often did, leaving Emily to suspect her private thoughts were displayed on her face as clearly as a tickertape racing its lighted message across a screen.

"The Gardners' home was the best place for Kari. I was only twenty-four at the time, not married. I loved my niece, but I didn't feel ready to make a home for her and the Gardners wanted a child so badly. If I came around too often, they'd feel as if Kari wasn't really their own daughter, that she had another family, her own blood relatives. They didn't want that." Lillian's mouth twisted with bitterness. "At first I didn't realize they meant it to be a complete break." Lillian sighed. Now that the floodgates had opened, she seemed glad to be telling someone, explaining why she had not kept in contact with her niece.

Lillian paused, looked down at her hands. "There was a stuffed rabbit that Kari loved. Its fur had worn off so her mother—my sister Julie—had stitched up a little felt jacket to cover its bald spots. I knew Kari would want it, so one day I brought it to the house. Kari came running down the path. I hardly recognized her. She was wearing a white sun dress with daisies embroidered on it and had yellow bows in her hair. Her mom had always kept her in shorts and a T-shirt.

"I hugged Kari and gave her the rabbit. She was so happy. She stood there with tears in her eyes, her cheek resting on top of that raggedy bunny, rocking it back and forth.

"Then Brent came out and stared at us. 'I thought we had a deal,' he said to me. "You weren't going to come around here."

"'Come on' I said. 'You didn't tell me I could never see Kari. Besides this is her favorite toy. She can't sleep without it.'

'She has a new one.' He reached out for the toy. 'Don't you, sweetie? A much nicer one.'

"Kari gave out a screech that would wake the dead and started stamping her feet. She pulled on the rabbit and screamed, 'No, no, no.' Then she began to kick Brent's shins."

Lillian chuckled. "The kid was always a little spitfire.

"Then Brent backed away, smiling uncertainly at me, not sure of how to handle this. The kicking must have hurt like hell but he didn't let on. Finally, he let the rabbit go and shrugged, making light of it. 'Kids!' he said.

"Sarah came out, alarmed by all the screaming and put her arms around Kari. She was torn between making me welcome and comforting the child so she tried to do both at once.

'Lillian, how nice to see you. Come in and have some lemonade.' She was kneeling on the ground, holding Kari who was starting to calm down by then. 'Kari, what's wrong?'

'My bunny. He wants to take it.' Kari glared at Brent, pointing an accusing little finger.

'Oh, surely not, honey,' Sarah said.

'I brought the rabbit Kari used to sleep with,' I explained.

'How kind of you.' Sarah said to me. Then she soothed Kari, 'Nobody will take away your bunny.'

"Brent didn't explain. He looked embarrassed. 'Mangy, goddam thing. Never been washed. She's going to get sick from all those germs.'

'I'll wash it when she's asleep,' Sarah said.

"I didn't try to make contact after that. I could see it would just cause trouble for Kari." Lillian sounded bitter.

"You don't care for Brent?"

"He's a nice enough guy. He just wanted Kari all to himself. I didn't fit into the picture."

"Why do you suppose Brent was so intense about Kari?"

"He was intense about everything. It's just his personality."

"Really? I didn't realize you knew him so well. Had you met before he adopted Kari?"

Lillian stared at her. "You don't know what happened then? You claimed to be such a close friend of the family. I thought you knew how Kari came to live with the Gardners."

Her tone was accusing. Emily suspected Lillian's free flowing reminiscences were at an end, but she need not have feared. Lillian could not resist shocking her.

"Brent was driving the car the night my sister was killed."

Emily was astounded. She had never heard the reasons for the adoption and had assumed Kari had been adopted through an agency.

"I didn't know Brent and Sarah knew your sister."

"Oh yes. Julie was a bookkeeper and all-around assistant in the Trust office. I worked there too in the summers when I wasn't teaching school."

"An accident...how dreadful." Emily searched her face, wondering if Lillian blamed Brent. How could she help it? But Lillian's face was impassive. "How did it happen?"

"Police blamed the weather. The night Julie died it was raining hard. Fierce winds were blowing off the ocean. Her car wouldn't start so Brent offered to drive her home. His car skidded on the slick road and hit a tree. Brent hurt his back, a very painful injury. My sister was killed instantly."

"I'm so sorry."

Sorrow clouded Lillian's eyes. She raised her chin, straightened her shoulders, a woman who meant to give nothing away.

Emily veered onto a less painful subject. "You must have been glad to hear from your niece after all this time."

"I was. But surprised. Kari called me about six weeks ago. She wanted to know 'her own real family.' I sensed trouble with that one. All the pains Brent had taken to raise her as their own child were going to backfire. But, hell, I didn't owe the guy anything. So I met her. She wanted to know all about her mom, see old photos, the whole nine yards. She particularly wanted to know about the accident.

"I didn't realize she didn't know Brent had been driving. Honestly. I wasn't trying to make trouble. How did he think he could keep it from her?"

Lillian clearly wanted to be absolved of any charge of deliberate troublemaking. Emily was glad to oblige. "It's amazing they kept the secret this long," she said. "After all, it must have been in the newspaper at the time. Someone was bound to mention it to Kari."

Lillian nodded. "That's what I thought."

"Kari seemed pretty cool to Brent when I saw them together," Emily said. "Do you think that's why? Because she blames him for her mother's death?"

"Maybe. She was awfully upset when she found out."

"No wonder. It must have been a shock to discover that the circumstances of her mother's death had been kept from her."

"I don't think it was deliberate. Brent and Sarah like to avoid 'unpleasantness.' Like most people I suppose. They just never got around to telling her." Lillian gave Emily a sharp look. "This can't be of much use for your article. We don't want to see family laundry hung out to dry in a newspaper."

"You won't see it. I write for a Minneapolis paper."

"Still it's old history. Kari and I talked a couple of times since she called me and that was that. It's not a big deal."

"Kari wanted me to take a look at some old letters and photographs your sister had left here. She thought it would be useful for the article." Even to Emily, this sounded a bit thin.

Lillian stood up, an unmistakable signal it was time to go. "I don't have anything that would interest you. Just old junk from the office. Kari is getting obsessed with tracking down information on her mother. I told her that."

That evening, Emily and Jack drove to the Maritime Center and dined at a bar decorated with fish nets, sailing paraphernalia, carved sea creatures and other odds and ends hanging from the walls and ceiling. They sat at a wooden picnic table near an open window where they could smell the sea and ordered Mahi Mahi and cold beer.

Settled in with a frosty mug of beer and delicious seafood, Emily gave Jack a vivid account of her conversation with Lillian. "Once Lillian got warmed up, she was quite the talker. She had total recall about the last time she had seen Kari, right after the Gardners adopted her, but when I asked to see any letters or papers that belonged to Kari's mother, Lillian was ready to press a magic button and make me disappear."

"So you think she's hiding something?"

"Why else would she want me out of there so quickly?"

"Maybe she has nothing to show you. Maybe Kari pushed too hard, demanding papers that no longer exist and her aunt was exasperated to have to listen to one more request, this time by a total stranger. Old junk is usually thrown out. Not by you, of course, but by many people."

Emily ignored his slight jab. "Maybe I should never have mentioned that I knew Kari at all, just stuck to the story that I was reporter who needed information about Julie for a newspaper article. At the time it seemed a poor excuse to pry into papers that are none of my business."

"That's never stopped you in the past."

"It's a reporter's natural instinct to pry."

"I suppose," Jack said. "How is your article coming along?" His innocent tone did not fool Emily in the least.

"You think I'm neglecting it, but that's far from being the case. I've written a good deal about the luxuriant rain forest where familiar potted plants, suitable for placing on a windowsill, have grown into massive prehistoric-type trees."

Jack gave a succinct account of his conference, then looked sadly at his empty mug. "Is it too decadent to order another beer?"

"Not at all. We're on vacation," Emily said, draining the last of her beer, secure in the knowledge that more refreshment was on its way. She returned to the subject that fascinated her. "Kari thinks Amanda discovered a secret about her birth mother that triggered her need to make a crucial decision. What could it be? And why did Amanda want to tell me, whom she hasn't seen in years, rather than Sarah who was her closest friend?"

"In the absence of any sort of evidence, you have a theory."

"Maybe Amanda discovered who Kari's father is. Kari talks a lot about being Polynesian, but like most people on the island she's a lovely mix of races. Maybe Todd is her father. That would explain why he gazes at her with such fondness. Also why Amanda was so angry. If she saw the Crumpet flirting outrageously with Todd right after she had discovered his long-ago affair, no wonder Amanda immediately suspected the worst and pounced."

"Todd has always looked guilty as hell to me."

"Or maybe Brent is Kari's father," Emily said. "Then it would be no wonder that Amanda couldn't talk to Sarah about it."

"And you think there's a clue in a box of memorabilia that Lillian is concealing for unknown reasons."

"That is my theory."

"Why would Lillian hide it? She could just throw this hypothetical document away and be done with it."

"Maybe she doesn't know what it is. What if someone was paying her to keep the whole box of stuff away from Kari—just on the off chance that it contained evidence of the relationship with Julie?"

"Apparently Lillian wasn't paid off too lavishly. If her home is as humble as you describe, it's hard to believe she's a successful blackmailer."

"Not blackmailer necessarily. Unwitting accomplice."

When they returned to the hotel, Jack switched on the television news and Emily closed the drapes.

The television announcer's voice startled her. "The medical examiner has determined that heiress Amanda Blake was not killed at Pu'uomahuka Heiau where her body was found."

Emily turned to see a grainy photo of Amanda in the upper right hand corner of the screen. Surely Todd could have done a better job of finding an attractive photo.

"Police now believe that Blake, a noted philanthropist, may have been murdered shortly after leaving a fundraiser for the Hawaiian Heritage Trust on Wednesday night. They are appealing to anyone who saw her after 10 p.m. to come forward with information. Police officials made this appeal to the public at a news conference this morning."

"Murkier and murkier," Emily said to Jack.

The phone rang. Emily expected it to be Sarah ready to talk about the latest developments. Instead it was Kari. She did not bother with polite preliminary remarks.

"So, did you get Lillian to give you the box of my mother's stuff?"

"Nope. I struck out. Lillian says she doesn't have anything."

"Oh, right. What do you think she's hiding from me?" Kari demanded.

"It's possible there's nothing to hide."

"If *your* sister were killed in an accident, would you toss out all her letters and photos? Of course not. Nobody would."

"The world is full of people who are not pack rats. If they don't use something in a year, they toss it out. Possibly, your aunt is of this persuasion." Emily was aware that she was using Jack's argument, which she still didn't buy, but she hoped to calm Kari.

"How did you approach her?" Kari asked. "Did you tell her you were a reporter? People always want to help reporters."

Emily had not noticed this, but she did not contradict.

"Oh, never mind." It was clear from Kari's snappish tone that Emily had failed to give satisfaction. "I'll just have to do it another way."

"How?" Emily asked, feeling a pang of apprehension.

"Matt will have to help out. He won't like it, but he'll do it."

Emily felt that, as the Voice of Reason, she should point out the obvious. "Lillian is unlikely to respond more warmly to a third request, especially from another stranger. What possible excuse would Matt give?"

"He won't need an excuse. He'll just have to take the papers when Lillian's not home. After all, those papers belong to me more than to Lillian. I'm the daughter, she's just a sister."

"That's breaking and entering. Surely you don't propose to involve poor Matt in a crime."

"If you had been able to talk Lillian out of the papers, this wouldn't be necessary." The line went dead.

"What an infuriating girl!" Emily turned to Jack for comfort. He was happy to oblige.

CHAPTER 13

The next morning, after Jack had gone off to his conference, Emily was luxuriating in a hot shower, singing a song remembered from a childhood talent show, "I throw the net out into the sea. And all the *ama'ama* come a swimming to me at the *hukilau*," This was a hula song that called for hand and arm movements so Emily took her time, a little soaping, a little singing and dancing. The pounding of hot water on her neck and back felt heavenly.

The minute Emily turned off the shower, she heard the phone ringing. Whoever it was didn't give up after a few rings. Emily leapt out of the tub, wrapped herself in a luxuriously thick bath towel and ran to answer.

She stood dripping in a puddle of water and gasped out, "Aloha."

"Emily, thank God. I have to talk to you. They've arrested Matt. Why? Why would he do it?"

Good Lord, breaking and entering. Emily felt a pang of remorse. She should have taken Kari's statement more seriously and put a stop to her crazy idea. Every time Emily refrained from meddling she regretted it.

"You probably don't even remember Matt," Sarah went on. "A nice young man who dates Kari. I always liked him, so polite, sort of quiet, he lets Kari do the talking. I could never have imagined him capable of anything so dreadful."

"Surely it's not as bad as all that. A first offense."

"Not so bad! What could be worse than murder? Emily, have you taken leave of your senses."

"Wait, hold on. What murder? I thought you said he was arrested for breaking and entering."

"Where did you get that idea? Matt was arrested for murdering Amanda. Emily, can you come over? Brent's not here. I have to talk."

Emily jotted a quick note for Jack. She didn't bother to dry her hair, just dragged a brush through her wet curls, pulled on shorts and a shirt and she was off.

Settled in an armchair in Sarah's living room, Emily still felt slightly damp. Outside she could see gray mist clouding the ocean, palm trees swaying, their fronds tapping relentlessly against the window pane.

Sarah handed her a cup of Kona coffee and placed a silver pitcher of thick cream on the table. Emily poured in a lavish amount, which she needed to keep up her strength, and took a sip of coffee.

"So tell me. Why do the police think Matt killed Amanda?" Emily asked.

Sarah leaned forward, her hands clamped between her knees. "There was a witness. A man who gets his nightly exercise by swimming up and down the beach before the Sheraton, recognized Matt's catamaran. You might have seen it. It has very distinctive turquoise sails. This guy saw Matt carrying a body from the shore. At the time, he thought it was a woman who had too much to drink, and a helpful friend was carrying her to the boat. Then later he began to wonder. When the police announced yesterday morning that Amanda wasn't killed at Puu O Mahuka Heiau and asked if anyone had seen anything unusual in and around the Sheraton where Amanda was last seen, this guy came forward."

"Surely he couldn't recognize Matt in the dark. Or even see the color of his sails."

"The guy claims to be absolutely certain. He said he swam close enough to see Matt in the moonlight. He knew the boat because he swims along this beach just about every night. The witness doesn't know Matt personally, but he knows him by sight. He'd seen him teaching surfing and windsailing on the beach. He swears it was Matt."

"How dreadful. Why on earth would Matt kill Amanda?"

"I have no idea. None of this makes any sense. I don't know what to think."

"How well do you know Matt?"

"Not very well. He seems devoted to Kari so I've always liked him. I can't believe he did it."

"Now let me get this straight. The police think that Matt killed Amanda on the beach and sailed away with her, then somehow transported her body to Puu O Mahuka Heiau. How strange to take a risk like that. Why not leave her on the shore?"

"There must be some significance to Puu O Mahuka Heiau, some point he was trying to make. But I don't know. It doesn't sound like him. Matt always seemed like a pretty level headed guy."

"How did you find out about all this? Does Kari know?"

"She was at Matt's apartment when he was arrested. She called me, sobbing and hysterical. I could hardly understand her. That was a couple of hours ago. I've been frantic ever since."

Emily heard the door burst open, a clatter in the hallway. Brent strode into the room, shedding drops of moisture. "I heard about Matt's arrest on the radio and came right home. Thank God this is settled. The police did a great job, wrapped up the case in record time." Brent kissed Sarah on top of her head and smiled at Emily.

"This calls for a Bloody Mary. What do you think? Anyone else?"

"At this hour?" Sarah asked.

Emily shook her head.

Brent opened the wood paneling to reveal a full bar. "How's Kari taking it?"

"She's terribly upset. Brent, she wants you to help Matt find a lawyer. She called me this morning. Kari was at Matt's apartment when they came for him. I don't know if she's going to the police station or coming over here. I was too shocked to ask for all the details."

"Kari was with him? Good Lord. Do the police know she was there? I hope she had enough sense to hide."

Emily didn't think that sounded like something Kari would do, but she kept her opinion to herself.

"If the cops didn't search the apartment, maybe they didn't even see her," Brent persisted. "What do you think, Sarah?"

"I don't think they could have missed her. Kari wouldn't hide under the bed like a criminal. She doesn't have anything to conceal."

"I just hope she hasn't gotten involved."

Brent's good mood was souring, Emily noticed. She wished she could be invisible for a while, able to eavesdrop on the family discussion without the embarrassment of actually being present.

"Kari made me promise to ask you about a lawyer," Sarah said.

"For her?"

"No. For Matt, of course. Kari's not under suspicion."

Brent took a long pull on his Bloody Mary.

"Brent, are you listening? Kari's counting on us to help."

"I'd be glad to recommend a criminal lawyer if I knew one, but I don't. We have to keep Matt at arm's length now. I don't want Kari getting involved in this police investigation any more than she already is."

"Why would she be?" Sarah asked.

"Think about it. Matt must have had an accomplice. How else would he get the body from the catamaran on North Beach up the mountain to Puu O Mahuka Heiau? Someone must have met him with a car, one that has four-wheel drive. The police are going to be looking very hard at Matt's friends and that includes overnight girlfriends. Especially girls with jeeps."

"You don't seriously believe that Kari helped Matt kill Amanda. She adored her. It's unthinkable. Kari isn't capable of murder."

"Don't jump all over me, Sarah. Of course, I don't think Kari did it. I'm just telling you what the police will say. Let's stay out of it."

"Stay out of what?" Kari's voice startled them. No one had heard her slip into the room. They turned to look at Kari. Strands of her long wet hair were plastered against her tear stained cheeks. Her shirt was crumpled and damp.

"Thank God you're here," Sarah said, rushing over to hug her. Kari briefly returned her embrace.

Brent put his arm around her. "Poor kid. You didn't know what you were getting into with that guy. He could have killed you as well as Amanda. There's a screw loose somewhere."

Kari shook free of him. "Don't be silly. Matt didn't kill anyone."

"Honey, there's a witness. You don't have to believe me. Just steer clear. Don't go to see Matt or draw any attention to yourself."

Emily felt increasingly uncomfortable in the middle of what threatened to turn into a family quarrel but, considering the gravity of the situation, she could hardly turn the conversation to the weather or current events, so she kept quiet. Outside, the palm trees were in a frenzy, the ocean had turned a dark gray.

"Do you think there could be a mistake?" Sarah asked, eager to find a compromise. "It was dark."

"What does Matt say?" Emily felt the calm voice of reasonable inquiry should be heard. "Has he admitted it?"

"So far he hasn't said a word," Kari said. "He needs a lawyer. Dad, we have to help him." Kari put her hand on Brent's arm and looked up at him.

"No, we don't." Brent turned away from her pleading eyes.

"Please, Dad," Kari said, gripping his arm. "I'm begging you to do this one thing."

"Let's not rush into anything." Brent drained his Bloody Mary. "The cops are pretty good at getting at the truth. Why don't we just let them do their job? The detectives will ask a few questions, tighten the screws. It'll all come out."

"Dad, just tell me the name of the lawyer you'd call if you were a suspect. I have no idea how to help Matt. It's not like I can start paging through the Yellow Pages and come up with someone really good."

"I know corporate lawyers, tax lawyers, estate lawyers. Fortunately I've had no occasion to know a criminal lawyer."

"Brent, isn't Tom Scanlon pretty good?" Sarah asked. "I've seen his name in the papers. He always seems to be on the winning side. We met him at a party over at the Miller's. Remember?"

"He'd be expensive as hell. Sure if Matt can afford Scanlon on his surfing-teacher salary, tell him to go for it. It would make more sense for him to ask for a public defender. If he's innocent, he'll be fine. If not, the faster justice is done the better."

Kari headed toward the hallway. Sarah started to follow.

"I'll be fine, Mom. Thanks. Scanlon's the guy."

"The money…"

"It's no problem; don't worry."

Brent was making another Bloody Mary

Later that morning, Emily was sitting on the beach, typing rapidly on her laptop, impatient for Jack to come back so she could tell him that the case appeared to be solved. The phone rang from deep inside her beach bag. Emily pulled it out and heard a bleat, which sounded like Todd's voice. There was too much static on the line to be sure.

"Todd, is that you? I can barely hear you. It's noisy here." In the background, she could hear the cry of seagulls, the happy screams of little children.

"The police have arrested Matt." Todd sounded exultant.

"So I've heard."

"Thank God. I always thought there was some connection between Amanda's death and those radicals who wanted funding. Remember what I was telling you?"

"So Matt is part of that group?" Emily lowered her voice, trying not to attract the interest of her fellow sunbathers.

"I didn't want to mention it before. Didn't want to get the poor guy in trouble if he wasn't really guilty. But sure, Matt's in tight with Mau Koolani and his friends."

"Kari thinks Matt's innocent," Emily said, pulling her striped beach towel over her head to give herself more privacy, constructing a little tent.

"Poor kid. This is going to be hard on her."

"Why do you think Matt did it? He barely knew Amanda, right?"

"I have no idea. Who cares? The important thing is he's behind bars. He must be guilty. I can't imagine anyone except Matt and one of his buddies putting Amanda on Puu O Mahuka Heiau."

"Kari says Amanda's murder had nothing to do with the old religion."

"Maybe. But those are the same guys who were yelling at Amanda because she turned down their grant request."

"Matt was yelling?"

"No, he didn't say much," Todd admitted. "It was Mau Koonani. Matt's a quiet guy, hangs in the background. But hey, aren't those guys always the ones who turn out to be guilty? The quiet ones? After a mass murder, neighbors say, 'He was kind of a loner, always kept to himself.'"

Emily had to agree that this was often the case. "What exactly did this group want?"

"It was a crazy scheme. They wanted money so they could look at ways to pay reparations to native Hawaiians for taking the land away from their ancestors. It was ridiculous. Amanda turned them down."

Hardly a reason for murder, Emily thought.

"So let's get together when this is all cleared up," Todd said.

"I'd like that."

As she turned off her phone, Emily felt her towel plucked from her head and looked up to see Jack.

"What on earth are you doing crouched on the beach with your head under a towel? I heard familiar sounds emerging and figured it was you."

Emily noted the stares of her fellow beachgoers. Apparently her attempt to be unobtrusive had not been successful.

CHAPTER 14

The next morning, Emily left the hotel and walked along a dense hedge of hibiscus, its dark leaves bedewed with raindrops. It felt good to be outside, breathing in the fragrant tropical air, heading out for a sightseeing expedition along the North Shore.

Now that Amanda's murder seemed to be solved, she was ready to concentrate wholeheartedly on her articles. Emily realized that she would probably never know what Amanda's momentous decision would have been and now with the murderer in jail, it didn't seem to matter.

Emily headed for the parking lot to find her rental car. When she opened the door, she drew back with a horrified cry.

Kari was sitting in the passenger seat.

"What are you doing here?" Emily slid into the driver's seat and glowered at Kari. The girl must have been stalking her.

"I have to talk to you," Kari said, tears brimming.

"Kari, I know you must be terribly upset. Matt's arrest came as a shock, even to me and I don't know him at all. But I can't help you."

"Sure you can. Just listen."

"I'm on a tight deadline. I have to work on my article." She should have stopped there, Emily later realized, but she went on to give a wholly unnecessary explanation of her plans for the day. "I need to make some notes about the beaches along the North Shore."

"I can help you," Kari said quickly. "I know exactly where the best beach is."

"I can't take you with me," Emily said firmly. She did not, however, know how to dislodge the girl, short of pushing her out of the car.

"We have to find a way to save Matt," Kari said. "He didn't do it."

"There's an eyewitness," Emily said, edging out into traffic.

"Who will be discredited quite easily by a sharp lawyer."

"I'll drop you at your home," Emily said.

"I've saved enough money over the years to take care of the fee."

"Maybe a lawyer will be able to cast doubt on the witness. After all, it was dark, but have you considered the possibility that Matt is guilty?"

"I know for sure that he isn't"

Emily felt her heart sink. "How do you know?"

Kari ignored her question. "The only way to prove Matt is innocent is to find the real killer. I'm convinced that we'll be able to do that if we can get the box of papers that belonged to my mother. Obviously, Matt can't get it himself now that he's in jail. You've got to try again."

"Absolutely not."

"You're a reporter. You can say that you want to interview both of us. A young girl finding her roots, uncovering the past. It's not a bad story. You might really want to write it. And then when we have Lillian hooked, you persuade her to show us the box of papers."

"You don't know this box even exists."

"You think Matt killed Amanda, don't you? That's why you won't help."

"I have no idea if he's guilty."

"If you knew for certain Matt was innocent, would you help me?

Emily was not going to allow Kari to manipulate her into another meeting with Lillian. They drove on in silence. Emily ignored the waves of disapproval emanating from Kari's rigid little body.

"You win," Kari said at last. She turned her angry face to Emily. "I'll tell you how I know Matt is innocent. I'll tell you everything. Then you'll realize how you have to help clear him. But you must swear not to tell a soul. We have to go somewhere absolutely private."

Emily drove along the coast as the sky lightened and a rainbow arched across the turquoise ocean. Curiosity and good sense had struggled within her and good sense had come out second best.

"I'll show you the perfect beach," Kari said. "You'll be glad you came. We'll be completely on our own. No one to overhear."

"You could tell me why you're so sure Matt is innocent right here in the car. Then I could drop you off at your parents' house."

"It's a long story. Let's head out toward North Beach. The waves are better."

One beach looked very much like another to Emily. All perfect.

They drove in silence, passing a number of perfectly fine sandy beaches. Emily grew weary of saying, "This one looks good," only to be told they weren't there yet.

Kari seemed to be pulling herself together during the drive, possibly becoming more accustomed to the strange turn of events, more in control of her emotions. Finally Kari cried out, "There! Take a sharp right."

Emily followed instructions and pulled into a parking lot lined by tall pine trees. Their car was the only one. No wonder. Cold drizzle and gray sky didn't make this an ideal beach day. Emily kicked off her sandals and followed Kari across damp sand toward the ocean. Waves crashed and foamed against black cliffs and swirled in craggy rock basins. The ocean was darker here than in Waikiki, more threatening and powerful. The sea misted Emily's face, salted her lips, made her hair curl.

"Now we're here," Emily said, "at the perfect beach," and she had to admit it was beautiful. "Now you can tell me…"

She turned around. Kari was pulling her shirt over her head.

"What are you doing?" Emily cried.

Kari stepped out of her shorts. Wearing a bright yellow bikini, she ran into the pounding waves and dove forward. She flipped over onto her back and bobbed for a moment, then dived into a huge wave and rode it in to shore, landing at Emily's feet. She stood up, shaking water from her hair like a dog. "Come on in. It's great."

"It's raining." Emily was running out of patience. She tried to indicate this by briskly tapping her foot, but the sand was too soft. Her foot just burrowed.

"You can't get much wetter than you are." Kari flicked her fingers at Emily shooting a fine spray of water into her face. "See how warm it is?" She turned and dove in once more.

Emily sighed. Even under gray skies, the water looked inviting after their long drive. No sense in missing a chance to swim at the perfect beach. Luckily she had had the foresight to bring her swimsuit just in case an opportunity to swim arose.

"Okay," she said to Kari and hiked back to the bathhouse near the parking lot.

After she changed into a swimsuit, Emily plunged in
and frolicked like a porpoise, diving under the waves
and breast stroking forward. She didn't dare to go out
into deep water as Kari was doing. The undertow was
frightening. As long as she kept near shore and let the
waves roll her about, she was delighted to play like an
otter. She dove into the waves and let them carry her in,
rolling her over and over in the frothy water.

After a while, she called out to Kari that she was
going to change.

Kari bobbed up in the water, nodded and waved.

Emily padded down the boardwalk to the bathhouse
where she showered away the sand under a thin rusty
stream of water, then put on her clothes and headed
back to the beach. No sign of Kari.

Emily ran along the shore, calling her. No answer.
She heard only the call of the gulls and the pounding
surf. Licking salt off her lips, she turned back, and
walked slowly, scanning the beach for signs of life.
Dread began to seep in, cold as ice. Where were all the
lifeguards? There must be at least one. She would have
to get her cell phone and call 911.

Then she saw Kari settled down with her back
against a cliff, sheltered in a rock crevice, looking out
to sea.

Relief and annoyance flooded Emily's mind in equal
measure. She was determined not to let Kari know she
had succeeded in worrying her. "Don't give her the
satisfaction," her mother would advise. Quite right.

Without a word of greeting, Emily sat down beside
Kari. She thrust her toes into the water, feeling the pull
of the current, watching the waves wash at her feet in a
rush of foam, then slide out again, leaving dimples in
the sand.

"Okay, Kari. Tell me what you know about the
murder." Sharpened by anxiety, Emily's voice sounded

more menacing than she had intended, as if, at this point, Kari's alternative to talking was to have her pockets packed with rocks and be thrown headfirst into the sea.

"I was there," Kari said, "on the beach when Amanda was killed."

"What? You saw it? You know who killed her? Who was it? Why haven't you told the police?"

"I didn't see who killed her. I was there. Let me explain."

Emily listened to Kari describe an improbable series of events.

The night of the murder, the hotel beach was deserted on the ocean side.

Kari and Matt were lying under a twisted tree whose tangled boughs arched down to the sand, making a secluded shelter. Through the branches, Kari saw Amanda walk past, stop to drop her high heels in the sand and hurry down to the sea. She wondered why Amanda was on the beach instead of at the party. Then Matt distracted her.

Later, Kari ducked out from under the tree and ran to the water with Matt close behind her. She splashed into the moonlit water, giggling, looking back to make sure Matt was following her. She felt something soft hit her leg and jumped back. Then she saw a body floating face down in a few feet of water, brown hair spread on the surface. "Not Amanda, please let it not be Amanda," Kari prayed, already knowing it was. She had recognized the filmy gray dress. Kari rolled the body over, hoping it was not too late to save Amanda. One look at the unseeing eyes, the slack mouth trailing seaweed, crushed her hope. Kari dropped to her knees in the water. She clung to Amanda's limp body. She couldn't bear to look at her lifeless face.

"Matt put his hands on her shoulders. "My God, this is horrible. It's Amanda Blake, isn't it?"

"We can't leave her here." Kari stood up and faced him. Amanda's cold body bumped against her leg like driftwood.

"I'll carry her up to the beach," Matt offered.

"That's not what I mean, Matt. We have to get Amanda away from here."

Matt put his arm around her. "You're upset."

"Damn right I'm upset. What do you think?" Tears streaked down Kari's furious face. "We have to give Amanda a proper send-off, the kind she would have wanted."

"Kari, that's crazy. What if she was murdered? We'd be destroying evidence."

"She wasn't murdered. That's ridiculous. "

"What do you think happened then?" Matt asked gently.

"It's obvious she killed herself. She couldn't take it anymore. I don't want to hear all the gossip and speculation. I don't want Amanda to be remembered in some grand society funeral, the kind her husband and my parents would arrange. You have to help me, Matt."

"What do you want me to do?"

Kari explained. Matt would carry Amanda Blake's body to sea in his catamaran and sail to a remote beach up the coast where Kari would meet him with her jeep. She assured Matt that since he had no connection with Amanda he would never be linked to the murder. Matt didn't seem entirely convinced, but the sobbing, ferocious look Kari turned on him carried the point. Together they would drive Amanda up to Puu O Mahuka Heiau and give her a proper Hawaiian funeral ceremony.

"Amanda is past knowing or caring," Matt said. "This is crazy."

"Whether she knows or not, I have to pay proper respect to her. Amanda was our friend. I have to make it up to her."

"What? Make up for what?"

"Are you going to help me or not? We don't have much time. Someone might see us."

Kari came to the end of her account. "We did what we had to do."

Emily was stunned. "So Matt agreed to go along with this?" she asked, reflecting with awe on the power of sexual attraction to dim the minds of young men.

"Of course he did. It seemed to go off without a hitch. We didn't know some nosy swimmer was out in the water, watching us."

"Surely you knew it was likely you'd be seen."

"No, not at that hour. It was late and very dark. Who could expect an insomniac swimmer to be out and about."

"Why take Amanda's body to the top of the mountain?"

"I wanted her to be laid to rest on the sacred hill. We surrounded her body with tapa and fragrant flowers. In the old days a Kahuna would have put her soul in a gourd and sung to coax her soul back into her body. I wished I could do that for Amanda. Matt and I sat beside her until dawn came over the ocean."

Emily found it hard to believe that this bizarre tale seemed to make perfect sense to Kari.

"You have to tell the police," Emily said.

"Not yet. They wouldn't believe me. I've got Matt into terrible trouble and now I have to find the real killer."

"It never occurred to you that Amanda might have been murdered? Didn't you notice bruises on her neck?

There must have been bruises. The police say she was strangled."

"No, it was dark. I just saw her blank, staring eyes. It was horrible. Don't make me remember. I was wrong, okay? It never occurred to me that Amanda had been murdered. Do you think I would have destroyed evidence if I had any idea she had been killed? I thought she just got fed up and walked into the ocean and drowned herself. I made a mistake."

"Why would Amanda kill herself?"

"She had reason enough."

"Why?" Emily persisted.

"I don't know," Kari admitted. "Amanda was awfully depressed those last few days. She told me she had been betrayed. So when I saw her floating there, naturally I thought…" Kari started to cry softly. "We have to find out who killed her."

"The police will do that," Emily said gently.

Kari's face was tear stained, her dark eyes glowing with intensity. "Look. I know you don't believe me, but the answer is in my mother's box of papers. I think Amanda looked through it and found some secret. We have to get the box from Lillian."

"It sounds farfetched. You've just latched onto that theory for no reason at all. Why hasn't Matt told the police the truth? He must realize it's his only hope."

"He promised me he wouldn't say a word. Matt's counting on me."

Emily stood up and brushed the sand off her shorts.

"Remember you promised not to say a word," Kari said.

"I didn't promise anything. I can't let an innocent young man be suspected of murder."

"Just give me one day. Half a day. Come with me to meet Lillian. Then I'll do exactly what you say."

"Not a chance. We have to get Matt out of jail now."

"I'll deny everything. Nobody will believe you. Matt won't give anything away."

"You can't be serious. How can you let the poor guy rot in jail for something you conned him into?"

"As soon as we have those papers, I'll go to the police and tell the whole story. Just meet me and Lillian."

"I'd be crazy to go along with this."

"You're right," Jack said that evening. "You'd be crazy to go along with her." They were sitting at the pool of the Sheraton, drinking tall, cold lemonades, watching the sun set. "If Kari won't go to the police, you should. Why give in to this young woman's unreasonable demands?"

It was just about time for the evening performance to begin and a drummer and guitarist were doing mic checks. A few children were still splashing about in the pool. Parents were holding out beach towels, cajoling them out onto dry land. Couples dressed to go out for the night were coming in to replace the afternoon swimmers poolside.

"I don't really want to explain Kari's peculiar story to the police," Emily said. "What if it's not true?"

"I thought you believed her."

"When I was with her, I did. Now I'm not so sure. If I went to the police I could be obscuring the truth, rather than revealing it."

"They'll sort it out. Police are not gullible."

"Also, I would feel as if I were betraying Sarah."

"Haven't you told Sarah? This is something a mother would want to know."

"No it's not. She'll hate knowing. Sarah has no idea her daughter was involved in moving a body, tampering with evidence, criminal activities that could land her in jail."

"That might not be the extent of her guilt. This is not the most believable story."

"No, and that's exactly why I want to get Kari to go to the police herself. I'll go to see Lillian if that's what it takes. But Kari is going to have to convince her aunt to hand over the box of papers." Her mind made up, Emily turned her attention to the stage. A beautiful young woman in a silver hula skirt with a lei of white flowers around her neck stepped forward. A golden spotlight illuminated her as she began to sing, "I throw my net out into the sea..."

"That's my song," Emily said, clutching Jack's arm. "The one I sang in the talent show when I was in seventh grade. Surely you've heard my rendition."

The singer paused. "Now I'd like to invite someone in the audience to step up and help me with the chorus."

"Are you going to reproduce your musical triumph?" Jack nudged Emily and grinned.

"Alas, those days of youthful disregard for the critics are long past."

A little girl in a paper hula skirt was pushed forward by her father, who had a video cam trained on her. "Here, honey, go on, go on, it will be fun," he said. The pale child looked as if she were being dragged to slaughter. The glamorous singer smiled as the girl edged up to stand beside her and adjusted the microphone to the child's height. Then she taught her a few graceful arm movements and began to sing, "I throw my net out into the sea and all the *ama'ama* come a swimming to me, at the *hukilau*..."

The child imitated her motions with awkward arms. Her father was crouching and leaping about, recording the moment for posterity from multiple camera angles. Emily was glad her father had not been armed with a similar device when she was in seventh grade. As it

was, she could remember her performance any way she
wished and who could contradict her?

CHAPTER 15

Despite Jack's warnings that it was a big mistake to give in to Kari's demands, Emily agreed to meet her and Lillian at the Royal Hawaiian Hotel, a flamingo-pink confectionary, built in a Moorish style that had its heyday in the 1920s. Emily felt a thrill of pleasure as she stepped onto the verandah. Everything was pink, the umbrella, the tablecloths, the napkins, the waiters' outfits. All this rosiness conjured up a playful mood that Emily found just right for a holiday hotel although it would be way too much of a good thing anywhere else.

She saw Lillian seated at an umbrella table facing the ocean, a glass of iced tea in hand.

"Lillian, I'm so glad to see you again. What a good idea for all three of us to meet!" Emily cried. She hoped her cheery tone would stimulate a little matching warmth and enthusiasm.

Lillian looked wary. "I don't know what Kari has in mind."

"I told you. She's trying to help with my article. Kari thought it would be a good idea for me to talk to you both at the same time, find out firsthand what it's like for a young girl to investigate her birth mother's past, and, at the same time, discover how it feels for an aunt to be reunited with a long-lost niece." Emily realized it sounded as if she were giving an implausible pitch for a TV movie.

"Hmph."

Emily didn't know exactly what this sound meant but was pretty sure it did not bode well. "Are you as interested in Hawaiian traditions as Kari?" she asked.

"A lot of nonsense, in my opinion. Leave it to the tourists. Only thing I'd like to see are those reparations Kari talks about."

"Tell me more." Emily leaned on her elbows and fixed a look of rapt attention on Lillian, hoping that Kari would show up soon or else that Lillian would have another bout of total recall. She seemed to have two conversational settings—pause and fast forward.

"Kari and some other folks she hangs around with think the *haoles* who took our land should pay for it. They say it's not too late to make reparations to the native people who were tricked out of their homeland. Seems like a crazy idea. It'll never happen. But if anyone wanted to hand me some money, fine." Lillian gave a mirthless chuckle.

A waiter asked if they were ready to order. Emily explained they were waiting for one more and ordered lemonade. She looked around, but saw no sign of Kari. Emily had no intention of asking Lillian for the documents herself. If Kari wanted them, she would have to show up and make the pitch. In the meantime, she would try to gather more information for her own real article.

"Kari tells me there's been a revival of interest in the ancient Hawaiian religion," Emily said.

"Couldn't tell you. I'm a Presbyterian."

"Then your church doesn't incorporate Hawaiian music and dance into the service? The hula that Kari and the little girls did at Amanda's funeral was lovely." Inevitably the conversation had swung back to Amanda.

Lillian nodded. "Kari thought the world of Amanda. Being part of the funeral service meant a lot to her. I think she was surprised the priest allowed it."

"Did you know Amanda well?"

"No. I knew her slightly and I heard a lot about her from my sister Julie but that was years ago. Kari talked me into coming to the funeral. So I showed up, paid my respects, humored my niece. Why not? After all, Amanda was a fine woman. She deserved a big turnout."

Emily agreed, wishing once again that she had known Amanda better.

"Good thing they caught her killer," Lillian added with surprising ferocity.

"If he's the right guy."

"Why wouldn't he be? He looks guilty as sin. I saw his picture in the paper."

"Did you know he's Kari's boyfriend? She doesn't believe Matt did it."

"This guy is dating Kari?"

"He was with her at the funeral. I'm sure you must have seen him."

"That thickset guy? Good Lord." Lillian looked toward the door. "Where do you suppose Kari is? She was supposed to be here a half hour ago."

"Has it been that long?"

"Yes," Lillian said with the precision of a heavy eater who has been waiting too long for nourishment.

"Let's give her ten more minutes and then order."

"I don't usually eat out. I just came because Kari insisted." Lillian's eyes were casting around for the exit. She looked as if she might bolt.

"Let's order. Kari can catch up." Emily caught the waiter's eye.

Emily ordered a chicken Caesar salad and Lillian a cheeseburger with fries and coleslaw.

While they waited for their meal, Emily fired off a series of questions intended to jump start the conversation. She found out that Lillian was a school teacher, taught sixth grade, liked it fine, but kids were getting out of hand these days, needed more discipline at home, parents expected her to teach manners as well as math and history. Emily ran out of questions.

The meals arrived. Conversation was allowed to languish as they ate. Emily found it difficult to eat leafy greens, spear croutons, and chat all at the same time.

She looked out at the turquoise ocean, where surf boarders skimmed along the waves. On the beach, a man with a parrot on each shoulder was apparently trying to talk a tourist into having her picture taken with the parrots.

"I hope nothing has happened to Kari," Emily said, as she finished her salad. Kari had been insistent on having this meeting. Why wouldn't she show up? Emily imagined her in jail, locked up next to Matt on a murder charge.

Lillian looked worried, but she said, "Maybe Kari forgot."

Emily thought that was highly unlikely.

Soon after Emily returned to her hotel room, the phone rang.

"It's for you and whoever it is doesn't sound happy," Jack said, holding out the receiver.

"You were in this together," Lillian shrieked into the phone.

"What do you mean?" Emily asked.

"Someone ransacked my place. You and Kari planned it together."

"Why on earth would I do that? I barely know the girl. She's your niece."

"You wanted those papers."

"The ones you don't have?"

She could hear furious breathing. Lillian was trapped by her own lie. "That damn Kari tore up my house."

"Was anything missing?"

"I can't tell yet."

"Talk to Kari. I had nothing to do with it." Emily felt slow fury creeping over her. Kari had tricked them both. She was a hideously Machiavellian young person.

After listening to more angry recriminations and false accusations, Emily finally succeeded in ending the conversation and turned to Jack.

"Why didn't I guess right away what Kari was up to?"

"Because you have a sweet, trusting nature. You would never lie, much less break and enter so you assume others are just as trustworthy."

"Now what? Do I accuse Kari, tell her parents, or leave her to her enraged aunt?"

"Stay out of it. Leave her to the enraged aunt and hope punishment will be swift and terrible."

There was a banging on the door.

Jack opened the door a crack.

"Quick, let me in." Kari weaseled her way through the door. She was carrying a large box.

"That was a nasty trick." Emily flew at her. "I don't want to be involved in your criminal activities. Your aunt just called me, furious, because she thinks I conspired to get her out of the house so you could break in and tear apart her home looking for the papers."

"It worked perfectly." Kari sat on the end of the bed, the box on her lap. She did not look repentant. She wore a lemon yellow tank top with spaghetti straps, a short white skirt, and high heel sandals with daisies flopping across the strap. Her toes and fingernails were enameled bright green.

Emily longed to shake the girl until her teeth rattled.

Jack stood over Kari, glowering down at her. "You are forgetting that Emily was not a willing co-conspirator."

Kari gave him a warm smile and thrust out her hand. "Do you remember me? Kari Gardner. We met at Amanda's funeral."

"I've heard a good deal about you since then, so the memory is still vivid."

Kari seemed to take that as a compliment.

"How did you find our room?" Emily asked.

"It wasn't hard," Kari said.

"Take that box and go," Emily said, barely controlling her anger. She feared that Lillian would burst into the room and find her with the ill-gotten gains. Nothing is more infuriating than being tricked into a false position and then wrongly accused.

"Please, let me leave this box with you," Kari begged. "I'm going to be picked up by the police for questioning any minute. You know I was in Matt's apartment when he was arrested, so they're bound to pull me in for questioning."

"You told me you'd go straight to the police and tell the truth if I met your aunt. Against my better judgment, I did what you asked. Now you fulfill your end of the bargain."

"I will. I promise. That's why I have to leave this box somewhere safe."

"Not a chance."

"I'm sorry that Lillian yelled at you and blamed you. She was exaggerating wildly about the place being torn up. I meant for her not to notice I had been there. I was trying to put everything back just so, but then I got worried about the time. I was afraid you'd guess what I was up to and cut it short. So then I started to move a bit faster, I didn't want to be interrupted and lose my chance. I got careless about putting everything exactly, precisely where it was, but believe me, her house was not a mess and Lillian must have been very suspicious to even notice I was there. She must have gone right to the place where she hid the box and seen it was missing."

"She had an excellent reason to suspect you. Just leave me out of this from now on. Whatever you do is your own business."

"I am truly sorry. I didn't mean to make you angry. I thought you'd be pleased I'd been successful. I never thought that Lillian would blame you."

"Do you spring from a family of half-wits? Of course your aunt would think I was part of a plot."

"Sorry, sorry. Please forgive me. Don't you see how much safer the papers would be here? I can't take this box home."

"I should think your own home would be much the best place," Jack said.

"It's not, trust me. If I put this box in my room, I'm sure my Dad would take it."

"Do you really think he's capable of violating your privacy like that?" Jack asked.

"Yes."

Emily reflected on how very much Kari and Brent had in common if he was such a prying sort of person. Perhaps he really was her father. Or perhaps Kari was lying about his nosy propensity.

"Find another solution," Emily snapped.

Fortified by fury, Emily resisted further attempts to persuade her. Kari finally lugged the box to the door. She paused and looked back, "You know you're curious, Emily. You'd love to go through this box."

CHAPTER 16

Jack was taking a shower when the hotel staff called to tell Emily she had a package at the front desk.

"Oh, no," Emily thought. "I should have realized Kari would never give up so easily." Emily knew it would make sense to refuse the parcel, say it was delivered by mistake, but curiosity overcame her. There could be a clue to the identity of Kari's father in those papers. Somehow that secret might be connected to the murder. She owed it to Amanda to find out even if it meant bending the rules. Emily said she would be right down.

The splashing sounds of a long, soothing shower were still wafting from the bathroom when Emily returned. She dumped the contents of the box on the bed and began to organize the papers.

In one large envelope Emily tucked letters, in another photos, in a third spreadsheets and business letters of some sort (heavens, the woman was a pack rat to save such boring stuff), and in the final envelope miscellaneous memorabilia. An organizing project usually made Emily feel virtuous, but she realized this particular project was drawing her into murky waters. By filing the papers, she was making it more difficult for Lillian to recover her property. If Lillian were to burst in unexpectedly—not impossible since security in this hotel was apparently not all it was cracked up to be, judging from the ease with which Kari had arrived at their doorstep—she would be unable to recognize her own box of papers and would therefore be denied the pleasure of hurling denunciations at innocent Emily. Or semi-innocent at this point.

Then Emily recalled that this box had actually belonged to Julie. Arguably her daughter had a better claim on it than her sister. Only possession had made it seem Lillian's property. Now possession had shifted, bringing along its nine-tenths of the law. Emily shoved two of the envelopes in Jack's briefcase for safe keeping and tucked the file of letters in her beach bag. She heard the bathroom door open and shoved the empty box under the bed with one foot.

Jack emerged clean and glowing, wearing khaki shorts and an Aloha shirt. "Our conference dress code has become more casual. Will you be staying in to write this afternoon?"

"I'll be more inspired if I'm on the beach. Plenty of battery power in my laptop, I'm ready for action."

"Who called?"

Emily had hoped the sound of water had drowned out the ringing of the phone. "The front desk."

"Are they offering us another promotional breakfast? If so, decline."

"No."

"So what did they want?"

"Kari dropped off the box at the front desk."

"Where you left it, I imagine, with a stern note, saying "Return to Sender." He cast a suspicious eye around the room.

"That might have been the wiser course."

"No question about it. Has it ever occurred to you that Kari is a danger to anyone who encounters her? A black-widow-spider kind of girl."

"You've captured her personality in a nutshell but she may point the way to important information."

"My advice is to avoid her. Don't let her suck you into her dubious adventures, especially ones that could land you in the slammer."

"Of course not. I am not that foolish."

Jack's doubting look was far from flattering.

Settled on a lounge chair on the beach, her laptop balanced on her knees, Emily typed rapidly. She covered three pages. Then her mind slid away from the task at hand.

How could Kari have resisted the temptation to go through those letters herself? Emily typed a few more lines. She glanced at the beach bag. Time for a little break. She pulled out a few letters and began to read. There was a series of letters back and forth between Julie and her sister, who had been on the mainland at college. The letters were filled with anecdotes of their daily life, gossip, comments about guys they dated. No passionate love letters, no confessions, no familiar names. Sadly disappointing. Back to work. Maybe she'd have better luck on her next little break.

Emily bent over her keyboard, trying to make up for lost time. Her cell phone's ring startled her.

Sarah sounded urgent. "I absolutely must get out of this house. Where are you?"

"Working."

"Where? Do I hear a seagull?"

"On the beach actually."

"Oh good."

Emily realized she had slipped up. The beach does not seem like a serious workaday spot where one cannot disturb a friend whose nose is to the grindstone.

"I can't sit here and wring my hands and stew about Matt and whether he is guilty and how Kari is involved for one more minute. The same thoughts run over and over in my mind and there's nothing useful I can do, absolutely nothing. Can we meet?"

Emily could not refuse. Sarah sounded too needy. "What do you have in mind? I really do have to write this article."

"You can easily combine work with pleasure."

"You intrigue me."

"This is going to sound crazy, but your readers will want to know where to shop."

"In Hawaii?"

"Not trinkets and junky souvenirs. Something really nice to remind them of their trip."

"I'm not so sure, Sarah. History, flora and fauna, yes, but shopping?"

"Shoppers' tips. Definitely."

"And you have some ideas."

"I'll pick you up in a half an hour in front of your hotel. Trust me. This will be very relaxing and will distract us from our troubles."

Relaxing? Hah! Emily was horrified at the prospect of keeping Kari's secret while spending an afternoon with Sarah. Should she tell? Certainly she had made no promises to Kari and felt no loyalty to the dreadful young woman. And yet, Sarah would certainly not like to be told that her daughter had confided in a virtual stranger rather than in her. Kari had said she would deny everything. Surely, Sarah would believe her daughter unless she had more insight into her nefarious character than she seemed to have. Emily felt she had become entangled in a hideous family situation through no actual fault of her own. What to do? There was no good answer. After some thought, Emily decided to try to cheer up her friend, say nothing until Kari could be persuaded to go to the police, and hope that her guilty secret was not emblazoned across her face for all to read.

Emily and Sarah spent the afternoon at a shopping complex across from the Aloha Tower. Sarah browsed through the shops, picking up and admiring, then discarding or choosing potential purchases, candles, earrings, scarves, sweaters. Apparently, she had no goal in mind, but swooped through like an invading army, taking whatever struck her fancy.

Emily reflected again on how much Sarah had changed since college. Emily remembered her as a tall athletic girl, with windblown cheeks, her hair tied back in an untidy ponytail that trailed down her back. She was at her best loping down the hockey field or basketball court, a strong young athlete. Off the playing fields, Sarah had seemed awkward, someone who was different in some slight, indefinable way.

Now despite the effects of the sun, Sarah was more attractive than she had been at twenty. *How could that be?* Emily wondered. Sarah's frosted hair was cut in neat, sharp layers, her makeup was subtle and flattering. She carried herself gracefully, not with galumphing strides.

"It's nice to be able to afford the things I want," Sarah said, gathering her purchases together. She had chosen a Lalique vase, a gold chain, a sandalwood candle, a paperweight, a paisley silk scarf.

That was the difference. Money. Sarah looked rich. And she was a whiz at spending.

Emily enjoyed being swept along on her friend's breathless, non-stop shopping spree. "This is like shopping with Martha Stewart. Such pretty things."

"Shopping relaxes me. After all these years it still surprises me to have money. Do you remember how I had to scrimp at college? I was a scholarship girl, waiting tables every night, never able to afford the things you all took for granted like going on a road trip or buying pizza. Those were huge extravagances for me."

Emily dimly recalled that Sarah was very studious, hardly ever leaving the library, refusing most invitations. Emily had never wondered why.

"Remember my sad clothes? I looked like a 4-H project gone awry. Homemade shapeless, dowdy outfits that my mother made, bless her heart. A woman with no taste and boundless energy at the sewing machine."

"I never noticed that you dressed any differently from the rest of us," Emily said.

"You were always perfectly put together," Sarah said.

"I dressed like everyone else."

"Exactly. I, however, stood out. I couldn't afford to buy a class blazer or class ring. Thank God those days are over. I could never go back to poverty or even a moderate income. Thank heavens I married a man who does very well."

Emily was surprised to find a contemporary who was pleased and proud to be supported by a man. This sounded like something her mother would say.

Apparently, Emily's surprise was writ large upon her face for Sarah added, "I know that makes me sound retro, but I feel my talent is to spend not earn. We all have our gifts."

Sarah flashed an ironic grin, but Emily believed she was telling the truth. Now she understood better what drew Sarah and Amanda together. Not just the experience of going to college together and a sense of isolation in a very small community. Here in Hawaii, they were both wealthy, drawn into a life of privilege, their fates intertwined through business connections and social life.

But Amanda had begun to pull away. More than ever, Emily suspected that the decision Amanda was considering would have led her away from the perfectly happy, serene life of their little band of friends.

"It may seem odd that I want to go shopping in a time of crisis," Sarah said, "but for me it's comforting. I was going crazy in that house. Thank you for coming with me, Emily. I hope I haven't cut into your workday too much. What's next?"

"I'm going home to write. Then tomorrow, Diamond Head, a place no tourist should miss."

"What a good idea! Shall I come with you? I'm a fabulous tour guide. Let's meet at the entrance at about 9 A.M. We'll have to wear sensible shoes and be ready for a good hike. It will do us both good."

Emily looked into her anxious eyes she couldn't refuse. "Sure, that's fine," Emily said without enthusiasm. Once more she would be faced with a dilemma. Should she tell Kari's version of what happened? Was it even true? Perhaps Amanda had found herself in the same situation, discovering information that could only hurt those she loved.

CHAPTER 17

After she returned from shopping with Sarah, Emily resolutely ignored the letters and memorabilia that Kari had given her, and devoted the rest of the day to writing her article. Early the next morning, she emailed it to George.

What amazing strength of character! Emily congratulated herself for her stern work ethic as she prepared to set off for Diamond Head. She glanced at the beach bag where she had tucked Julie's letters and postcards. Regrettably there was no time to read more of them. Sarah had stressed the importance of getting to Diamond Head early. There was no shelter from the sun and by noon it would be unpleasantly hot. Nevertheless Emily felt the letters' magnetic pull from deep within the beach bag. Perhaps Julie had written a letter that revealed the father of her baby and suggested a motive for Amanda's murder. Emily grabbed her beach bag and took it along. Sarah might be late. Then Emily would have time to read a few letters while she waited.

She turned on to Diamond Head Road. The Hawaiians had named the volcano Laeahi, brow of the tuna. Since Emily had never seen the profile of a tuna and knew the fish best in its tinned condition, she took on faith the appropriateness of this ancient name. British sailors renamed the volcano Diamond Head because, seeing it from a distance, they had noticed calcite crystals in the lava glittering in the sun and mistaken them for diamonds.

Emily drove up into the crater, parked the car and walked toward the trailhead marker where she had arranged to meet Sarah. Wearing a baseball cap to keep off the sun, camp shorts and a T-shirt, Emily was sensibly dressed for the climb. She looked up toward the rim. Long ago lava had shot up from this very spot, spilling over the sides of the crater high above her. Now the crater looked dry and dusty. The volcano had been extinct for 150,000 years.

Keeping her eyes peeled for Sarah, Emily came to a booth where two young people were handing out bottles of water. Returning hikers were snatching them and gulping water as if they had just crossed the desert. Emily was glad she had tucked a water bottle and her cell phone in a knapsack. Like a scout she was prepared for whatever might befall her.

To her surprise, Brent was waiting for her on the path just past the booth. Deeply tan, wearing climbing boots and khaki shorts, he stood with his profile toward her, one foot on a rock, gazing up at the rim, as if he were posing for a photo in an adventure magazine.

"Hi," Emily called out to him. "Where's Sarah?"

"Something came up. She asked me to take her place. I'll be your guide for the day."

"That's odd," Emily said, realizing, as she spoke, that Miss Manners would probably advise her to show pleasure, not astonishment, at greeting a friend, or even an acquaintance.

"I've brought you chocolate to make up for the disappointment of finding such a poor substitute for Sarah." He held out a Toblerone bar. "You'll need sustenance for the climb."

"That is kind. White chocolate with almonds is very nourishing. What came up?" Emily peeled off the wrapper and took a bite.

"More trouble with Kari. Sarah's dealing with it." Brent marched on ahead.

Emily hurried to catch up. She wondered why Sarah hadn't called.

"Sarah tried to call, but you must had already left," Brent called back.

How could that be? Emily's cell phone had been lying quietly in her knapsack all the while. Perhaps it had malfunctioned.

A few people were walking up ahead. On the trail going down, she saw a long line of hikers, who looked like refugees on a forced march. Women wearing short skirts teetered on stylish chunky platform heels. Parents carried toddlers in packs on their backs.

Traveler's Tip: Do not wear high heels if you plan to hike to the top of Diamond Head! After a rigorous uphill climb, you must walk up 99 stairs and then after a bit, another 100 stairs. Do not let this deter you. The fabulous view makes your effort well worthwhile. But dress sensibly.

At this point, Emily was taking the fabulous view on faith, but she could always erase her mental note if it didn't live up to advance notices.

"I'm glad to have this chance to talk to you alone, Emily," Brent called back. He was striding along the paved trail at a good clip.

"Really?" Emily picked up the pace. Brent's long legs were churning relentlessly forward. She was determined not to fall behind.

"I have something important to tell you." Brent glanced back over his shoulder. "But I must ask you not to repeat it to Sarah."

"I can't help you keep secrets from your wife. Sisterly solidarity forbids it."

"I understand your scruples, Emily. But I have very good reason for asking you to keep this particular secret. I'm only thinking of Sarah's welfare. I'm trying to protect her."

"Do you really think Sarah's such a delicate flower that she needs protection?" Emily asked.

There was a pause. Brent stopped and turned to her, his brown eyes softened with concern. "You don't want Sarah to be hurt, do you?"

"Of course not. Secrets between couples always cause pain."

Brent dropped his eyes. "Not always. Confession can unburden the guilty and, at the same time, inflict painful knowledge on the innocent. Don't you agree?" He scuffed the ground with the toe of his boot.

Emily had read too many letters in advice columns from unfaithful, repentant spouses not to see where he was going. She felt the snare tighten, and gave a last fluttering attempt to escape.

"I am not advising you to confess to anything, Brent. I am simply refusing to be your accomplice."

He didn't answer. His lips compressed into a tight white line. He turned from her and moved forward. Emily had not meant to put Brent in his place quite so firmly but there was a limit to the number of secrets she was prepared to keep from Sarah. Kari's unwelcome confidences were entangling enough.

She could hear Brent's labored breathing as they hiked along through the barren, bowl-shaped crater. Dry grass, dusty earth and scrub Kiawe trees made a stark contrast to the lush version of Hawaii she had seen so far. They reached the first set of stairs and walked up in silence. The hike was less than two miles but it was straight up and even at Brent's brisk pace they had been climbing for more than an hour.

Up ahead Emily could see the entrance to the unlit tunnel. Brent was waiting for her. "Did you bring a flashlight?" he asked when she loped to his side.

"I knew I'd forgotten something." She wondered why he didn't have one. He looked like such a mountain man.

"That's all right. I'll watch out for you." Brent grinned, flashing large, perfectly white teeth. He seemed to be over his snit. Stepping back, he let her enter the tunnel first. Emily was glad. She didn't want Brent to go barreling ahead and leave her all alone. The tunnel was pitch dark and she knew from her reading it led upward for 225 feet. Emily ran her hand along the rough wall to steady herself. They climbed in silence. Suddenly, Emily was grabbed from behind and pulled off balance. Teetering, she cried out in shock, her cry echoing in the darkness. In a moment, Brent was holding her upright, his fingers gripping her ribcage so tightly that it hurt.

"I thought you were going to fall. Thank God I caught you, Emily. This is a treacherous climb." She could feel Brent's breath in her ear.

"Nonsense. I was doing just fine." Emily shook him off and continued forward, moving gingerly now, her hand clinging to the wall. Brent's sudden fits of manly protectiveness could drive a woman crazy. How on earth did Sarah stand it?

Traveler's Tip: *Bring your flashlight. You'll need it. I know you didn't take it on vacation with you so stop at the ABC Store. You won't regret it.*

Gratefully, Emily emerged into light. They were at the top of Diamond Head. Howling winds whipped around the tower, blowing her hair in her face. Leaning out over the parapet she could see for miles in all directions.

"You can see all the way from Kapiolani Park to Koko Head," Brent yelled.

Emily clung to the metal railing. Looking back toward Waikiki, she saw the undulating coastline, the changing colors of the sea fading from dark blue to turquoise, hundreds of skyscrapers for miles and miles, and away in the distance puffs of white clouds drifting over the mountains. There was no need to amend her traveler's tip. This spectacular view was well worth the climb.

Emily looked straight down at lush vegetation, the palm trees along the water's edge, exposed reefs poking up in the turquoise sea. It was breathtaking. She pushed her hair back from her face and leaned into the wind.

"Emily, I have not been completely honest," Brent bent close to her, his voice a hoarse whisper. "I'm afraid you'll find out my secret on your own and tell Sarah. Or Kari. That's why I'm trying to make a preemptive strike, extract your promise and tell you the truth before you discover it. Believe me, it's to protect Sarah, not just to save my own skin."

"You give me too much credit for unearthing secrets." Emily edged along the parapet, dazzled by the view, not wanting to hear an outpouring of confidences.

"You'll find out all right," Brent snapped. "You have papers that belonged to Lillian. Papers that were stolen."

"What makes you think so?" Under pressure, Emily stalled for time, using a stock reply that had served her well since childhood.

Brent brushed past this question, his voice bitter now. "I know all about your involvement in this incident. There are a couple of areas of concern. First, encouraging my daughter to steal property that is not her own and then to conceal it. You have been an accomplice. A receiver of stolen goods, if you will."

Emily felt a pang of guilt. She should have called Lillian and given the box back instead of organizing it out of all recognition. For a moment, Emily was tempted to advance Kari's own slightly shaky arguments about having a better claim to her mother's property than Lillian, but decided to admit nothing. How could Brent be so sure she had the documents? Kari wouldn't tell him. Maybe Brent was just guessing.

The wind was howling. A family of tourists emerged from the tunnel. A little boy ran for the railing and climbed up. Emily waited in vain for his parents to yell, "Get down, you moron, that's dangerous." They had nerves of steel. Or else this kid was expendable.

The father had his camera out and began herding the kids into a family photo. The mother balanced a plump baby on the railing. The three children gathered around her.

The anger had faded from Brent's face as suddenly as it had come. He switched to tour guide mode, speaking loudly enough for the family to be edified. "Did you know that Diamond Head was sacred to the wind god? Human sacrifices were carried out here."

Like Puu O Mahuka Heiau. Emily shuddered, remembering the site of Amanda's murder. For a peaceful island, there were quite a few places with grim and violent histories. She tried to tune out the family's voices and gazed out at the mist drifting across the panorama below.

Brent came up behind her. She remembered his hands on her waist in the tunnel and backed away from the edge, bumping against him and dodging sideways. Her move was instinctive.

"Are you afraid of heights?" He seemed surprised.

"Not usually. Can we go down?"

The family had completed their photographs and ducked back down into the tunnel, their voices receding as they climbed down.

"In a minute. I want to tell you about my second area of concern."

As he became frustrated, Brent's language became more pompous.

"There may be letters in that box that are compromising. I didn't want to tell you this, but apparently, I'll have to."

An edge of resentment was seeping back into his tone. Brent seemed be waiting for Emily to say, "No, no, you don't have to tell me anything. I'll give you whatever you want." How Sarah must spoil him! Emily had no intention of making the same mistake. She waited to hear what the "compromising" content might be.

Brent sighed. "All right, you win. I'll tell you the whole story."

"Let's go down first," Emily said. "It's too windy up here. I feel as if I'll be blown away."

"Okay. Fine." Brent took Emily's elbow, and led her toward the tunnel.

"You first," Emily said, stepping back. She didn't want to be subjected to any more grabbing from behind.

Brent stepped past her. Emily could hear him clunking down the steps in front of her, but couldn't see a thing. They continued in silence down 99 steps and came out at last into hazy sunlight.

"What a good place for a rest stop," Emily said. She sat down on a boulder and patted the space beside her. Brent leaned back against the rock, stretching out his legs.

"So, you have something to tell me."

Brent sighed deeply. "Okay. I guess I have to."

"Not necessarily. This was your idea."

Brent ignored her comment. "You have to understand that Kari's mother Julie was a beautiful woman," he said softly, looking down, his boot rubbing the dust into a circle. "We worked very closely together. At first, I pretended not to notice how she was flirting, brushing up against me, coming closer than she needed, her intimate smiles. I tried to make a joke of her little crush on me. Finally, one night, we were alone at the office, working late. I told Julie to go home, I didn't need help, but she insisted it was no trouble."

Brent looked up, gave a boyish grin and spread his hands. "What can I say? Nobody is perfect."

"So you had an affair?"

"No, no. Just one night."

"I don't get it. Why is this so significant after all these years? Are you Kari's father? Is that what you're saying?"

"Possibly. I never knew for sure."

"And you think there are letters from you to Julie that would reveal this?"

"Maybe. I don't know. I never even thought about it until Kari tried to find out more about her birth mother. Then I remembered letters I'd written to Julie. I had asked her to destroy them, but I don't know if she ever did. Kari told me that her aunt Lillian had a box of Julie's old letters. She was very excited. Clearly she would read every word. I began to wonder what was in those letters. I asked Kari to leave them alone, forget about her birth mother. She thought I was just being possessive."

No wonder Kari was afraid to leave the box where Brent could find it, Emily thought. Brent was determined to protect his secret and must have been unable to conceal his intention from Kari.

"Why did you write to Julie? Didn't she work in your office? What did you do—pass notes back and forth like middle schoolers?"

"Julie found out she was pregnant while Sarah and I were in Kansas, visiting my folks. My Dad was sick at the time. He'd had a heart attack that scared us badly. Julie kept calling me. I couldn't talk to her. I was never alone. I told her I'd write if she'd just get off the goddam phone and stay off. Anyone could have picked up the extension and heard her ranting at me. Sarah. My mother. My poor Dad. Then I wrote to Julie, making promises, whatever she wanted as long as she didn't tell anyone, not a soul, not even her sister. I'd support her if she wanted to keep the baby, and if she made another choice, fine. But if anyone found out, all deals were off. At the end of the letter, I wrote, 'Destroy this!' in capital letters. But did she? Or did she keep it as insurance, a written contract? I have no idea. Julie was a mystery to me. We weren't lovers. We had an encounter."

Brent's voice trembled with emotion. "Please, Emily. It would kill Sarah to know the truth. She adores Kari and this would ruin their relationship. Sarah wouldn't be able to look at Kari without feeling resentment and anger. I made another woman pregnant in a meaningless one-night stand, while my own wife never could conceive a child."

Emily suspected that Sarah's "resentment and anger," would be directed at Brent, not Kari. Still, the knowledge would cause Sarah great pain.

Brent touched Emily's arm. "I need your help, Emily. I can't tell Sarah. I can't let Kari find out. It would be cruel. Secrets are sometimes the best way. The truth could only hurt."

Emily felt herself wavering. Brent was right. There was no point in hurting Sarah to satisfy Kari's curiosity. It wouldn't do anyone any good.

"What do you want me to do?"

"Give me the box of papers. I'll sort through them and take out anything that incriminates me. I'll give everything else back to you."

"Let me think, Brent. Let's go back." Emily stood up, brushed the dust off the seat of her shorts and started down the path. How had she become so entangled in this family's secrets? There seemed no honorable way out.

Brent came up beside her and took her elbow, tightening his grip. "What is there to think about? It's pretty clear what you must do."

He was getting testy again. His boyish charm was a thin veneer over an exasperated, angry determination to get his own way.

"Kari made me promise." Emily jerked free. Actually she had never promised Kari anything but this seemed like an excellent excuse to hold onto the letters long enough to find out if there was anything that could shed light on Amanda's murder, unlikely as that was under these new circumstances. It was hard to let go of her theory.

Brent walked beside her. They were both moving downhill quickly now. "Kari doesn't even have to know the papers were out of your hands. I'll give them right back."

"I have a better idea. I could skim through them and give you any letter that reveals your secret." Emily turned to face him. "That way I wouldn't break my promise to Kari." Emily thought of the letters tucked in her beach bag, locked in the trunk of the car. She hadn't even had a chance to read them. How foolish her restraint seemed now.

"I'd prefer not to have anyone else read my intimate, personal correspondence." Brent's tone was as icy as a Minnesota winter.

Emily blushed. Her offer did seem presumptuous. She should have denied having the letters. Damn that knee-jerk reflex of honesty.

"Come on, Emily. You know what you have to do."

"Let me talk to Kari first," Emily said.

"Impossible," Brent snapped. "She's at the police station."

Emily gasped. Brent was clearly enjoying his dramatic way of revealing the news but she saw that he was truly upset. "What happened? Have they arrested her?"

"The police pulled Kari in for questioning. If she doesn't cooperate, she's going to find herself charged as an accessory in a murder."

"So that's why Sarah didn't come." Now Emily could understand Brent's tension and his strange mood swings. It was more than just trying to cover up his somewhat shady past.

"Exactly. She hurried off to be with Kari. I thought this would give me an opportunity to talk to you alone, Emily. I simply cannot have my wife and daughter hear the painful story of a two-decades-old indiscretion right now. Yes, I was wrong. A sinful, lustful man. I succumbed to snares of the flesh for one night and I have spent years making amends. I've taken in my daughter and I have loved her." His voice broke and he ran his hand over his eyes for a moment before he continued, "Sarah is shattered by this. First her best friend is murdered by our daughter's boyfriend. Now Kari's been drawn into the whole sordid mess. You can't allow them to be hurt any more, Emily." His brown eyes revealed a world of sorrow; he was leaning toward her, his voice barely a whisper.

Emily realized she had to give him what he wanted. There was almost no hope that the letters would shed light on who had killed Amanda. Besides, Brent would give them back to her and she could skim through them, looking for clues.

"Emily, please," he whispered, his eyes brimming with unshed tears.

"All right. I'll give them to you."

Brent relaxed, smiled. "I'll follow you back to your apartment and take the letters off your hands."

"No need for that. They're in the car."

"Even better." Brent was grinning at her.

He was in a jovial mood as they continued on down to the bottom of the crater. Emily stopped for a minute, rummaged around in her knapsack, pulled out her bottle of water and held it out to Brent. "Want a swig?"

"Nope." He shot a quick look at his watch.

Emily took the hint and walked along. Back at the car, Emily popped open the trunk, pulled out her beach bag, dug around for a minute, then pulled out the manila envelope. "Here it is," she said holding it out to him.

Brent's smile faded. "There was a box. A large box of Julie's papers."

"I organized it. These are the letters. Much simpler for you."

Far from being grateful, Brent was looking at the envelope in his hand in stunned disbelief.

"They're all there. I haven't even read them." At least not all of them. Emily wished there had been time to find his letter. She was curious about the tone. Had his letter to Julie been written in a lover's voice, or that of a threatened employer who had slipped just that once?

"It would be best to give me the box, everything." Brent's voice was cold.

Emily could see that he didn't believe she had given him all the letters. Offended that he didn't see how trustworthy she was, Emily banged the car trunk car closed and snapped, "Brent, the box is gone."

"Gone? What do you mean?"

Emily walked around and slid into the driver's seat. "I had a bout of tidiness. You have all you need in that envelope. Nothing more to fear." She pulled the car door shut.

Brent had one hand on top of her car. He was leaning over, glaring at her.

Emily rolled down the window. "Your secret is safe with me. But remember, you said you'd give the letters back so I could keep most of my promise to Kari."

Emily turned the key in the ignition and revved the motor. Brent stepped back quickly.

He should be whooping in triumph, Emily thought as she drove away. *Why isn't he?*

CHAPTER 18

Emily burst into the hotel room, eager to tell Jack the tale of her adventure at Diamond Head. "I must tell you about the latest developments. Most interesting news." She plopped on the bed beside Jack and kissed him.

Jack was reclining on the bed, watching television. On the screen a man in an Aloha shirt was teaching the Hawaiian word for the day, "*Pua,* flower," he said, brandishing an orchid.

"Kari is not the only one to be captivated by traditional ways," Jack said. "Today I have learned that *pua,* meaning flower, is not to be confused with *pupu,* a snack."

Emily did not feel guilty for cutting his language lesson short for she could not imagine when he would find himself called upon to speak Hawaiian.

"Jack, listen to this. Brent is Kari's father. He admitted it, more or less, claims he isn't absolutely certain, but he has reason to believe. I'm not sure what this means to the investigation, however."

Jack switched off the television and gave Emily his full attention. "What investigation? I thought you were staying out of it."

"I am. But somehow I—all unwittingly—find myself in possession of information I can't share with anyone. Brent begged me not to tell Sarah. Poor soul. She's in the dark about most of her family's nefarious activities."

"Why on earth does everyone keep confiding in you?"

"I'd like to think it was because of my wise and sympathetic nature, but Brent only told me because he thought I'd find out by reading the letters."

"Why was Brent at Diamond Head anyway? I thought you were meeting Sarah?"

"That was the plan, but the police pulled Kari in for questioning so Sarah rushed to the station to be at her side. Brent showed up instead and he persuaded me to give him the letters."

"I'm surprised you gave in so easily."

"Brent played on my finer feelings. He pointed out that discovering the truth could only hurt Sarah and damage her relationship with Kari. They were his own letters after all. And since Brent is Kari's father, the letters are not likely to reveal a motive for murder. It would be significant if Todd were the father. At a time when their marriage was shaky anyway, if Amanda found out ..."

"Todd might kill to suppress the secret."

"I can't believe it, but, arguably it would give him a motive. Or anyone else whose career or marriage could be damaged by such a discovery."

"Maybe Brent killed Amanda to cover up his secret. Did you think of that?"

"No. Too thin a motive. Brent wants to spare Sarah unnecessary pain, but killing her best friend would hardly accomplish that. He was in an odd mood today. He veered between pleading with me, his eyes swimming with tears, which is always disconcerting, and heaping me with bitter reproaches. Once he grabbed me in a dark, scary tunnel. I don't know if he was trying to show off his manly power or what."

"Good lord. Grabbed you?"

"He thought I was going to fall. Why, I cannot imagine."

"Well you do teeter about sometimes." Jack looked relieved. "Especially when you've lost a contact lens."

Emily glowered. She considered herself as surefooted and nimble as a mountain goat and was slightly miffed that neither Jack nor Brent seemed to recognize this. Tactfully, she changed the subject. "You came in so late from your dinner with the other docs last night that I didn't have time to show you what I bought on my expedition with Sarah." Emily pulled a large shopping bag out of the closet and dumped an array of souvenirs onto the bed. The sight of her small treasures dispelled her irritation. One by one, she held up small plastic bags of leafless sprouts with pictures of magnificent tropical plants on the label. "Look at this, Jack, a Ti plant, White Ginger, Bamboo, Bird of Paradise."

"They're awfully small. Sticks really."

"They'll grow. And look what else." She displayed jars of mango, pineapple and papaya jam, coconut syrup, cans of Macadamia nuts, plain, candied and chocolate coated, White Ginger bath oil and powder, coral earrings.

"You're going to haul all that stuff home on the plane?"

"You don't sound properly impressed by my souvenirs."

The phone rang. Emily paused, regarding it with deep, well founded suspicion and let Jack answer.

He held out the receiver, mouthing the words, "Another crisis."

Emily groaned, but she took the phone. "Emily, this is a nightmare," Sarah gasped. "It just keeps getting worse and worse."

"What happened?"

"Did Brent tell you? Kari was picked up for questioning."

"That's not so terrible, is it? After all, Kari was discovered in the apartment of the suspected murderer. They'll just ask a few questions and let her go, right?"

"If she would give anyone a straight answer, maybe it would be like that," Sarah said. "But she won't. The police think she's an accomplice. Brent wants to get Scanlon as her lawyer, but Kari refuses."

Emily cursed Kari for putting her in a position where she knew secrets that were kept from her own mother.

"Have you asked her if she was on the beach the night Amanda died?" Emily asked.

"Of course, I have. Many times. Kari says, 'No comment,' a horribly annoying answer. I think she's trying to protect Matt. Maybe Brent's right. Maybe Matt did kill Amanda. Otherwise I have no idea why Matt and Kari wouldn't simply explain what happened. Is it a case of mistaken identity or are they hiding something?"

Should I tell her? Emily wondered. If she did, would Sarah feel better or worse? Worse probably. She would hate knowing that her daughter had turned to a stranger and would be appalled that Kari had been involved in moving Amanda's body and disturbing evidence.

"What are you doing tonight?" Sarah asked.

"Jack and I are going out to dinner." Emily noticed Jack was rooting around the room, lifting up his jacket, newspapers, a beach towel, apparently in search of something.

"I don't suppose you could stop over for a drink first. Just for a minute."

Emily didn't want to see Brent; she knew far too much about his wayward past. Groping for an excuse, she asked, "Jack, do we have plans for tonight?" She tried to position herself in Jack's line of vision, nodding her head vigorously and mouthing "yes."

Intent on his search, Jack did not look up. "No, I don't believe we do," he called out in a loud, clear voice.

Emily sighed. "Just for a minute then. We're planning an early night." She turned off her phone and turned to Jack. "Why didn't you pick up on my signal? Dr. Watson would have been quicker."

"I don't like to be cast as Watson, a dimwitted sort of fellow."

"I was giving unmistakable visual cues as to the right answer."

Jack laughed. "It didn't occur to me to look for my cue like a well-trained seal."

"What were you hunting for so avidly anyway?"

"A most interesting article in the *New England Journal of Medicine*. I must have left it in my briefcase in the car. Remind me to bring it in tonight."

On the drive over to Sarah and Brent's house, Emily gazed out the window at the crowded bright streets of Waikiki. With the car windows rolled down, she heard horns honking, tires squealing, the hubbub of city life. They were traveling along the shore road in the direction of Diamond Head just as the sun was setting. Emily wished she had been firm and turned down Sarah's invitation.

"Horrible as it is to imagine, until this afternoon I really did wonder about Brent just a little," Emily said.

"And now you don't?"

"No. I think he was just trying to hide his tracks, cover up his old affair. Diamond Head is the sort of place that stimulates horrible fantasies. People were sacrificed to the wind god, cast down into the fiery volcano. It chills my blood just to think of it."

Jack turned the car into a narrow road flanked by palm trees." Didn't you say Kari's mother died under mysterious circumstances? Is Brent off the hook for that too?"

"He was never on the hook. Lillian says there was no question of Julie's death being anything other than an accident. I admit I had my doubts. But nobody would kill to cover up an affair. They're far too common."

"I thought you had very strict views about infidelity."

"For my near and dear, I do," she said, patting his knee. "To the rest of the world I'm quite lenient, recognizing men are often weak and prone to vice."

"What about Sarah? Does she share your strict or your lenient view?"

"Hard to say." Emily wondered about that. She couldn't imagine Sarah leaving Brent; she was far too comfortable, reveling in her life of ease and riches. But surely she would be crushed, not to mention mad as hell, if she found out about his indiscretion. All in all, Emily was glad she had given Brent the letters and kept them away from Kari's prying eyes. Perhaps Brent would have already found the incriminating letter and would give back the envelope tonight. If he didn't say anything, she would be sure to pull him aside and ask.

They pulled into the driveway and parked by the front door. Gentle breezes wafted the fragrance of unseen tropical flowers. In the distance, Emily could hear the sound of surf pounding on rocks.

Brent answered the door. "Come on in. Sarah's in the pool. She was afraid it would take you a good while to get here and she wanted to work off her anxiety." Barely glancing at Emily, he greeted Jack with hearty, man-to-man good will. Emily was glad. It was embarrassing to know his secrets.

Brent led the way through the living room out French doors to an oval pool. The turquoise water, brilliantly illuminated by spotlights, was shimmering like a jewel in the darkening night. Sarah was churning through the water.

"Hey Sarah," Brent yelled.

Sarah bobbed up and shook the water from her hair. "You were so kind to come, Emily." She swam to the side and pulled herself up. Sarah was still a strong, powerful athlete, Emily noticed, making a firm resolve to use her barbells every day.

Sarah dried off rapidly.

"What can I get you?" Brent went over to a poolside bar and stood ready to dispense drinks.

"Something plain," Jack said. "No umbrellas or tropical fruit garnish please."

Brent handed him a single malt scotch and filled requests for white wine from Emily and Sarah.

Sarah pulled a yellow caftan over her head and rolled her hair into a towel turban. "Shall we go inside, or would you rather sit by the pool?"

"It's lovely outside," Emily said.

Brent flicked a switch activating lily-shaped lights that lit the patio, glimmering on plants that flanked the tile verandah. He motioned to chairs around a rattan table and lit a citronella candle.

"Scanlon will sort this out," Brent said. "Kari will be out by tomorrow. The police can't hold her longer than twenty-four hours unless they charge her."

"There's no evidence," Sarah cried. "How could there be?"

"So it's just the word of this one witness?" Emily asked.

"At this point, yes," Brent said. "They're running forensic tests on Matt's catamaran and now they've impounded Kari's jeep. They'll be able to determine once and for all whether Matt's guilty. Thank God. I'm inclined to think he did it. Who else? He's the only real suspect."

Emily's heart sank. Of course, the tests would show that Amanda's body had been in the boat and the jeep. Why didn't Kari explain now?

"Did Matt have a motive?" Jack asked, sipping his scotch.

"None that was apparent," Brent said.

"And certainly Kari didn't," Sarah added. "She likes Matt, but not enough to conspire to murder Amanda who has been a friend all her life. She'd have to be a monster to do such a thing." Sarah pulled off the towel and drew her fingers through her damp hair.

"The witness recognized the boat and I imagine he knows it belongs to Matt so he thinks he saw him. He didn't say anything about Kari. Just mentioned another person, possibly female," Brent said.

"They arrested Kari right in this house. When she wouldn't tell them anything, they read her her rights, then handcuffed her like a common criminal."

Emily and Jack exchanged a look. It didn't sound as if Kari had just been pulled in for routine questioning. She was probably "a person of interest."

"I followed them down to the station, but the police wouldn't let me see her." Sarah's voice faltered.

"Tomorrow," Brent promised. "Scanlon will take care of it."

"After I'd waited for hours and hours at the police station, I came back here and Kari called me. I was so relieved to hear her voice. She sounded scared. The cell is filled with women from all walks of life." Sarah paused to let the enormity of that statement sink in.

"You didn't expect her to have a private room, did you?" Brent asked. "This is serious. Kari has to wake up and realize that."

Emily wished she could barge into the police station and set this all to rights. If Kari didn't explain soon, Emily would have to tell Sarah and Brent, and possibly the police as well. But it would be much more convincing if Kari spoke up herself. At best, her story sounded implausible.

"Did Kari tell you why she won't talk to the police?" Emily asked.

"She very wisely wanted to consult with a lawyer first," Sarah said. "And she wanted to make sure that Matt was represented as well." Sarah looked at Brent, waiting for a response. "Brent, she must have told you. When she called earlier, she must have asked if Scanlon could represent them both."

"Why the hell would I arrange that? Matt is probably the killer. Kari's interests and his are not the same. Matt has access to a public defender. It's a lot more than he deserves. Kari is not going to blackmail me into paying for legal counsel for Matt."

"She's not trying to blackmail you," Sarah said. "Kari is understandably concerned about Matt and she's a stubborn girl"

"She'll be more flexible after a few days in jail." Brent went to the bar, rattling the ice in his empty glass. "Anyone want another?"

"No thanks. We have to go," Jack drained his scotch and stood up. A pall had settled over the company.

"We could send out for Chinese," Brent said quickly.

Emily saw that Brent was as eager as Sarah to have company, possibly as a distraction from their troubles, or as a buffer between them.

"I wish we could," Jack said. "Unfortunately, I told one of my colleagues at the conference that we would join him and his wife for dinner."

Brent clapped him on the back. "Enjoy your evening."

On the way out, Emily put her hand on Brent's arm to detain him. She spoke softly while Sarah was talking to Jack. "Have you had a chance to …?"

"I'll get them back to you tomorrow," he said, propelling her toward the door.

Settled into the rental car, Emily asked, "Is this colleague fictitious?"

"Yes, he is. I was stung by your earlier criticism of my failure to abet your phony spur-of-the-moment excuse."

Stars were coming out as they drove along the ocean back toward downtown Waikiki.

"I was hoping Brent would have already found what he was looking for so he could give me back the rest of the letters tonight," Emily said.

"Perhaps he's a slow reader."

"Tomorrow, he said. I just hope he turns them over before Kari gets out of jail."

"Don't let that dreadful girl bully you. You did not ask to be the custodian of her stolen goods."

"No, but when Kari gets out, she's bound to come to me, brimming with hope that I've found a clue, which, of course, I have not. And then she'll want to see the letters, and look for herself. She's desperate for any information that will prove who the real killer is and I can't explain why this is a false trail."

"I don't think you have to worry about Kari getting out any time soon. Are you convinced that she's telling the truth? Maybe she and Matt were both involved in Amanda's murder after all. Her story is a bit preposterous."

"Kari was devoted to Amanda. Unpleasant as she is, Kari is trying to do the right thing, to protect Matt and make sure he has legal counsel. She feels guilty for getting him involved in all this. I'm not so sure about Matt. Maybe he's not as innocent as she thinks."

"Matt has an alibi, as you well know. If Kari's story is true, they were locked in a passionate embrace while Amanda was being murdered."

"Maybe Matt knows who did it. Perhaps he was part of the group that wanted something from Amanda that she refused to give. Kari could have been fooled into acting as an accomplice."

"Matt could not anticipate that Kari would come up with the ridiculous and dangerous plan to move Amanda's body to Pu'O Mahuka Heiau. No, either they're both innocent or they're in it together."

Emily offered an alternative. "Maybe Matt planted the idea of the traditional ceremony in her mind and Kari is presenting it as her own."

"Why are you defending this young woman and trying to pin the rap on her hapless boyfriend?"

"Probably because I don't really know Matt and I do know Kari." Emily wondered how close Matt was to Mau Koolani and his group. The link to the old religion seemed to hold the key to the mystery. Then she remembered that she had said the same thing about the letters.

CHAPTER 19

Later that night, relaxed and revived by good food, Emily followed Jack down the corridor to their hotel room, humming happily. She would soak in a White Ginger bubble bath, paint her toenails red, and put on the white lace camisole that Jack found so fetching.

Her mellow mood was not destined to last. Jack started to open the door, then stopped and reached back for her hand. He turned to her, his face ashen.

"What is it?"

"Wait, Emily. Someone might still be inside. Don't go in there." Jack tightened his grip on her hand.

Peering past him, Emily saw a scene of devastation. The tropical sprouts had been ripped from their bags, snapped and scattered in green shreds about the room. Macadamia nuts were scattered everywhere. Chocolate-stained sheets were ripped from the beds, the mattresses hung off the box springs. Clothes were dumped in a heap on the floor. Coconut syrup ran in rivulets, forming sticky puddles in the creases of a crumpled dress.

Emily didn't see anyone lurking. There was really no place to hide in such a small room so she edged inside. Jack swiftly moved forward, flung open the closet door, then the bathroom door. He sighed with relief. "All clear."

Emily ran to the closet to look for her laptop computer. "Thank God my computer is still there," she cried, hugging it to her it as if it were a child. A small miracle. Why didn't they steal what was easily the most valuable item in the room? Still she was grateful for small favors. Her computer was an extra brain where her thoughts, reflections and articles were stored. Her moment of relief was followed by panic. "Where are the letters from Amanda's family?"

"They must be here someplace. No burglar would want them."

But Emily soon realized the letters were definitely gone. "What will I tell Todd?"

"That they were stolen. It's not your fault. I suppose we looked like rich tourists to some misguided thief."

"Luckily, we don't travel with anything of value. The only jewelry I have with me is this bracelet. There's no money in the room and the souvenirs didn't cost much. They were just for fun. But I do feel terrible about Amanda's family papers."

"Whoever did this sure made a hell of a mess." Jack picked up a shirt that had been ripped in half. "It's vindictive. Frightening really. I suppose we'd better call the police." He slowly stood up and began to pick up the papers and magazines that had been ripped apart and strewn on the floor.

"Let's move to another hotel, Jack. One with a security system like Fort Knox. What if we had been here when these goons broke in?"

"I would have taken care of it," Jack said, but he looked as upset as Emily felt by this invasion.

Emily lifted the phone and dialed "911."

A short time later, two uniformed police officers stood among the wreckage. The hotel manager hovered in the background, wringing his hands and blinking rapidly.

"Man, this is one sorry mess. I'm Sergeant Kau and this is Officer Blum."

Blum, a thin man with strands of hair combed over his bald head nodded and gave a brief, frosty smile.

"Sorry this happened to you folks," Officer Kau said. He glanced around the room, his report form and a pen in hand. "What's missing?"

"Some historic documents that belong to a friend," Emily said.

"That's it? Papers?"

"It's hard to tell in all this mess, but I think so."

Both officers looked to Jack for confirmation.

"As far as I know," Jack said, "perfect strangers invaded our room just to smash souvenirs and steal personal letters."

"Whoever did this was probably looking for money and jewelry and was seriously pissed off when he didn't find them," Officer Blum said.

"I know this doesn't seem too serious, and you must see truly terrible crimes." Emily began to apologize as she realized that what to her seemed like a horrible violation was small potatoes to the police.

The hotel manager, a plump man with a smile that faded in and out like a light bulb in its last moments, offered his own apologies. "Our security system is excellent. I have no idea how they got in. This has never happened before."

"These guys weren't the first to foil your security system," Emily snapped. The prospect of cleaning up the horrible mess was making her crabby.

"This has happened before?" Sgt. Kau turned to her with sharp attention and Emily realized she should have kept her mouth shut.

"No, it's nothing. A friend, a girl I know, was able to slip past the front desk and come up here and knock on our door. She didn't break in."

"We'll be happy to have our cleaning staff put your room back in shape," the manager intervened, his smile twitching.

Emily gave him a grateful smile. "That is very kind of you." She was willing to drop any complaints about security just to have her room restored to normal.

"Where is this girl now?" asked Officer Blum.

"Oh, she's out of the picture," Emily said. "She couldn't have been involved."

"Maybe not. We'll just check. What's her name?"

"Kari Gardner."

"That sounds familiar," Blum said, frowning.

"Why do you say she's out of the picture?" Kau asked, glancing up from his report pad, fixing flinty eyes on Emily. "Where is she?"

"In jail, actually," Emily admitted.

Both officers were now paying Emily keen attention.

"On burglary charges?"

"No. She couldn't have done this."

"Not directly perhaps, but it's possible she's part of a crime ring. We've known criminals to operate from a jail cell," Sgt. Kau said.

"Do you know if she's a drug dealer?" Officer Blum asked, scanning the room with his pale watery eyes.

"No, no, let me explain. Kari's been pulled in for questioning in connection with a murder."

Seeing the police snap to attention, Emily realized she was beginning to look less like a typical tourist and more like someone with underworld connections.

"Probably a drug-related murder," Blum muttered. "Have you ever been arrested on a drug charge yourself, ma'am?" he asked.

"Certainly not," Emily snapped. She noticed that Jack looked amused and silently vowed revenge.

"Do you have a police record of any kind?"

"No, I'm the victim here, remember?"

"How about you, sir? Any convictions?" Emily was pleased to see Jack's look of shock and surprise.

"Of course not. I'm a physician."

The magic word failed to have the desired effect.

"We'd better run a check on them," Blum said, glancing at his partner.

"Right." Kau turned away to speak into his phone, then strode back toward them. "I knew that name sounded familiar. Just talked to Homicide. Kari Gardner is a person of interest in the Amanda Blake murder. She's been pulled in for questioning and is stonewalling."

"I didn't realize the Blake murder was drug-related," Officer Blum said. "But it makes sense."

"No, no. Drugs have nothing to do with it," Emily said. She saw Jack's warning glance and realized she was protesting too much. "At least, I've never heard that they did," she added.

"This wasn't much of a robbery, was it? They just tossed this place. What were they looking for?" Officer Blum didn't have to say "drugs." Emily knew he'd made up his mind.

"Now, look here, Officer, we're the victims," Jack said. "Please do not lose sight of that key fact. Our privacy has been invaded and our personal belongings destroyed. We should be able to ask police officers for help without falling under suspicion ourselves."

"Of course, sir. Don't take it personally. I think we're getting off the track myself," said Sgt. Kau with a quick glance at his colleague. "This looks like a professional robbery. They knew how to work it. Just guessed wrong about jewelry and valuables being in the room. They should have known people like yourselves would have them locked away in the hotel safe. Very sorry about this."

"You will take this vandalism seriously?" Jack asked, still testy.

"We take all crimes seriously. We want tourists who come to Waikiki to enjoy themselves, no problems."

"We'd better test for drug traces. Just in case," Officer Blum muttered.

Sgt. Kau nodded to his partner, then turned and smiled at Emily. "Just a formality. Officer Blum goes by the book. I can see that you were innocent victims of a particularly nasty burglary."

"I hope you'll find whoever did this," Emily said, not mollified by his feeble attempt to make amends.

"We'll do what we can."

Emily suspected this might be nothing.

"You can wait in the lobby while we examine the room. You'll be more comfortable there."

The hotel manager was looking at her with less favor now that she had been revealed as a drug lord.

Despite the manager's halfhearted offer to move them to another room, Emily and Jack sought shelter in the nearby Sheraton Waikiki.

Emily unpacked what was left of her belongings, happy to be away from the scene of robbery and mayhem.

"It's a good idea to stay at more than one hotel anyway," Emily said. "I can let my readers know about their choices, what's available in various price ranges."

Jack had already finished unpacking and was sitting at a small desk by the window, jotting notes on a legal pad.

"How can men pack and unpack in the blink of an eye?" Emily asked. "Most unfair."

"We're methodical and well organized."

"More likely you have lax folding standards."

Unlike their previous hotel, the Sheraton was right on the beach. If Emily stood at the window of their room, positioned just right, she could see a sliver of ocean between tall hotels.

"I was not favorably impressed by the police," Emily said, laying out her swimsuit for easy access in the morning. "I just hope they will put their shoulders to the wheel and find the perpetrators."

"Unfortunately, you distracted the officers by convincing them you're a drug kingpin. We're lucky not to be in jail ourselves. "

"Officer Blum had his own private hobbyhorse. I could have said anything and he would have replied, 'drugs.' Perhaps he's jockeying for a spot on the drug squad instead of on the minor-crimes-and-misdemeanors squad."

"Unless they thought the break-in was drug-related, the police wouldn't bother to prosecute even if they did find out who did it. Not worth the trouble unless there was a pattern of similar crimes attracting bad publicity and threatening the tourist industry."

"This crushes my faith in our criminal justice system. I want perpetrators to pay for their crimes, and, while I'm fuming, I must also blame the hotel. Very casual about security."

"It wasn't their fault."

"Are you kidding? Our hotel room was wide open day and night; Kari wandered in unannounced, burglars made free with our possessions. Surely fault must be assigned to someone."

"Professional criminals know how to outsmart hotel security systems."

"That does not make me feel better."

"The police thought they were looking for something."

"Money and jewels most likely."

"There are slim pickings in these days of credit cards, cash machines, and hotel safes. Burglars cannot reasonably expect to find socks stuffed with hundred dollar bills under the mattress. So failure to find treasure-stuffed socks should not arouse such keen disappointment that they would trash a room."

"Jack, do you suppose they were looking for something else?"

"I've never believed you were a drug lord."

"Seriously. What about the papers Kari took from Lillian? Do you suppose someone wanted them enough to search our room and make it look like a deranged burglar had done it?"

"Who knew you had the papers? And who would want them?"

Emily was a little frightened that Jack was taking her suggestions seriously instead of cracking a joke. "Only Kari and Brent. Kari's in jail and it couldn't have been Brent. I gave him the letters."

"But you said he looked dissatisfied. Perhaps he thought you had extracted the very letter he wanted."

"We were with him last night."

"He could have slipped out of the house after we left, while we were at dinner. Or he could have hired thugs."

"Thugs? What an outlandish idea!"

"Perhaps, and yet we know that thugs are hired right and left. Otherwise the bottom would have fallen out of the large scale breaking-and-entering market and we know this is not the case."

"Brent is not a crook with criminals-for-hire at his beck and call."

"We don't know much about him. Or about Sarah for that matter."

Emily was taken aback. "I suppose you're right," she admitted. "It feels as if Sarah and I are close friends, but really it's the intensity of our experiences during this past week that makes our relationship seem intimate. Still, I can't believe that she or Brent would hire someone to rob us and smash our belongings."

"It depends on what they think was in that box."

"Sarah is the one Brent is trying to keep from reading the incriminating letter. She couldn't be involved."

"Maybe it was Todd," Jack said. "For all we know, Julie could have been having an affair with him as well as with Brent and one of the letters revealed their sordid liaison. Maybe Julie was blackmailing them both."

"That's pretty farfetched. Besides Todd doesn't know I have the letters."

"As far as we know."

"You just don't like Todd."

"Okay, let's consider other possibilities. If it isn't the letters, what could it be? And who wants it? You had a whole box of Lillian's miscellany. What happened to it? Do you suppose the burglars found it and we just didn't notice in all the chaos?"

"Oh, dear. You have the rest of the papers, Jack. They're in your briefcase. I tucked them there to keep them out of temptation's way, so I would write my article instead of pawing through fascinating papers that are no business of mine."

"Perhaps we should investigate them more closely," Jack suggested. "Let's bring my briefcase in from the car."

Emily leaped to her feet. Jack caught her hand. "Not now, my beauty. They'll be there in the morning."

Emily laughed and tumbled onto the bed.

CHAPTER 20

The next morning, Emily was lounging on the beach with Jack beside her, listening to seagulls' cries and children's shrieks of joy as they splashed in the waves. She was holding a photo of Julie and her sister, taken long ago. The two girls were standing under a palm tree, squinting into the camera. Julie wore a white bikini that looked spectacular against her golden skin. She was grinning as if she'd been caught in mid-laugh. Lillian wore a one-piece suit and a scowl.

So far the purloined photos and memorabilia had been a sad disappointment. With high hopes, Emily had retrieved the more promising of the two remaining files from Jack's briefcase and taken them down to the beach where she could methodically pore over their contents. So far she had learned nothing. There were no incriminating photos of Todd or Brent leering at Julie.

Emily shook out the last photo and peered at it carefully. In the posed group photo, Brent stood in the back row beside Sarah. She was gazing up at him with an adoring look that Emily had previously supposed was used exclusively by politicians' wives wearing expensive red suits. Scanning the faces in the photograph, Emily found Todd with an arm around Amanda and Julie, who was holding her long, black hair away from her face with one hand. Her resemblance to Kari was striking. Lillian wasn't in the picture. Emily let the photo drop in her lap, and leaned back, enjoying the warmth of the tropical sun, the taste of sea salt on her lips.

The phone rang. Jack grunted and twitched. Was it her imagination or was he already darker than he had been a few minutes ago? How unfair that he should turn golden tan with no effort at all.

Emily reached in her beach bag for her phone. She heard an excited gabble that sounded as if it might be Todd.

"Todd, is that you? I can barely hear your voice. It's noisy here."

"Emily, the police found proof that Matt's guilty. I'm in the clear. I can invite you to visit me without worrying that you'll be afraid to be alone with a murderer."

"Don't be silly, Todd. I never suspected you," Emily assured him.

"If so, you were the only one. Even Brent, my best friend, seemed to have his doubts. So I've been keeping to myself."

"Poor you."

"Now I would like to invite you and Jack to visit," Todd said with sudden formality. "Could you come this afternoon?"

Emily sucked in her breath. She was not looking forward to telling Todd that his wife's family documents had been stolen. "Jack has only an hour before he has to go to a meeting," she stalled.

There was a long pause. She could hear Todd's ragged breathing over the phone. Maybe he thought that even now she was afraid to be alone with him. "I suppose I could come by myself," Emily said slowly.

"Good girl!" Todd cried.

Girl? Emily already regretted giving in.

Dreading the revelation she had to make, Emily drove up the steep, twisting mountain road to Todd's home. The Blake family documents had been in her possession only a few days before they had been stolen. Unlikely as it seemed, perhaps they were the real reason for the robbery. Emily wondered if there was a clue she had overlooked.

Musings and misgivings occupied her mind until Emily arrived at Todd's front door. An elderly housekeeper showed her into the living room where Todd was sprawled in a Barcalounger watching a surfing competition on a large-screen TV, the volume on high. He clicked the remote, shutting off audio, then leapt to his feet and came forward, enfolding Emily in a hug.

"Thanks for coming. I haven't had many visitors these days."

Emily glanced over his shoulder at the unsightly red lounge chair he had just vacated. Surely it was a new addition.

"Maud, would you bring us some iced tea? You'll have some, won't you, Emily?" Todd grinned and ran a hand through his blonde hair. He was unshaven, but his eyes looked clear and bright.

"Yes, iced tea would be wonderful. How are you holding up?"

"Much better since the police caught Amanda's killer. I hated being the prime suspect. It's bad enough losing my wife without having everyone believe I murdered her."

"You weren't the only suspect. I heard the police questioned Sarah and Brent as well. She seemed okay about it, but he was furious."

"He's a touchy guy, but salt of the earth, a good friend to me and Amanda. Come on, let's sit down and talk."

Todd padded on bare feet over to a seating area by the window. He was wearing wrinkled khaki shorts, a loose, slightly soiled T-shirt and no shoes. Was he enjoying a loosening of the dress code or too depressed to look preppy?

Emily sank down into a chair and gazed out at the sun-sparkling sea. She wondered how to introduce the subject of the stolen papers.

Todd didn't give her time to raise the issue. "Matt sure had me fooled." he said, rubbing the stubble on his cheek. "He seemed like an okay guy. You never know, do you? The son of a bitch turns out to be a killer."

"So you think he's guilty?" Emily said.

"No question. The forensic report came back showing that Amanda's body was in Matt's catamaran and in Kari's jeep. I still can't believe Kari was in on it. I've known that girl since she was a baby."

"Maybe there's an explanation," Emily suggested, wishing she could be more frank.

Todd was starting to answer when Maud returned with two tall, crystal glasses of iced tea on a silver tray.

Emily took a sip of tea so cold it made her forehead ache.

As soon as the housekeeper closed the door, Todd said with sudden ferocity, "The explanation is: Matt's guilty as hell."

"What motive could he possibly have?" Emily asked.

"That's easy. He was pissed at Amanda for turning down the grant request. Plus he thought he was doing something that would make Kari happy."

"That doesn't make sense. Kari adored Amanda, or so I hear."

"She did. Absolutely. But she and Amanda had quarreled and I think Matt took it too seriously. Amanda was considering cutting off money to the Trust and giving it to some orphanage in Thailand instead. Kari was furious. Amanda was the one who got her interested in her Hawaiian heritage in the first place. So these past couple of years, Kari has been learning the Hawaiian language, teaching hula classes, finding out more and more about the ancient culture. Everything was going along fine until Kari met Matt and that whole crew. Matt sold her on the idea that Hawaii should be a separate independent nation, Hawaiians should be practicing the old religion, and they deserved to be paid reparations. Amanda did not approve." Todd shook his head and laughed in disbelief.

"So Amanda was ready to cut off the money?" Emily prompted.

"She hadn't decided, but she certainly wasn't going to give any of the Trust's money to this group."

"Could Amanda make the decisions about the grant proposals by herself?"

"No. There are three trustees: Amanda, me, and Brent. We meet as a group to consider the proposals, but it was Amanda's money and she really called the shots. Brent and his staff deal with the day-to-day administration of the Trust, the paperwork, taxes, tracking how the money is used, that sort of thing."

The phone rang. Todd looked at it for a long moment before picking up. "Hello?" he said cautiously. A smile lit his face. "Not now. I'll call you back, okay?"

The Crumpet. It had to be. Emily felt her sympathy for Todd eroding.

He hung up the phone and turned to her. "Business. You can never get away from it, can you?" Todd gave Emily the benefit of his most winning smile.

Sternly, Emily directed the conversation back to the Trust. "You told me Matt was there but it was Mau Koolani who yelled at Amanda."

"I told you about that, did I? Hell, I'd forgotten. Yeah, Mau Koolani wrote the grant proposal asking for funds to look for ways to pay reparations to native

Hawaiians for taking the land of their ancestors. Kari
had told him that it was a done deal because of her
relationship with Amanda. Kari never doubted for a
moment that Amanda would think paying reparations
was a terrific idea." Todd shook his head. "Can you
believe it? When Amanda told Mau it was unworkable
he got angry.

"Kari was embarrassed in front of her friends when
the grant was turned down. She and Amanda had a hell
of a fight. Well, not a fight really because that implies
two people, and this was a one-sided match. Kari was
shrieking at Amanda who was sitting very still, not
saying much. Finally, I had to step in and stop it. Kari
was really abusive. That girl has a terrible temper.
Finally, I took her by the arm and told her to knock it
off.

"Her relationship with Amanda went downhill from
there. After the argument over the grant proposal,
Amanda began rethinking the whole purpose of the
Trust, said there might have to be some major changes.
That set off another round of abuse from Kari. Last
time I saw them together, Kari looked ready to throttle
Amanda."

Emily flinched at the word "throttle." Did Todd
believe Kari had been angry enough to kill Amanda?
Emily wondered. She couldn't bring herself to ask. It
was too horrible.

Todd drained his glass. His face was flushed.
"Maybe Kari lashed out at Amanda. Not meaning to
hurt her."

Emily couldn't imagine a flash of anger sustaining
itself in a prolonged strangling episode, but she didn't
say so.

"Then that bastard, Matt, pitched in and finished the
job." Todd poured a couple of ice cubes into his mouth
and crunched down on them. "More likely though, Matt

killed her all by himself. He probably thought he was doing Kari a favor. The dumb shit."

"Did you tell the police about the argument?"

"Sure. I had to. The police asked if anyone had quarreled with Amanda recently so I told them. It didn't seem important at the time. Everyone has a flare-up once in a while. Now with the physical evidence, it looks black for Kari and Matt. The police figure that if she didn't do it herself in a fit of rage, maybe she convinced her boyfriend to do it."

Emily drained her glass of tea in two gulps. Perhaps Kari was guilty. The cover-up story had always sounded preposterous and yet she had accepted it on faith from a young woman she had just met and didn't particularly like.

"I can't imagine anyone except Matt and one of his buddies putting Amanda on Puu O Mahuka Heiau," Todd said bitterly. "Kari wouldn't do that. It's sick." Todd's blue eyes filled with tears and his voice shook.

If Todd killed Amanda himself, he's a hell of an actor, Emily thought. But then the world was full of talent.

"God, I miss Amanda," Todd moaned.

Emily patted his arm. Todd looked at her gratefully, put his hand on top of hers and drew in a deep breath. He blinked to clear his eyes.

Emily steered the conversation to memories of Amanda in happier times, trying to comfort and divert him.

Emily's own bad news seemed so insignificant compared to Todd's loss that she was reluctant to bring it up. She waited until it was time to go, then on the way to the door, Emily said, "Todd, there's something I have to tell you."

"I know, I know," he murmured, squeezing her arm.

Emily took a deep breath. "It's not related to Amanda's death. I have a confession to make."

Todd looked surprised. Emily forged on.

"Jack and I were robbed last night."

"Robbed? At gunpoint?"

"No, luckily we weren't home when they broke in."

"Thank God! What happened?"

"Our hotel room was ransacked."

"What did they take?"

"That's the terrible thing. Todd, I'm so sorry, but they took the letters you lent me, Amanda's letters."

"What the hell." Todd gave a relieved laugh. "Who would want Amanda's family papers?"

"The police think it was a drug-related crime. Why we would be expected to have drugs, I have no idea." Emily spoke sharply, for the memory of the police's suspicions still rankled.

"It's a blessing they didn't take anything really valuable."

Perversely, Emily felt a flash of irritation. Amanda would have been devastated to lose her family's letters. "I'm just glad I had a chance to read the letters before they were stolen. A fascinating look at history. Did you read them?"

"Sure. Amanda insisted. As I told you, those letters were the reason Amanda felt so guilty about her family's role in taking over Hawaii. She believed the missionaries destroyed the native culture, and she wanted to restore it. That's why she started the Trust."

"After reading the letters, I can certainly see why. What I don't understand is why she was wavering. Was her experience with Mau Koolani distressing enough to make her change her mind?"

"Something changed the way Amanda felt about the Trust. I don't know what it was; she didn't tell me." His face clouded.

Was Todd bitter that his wife hadn't confided in him? Or remorseful that he had been otherwise engaged and wasn't around to hear her confidences?

"I suppose any decision about the Trust would have affected Brent," Emily mused. "Was Kari worried about that?"

"I doubt it," Todd said. "Young people usually think their family will be just fine. I certainly never looked back after I met Amanda and came to Hawaii."

Emily had no trouble believing that.

"Brent wouldn't have been affected much anyway. The Trust would have continued and the money would still need managing. Amanda was just considering not adding more to the principal."

"So Brent would still have his job?"

"Definitely. Amanda relied on him completely. Right after her father died, Amanda came up with this idea of setting up the Trust. We'd only been married a year at the time. Brent offered to set up the whole deal and manage it for us. He's only a couple of years older than I am; we were fraternity brothers at Cornell, but Brent always seemed to know more than anyone else. Maybe it's his self confidence that makes everyone trust the guy. Anyway, I knew that he'd been a business major with top grades so I figured there was a lot of substance behind his bragging. The only one who can puncture Brent's ego is his Dad. Sarcastic old bugger. He told Brent he'd cut off his tuition if he ever slipped off the Dean's list. The old bastard said there were two grades a guy could get: an "A" or failure."

"Sounds like a sweet fellow."

"He sure lit a fire under his son. Brent's always been a go-getter, the kind of guy who inspires confidence. That's why Amanda was so glad to have him take on the business administration of the Trust. She would never have done anything to undermine his position at the Trust."

"What will happen now that Amanda…now that she won't be making any more decisions about the Trust? Can you and Brent do whatever you like with the money?"

"I hadn't really thought about that. The Trust is the least of my worries. Right now I just want to see that Matt's convicted."

"If he's guilty," Emily added.

"Right, right. There's not much question, is there? I just wonder who else was in on it." Todd's face collapsed into sadness.

Emily knew he couldn't help suspecting Kari. She shuddered. Maybe he was right.

CHAPTER 21

That evening Emily suggested to Jack that they go back to the Aloha Tower where they could walk along the harbor and look at the glorious yachts. Settled in a restaurant at the end of Pier 9, fortified with a glass of wine, Emily told Jack what she had discovered during her visit with Todd.

"Todd thinks Matt is definitely guilty, and although he says he doesn't believe Kari was involved, he did give her a motive."

"Eager to help pin the guilt on someone else, was he? I'm not surprised. What did Todd say?"

Emily took a bite of her salad. "Apparently, Amanda refused to fund a proposal to make reparations to native Hawaiians for the land taken from their ancestors and Kari was furious."

"Was she, indeed?" Jack raised one eyebrow. "Furious?"

"It's hard to believe anyone would kill for such a flimsy reason."

"People have been known to kill their best friend for eating the last of the Grape Nuts," Jack said. "It's not a rational world."

Emily eyed him skeptically. "Evidently medical circles are more dangerous than I thought if your acquaintances kill because of limited cereal choices."

Jack looked pained. "'People *have been* known,' I said, not 'people *I have known*.'"

"What people?" Emily persisted.

"Those in *News of the Weird*," Jack admitted with a grin.

Emily smiled and returned to the topic at hand. "Todd surmised that Kari might have killed Amanda in a moment of fury, then he began backpedaling and said it was probably Matt. Somehow Matt got the idea that Kari would be extremely grateful if he killed Amanda for her."

"Kari did remind me of a young Lady Macbeth."

"There is a striking resemblance," Emily agreed. "I can't help remembering how fierce Kari looked when she quoted Queen Lileohalani, something about the punishment of Ahab falling on your children if you coveted the land of the Hawaiian people."

"Yet you seem to believe Kari's explanation for placing Amanda on the altar."

"I don't believe or disbelieve Kari at this point."

"Does she strike you as a true fanatic?"

"I don't know. She definitely has strong opinions."

A waiter snatched up Emily's empty salad plate and set a feast of coconut prawns before her. "Fresh air stimulates the appetite wonderfully," she said, squeezing lemon on her shrimp. "I told Todd about the letters being stolen. He's not much of a history buff, so he took it calmly."

"Since he is a bereaved widower, he may have put it in perspective."

"I wonder how bereaved he is. Apparently Todd and Brent now control the Trust money."

"Surely they can't just pocket it."

"I assume not."

"You were so sure Todd was innocent. Are you wavering?"

"No. I'm stumped. So much depends on what Amanda would have done. Would she have divorced Todd because of the Crumpet? Did she find out that

Brent was Kari's father? And, if she did, would it have jeopardized his position in the Trust? Would she have completely abandoned funding for Hawaiian cultural projects? It's been years since I spent much time with Amanda and I never knew her well. I've been trying to remember more about her, but it's no use. But do you know who might remember something useful?"

Jack shook his head.

"Mindy," Emily said. "I could call her." Mindy, her former college roommate, was a treasure trove of information about their classmates. "I don't know why I didn't think of this before."

"Because you were busy writing your articles instead of engaging in fruitless speculation about what Amanda would have told you," Jack said. "It's no use trying to figure out what Amanda would have done unless you plan to conduct a séance."

When they had finished dinner and were walking back along the pier, Emily punched in Mindy's number and heard her friend cry, "Emily, how are you? What's going on? I heard about Amanda. My God, how horrible."

"That's why I'm calling. I'm trying to remember everything I can about Amanda. Don't ask me why. I'll explain it all later. What do you remember about her?"

"Not much. I didn't know her that well. A nice girl. Smart."

"That's no help. Can you get our yearbook? Tell me everything you can find out about her."

"Okay, just a sec. I'm walking into the den. Here's the yearbook. I found Amanda's senior picture. She's sitting on the dock, looking out at the lake. Oh she looks so young!"

"What else?"

"Her quote is: 'The peacefulest, restfulest, balmiest, dreamiest haven of refuge for a worn and weary spirit the surface of the earth can offer,' Mark Twain. Do you suppose she meant Aurora, New York?"

"Twain was writing about Hawaii," Emily said with the authority of a writer who has done her research. "Poor Amanda. What else? What kind of activities?"

"Okay, I'm flipping through. Hah, this is a pretty hilarious picture of you wearing furry slippers, eating a sundae in the dorm. Hee hee. Your cheeks look like squirrel cheeks."

"Stick to Amanda." Emily did not like to be reminded of the freshman fifteen she had put on, wolfing down ice cream that was brought to the dorms each night to keep up students' spirits.

"Okay, okay. Here she is. Philosophy club. Amanda's sitting by the fireplace in MacMillan, looking thoughtful and wise, along with the two other members of the club. And here's another picture. Judiciary Committee. Oh, Em, I do remember her on Judiciary. She was a grim reaper sort of person. Very much by the book, no excuses. Once I had stayed out very late, past curfew—what an antiquated concept; nobody has curfews anymore, but you remember what a big deal it was in our day?—and I had to come up before Judiciary. So did Dede, a great friend of Amanda's. We went to Cornell in the same car and it ran out of gas and we'd had several too many beers. Oh, lord, we had to walk for miles in the snow. And then we were late, late, late. I didn't think it was too bad since we didn't stay out on purpose, it was the car's fault really, but Amanda looked so stern, her mouth set in a tight, straight line and I took that as a very bad sign, which it was, because we were given zillions of demerits and lost all our 2 o'clock privileges and I couldn't go away for Dartmouth's Winter Carnival and

I was in despair and so was Dede, her best friend and roommate, who never, ever forgave her for being so ruthless. Years later, Dede cut her dead at the reunion and I saw how Amanda winced. Of course, Amanda wasn't the only member of the committee but her expression gave us the fearful feeling that she would persuade the others not to cut us any slack. Oh dear. We recited, 'The quality of mercy is not strained, but falleth like the gentle rain from heaven,' but cruel Amanda paid no attention. You see it all comes back to me now that I see this picture. How I wish you hadn't reminded me because now I've spoken ill of the dead and God only knows what my punishment will be. Does this help at all? Is it what you're looking for?"

"Yes, yes, it might be. Thanks, Mindy." Emily hung up, ignoring Mindy's pleas for more information.

"What has Mindy told you that makes your eyes light with the fire of intelligence?"

"Just that Amanda was a stern judge. She did not let even her best friend off the hook when she thought justice demanded punishment. And Amanda suffered for it. Her friend never forgave her. If she had found out something terrible—about Todd's infidelity or Brent's paternity secret or if she no longer believed in the mission of the Trust—she probably would not have shown mercy or been swayed by personal feelings. But she would remember how it felt to stand firm and lose a friend. Oh heavens, poor Amanda. What did she find out? I wish I had been here a few days earlier."

Her cell phone rang. Emily snatched it out of her purse. She heard Sarah's voice, light with relief. "Kari finally told the police what happened," she said. "It's all a misunderstanding. Those kids were just trying to give Amanda a traditional burial of some sort. They didn't mean any harm."

Emily doubted that the police would consider a young woman in her early twenties to be just an innocent kid who knew no better than to tamper with a murder scene, but she didn't say so. "Will the police let Kari and Matt go?" she asked.

"If they had any sense, they would. But the police don't believe her. Somehow Scanlon found out that the police think Kari concocted a fantastic story to cover up the murder. When Matt heard that Kari had explained everything, he confirmed it. He told the police the exact same story as Kari and, of course, the kids had no opportunity to compare notes. Yet, the police are skeptical and so, surprisingly, is her lawyer. Scanlon snorted in an offensive sort of way and rolled his eyes when Kari finally explained. Brent and I insisted on being present when Kari talked to him."

Emily was relieved that she was no longer the only one who knew about Kari's bizarre version of events on the night of the murder.

"Do you believe her, Sarah?"

"Of course I do. But she's in real trouble. The police have made up their minds that she and Matt are guilty. I'm afraid they won't even consider other options. Emily, you're so good at figuring things out."

Emily could hear the longing in Sarah's voice. She ignored it.

"Maybe you could look into it," Sarah persisted. "I remember how you caught the murderer on Madeline Island. It was highlighted in the *Alumnae News*."

Emily could hear Brent bellowing in the background. "Leave Emily out of this, goddamit. It's not her problem."

"Kari will be home tomorrow. Scanlon has arranged for bail. It's exorbitant, of course, but we'd do anything to get her out of there. Would you come over and talk to Kari?"

Emily fumbled for an excuse.

"I don't know how else we can start figuring out who the killer is," Sarah went on. "It must have been a stranger, roaming the beach. If you talk to Kari, you might get some ideas. After all, she did discover the body. You're a reporter. You know how to interview and get at the truth."

"This is a job for the police," Brent bellowed in the distance.

"The police are asking all the wrong questions." Sarah ignored Brent's interruption. "They don't want the killer to be a stranger. Think how bad for tourism."

"Sarah, that's ridiculous," Brent roared.

Sarah seemed oblivious to Brent's fits of temper. Like a boat upon the sea, she skimmed along, bobbing untroubled upon the waves of his displeasure.

Emily knew she could never be so restrained. Luckily, Jack was far too polite to bellow.

"Unlike the police, you will not be blinded to clues that could be lying right under our noses," Sarah persisted. "Clues that could clear Kari."

"I have no idea how to solve this case, Sarah."

Sarah heaved a sad sigh and fell silent.

After a long pause, Emily relented. "But I would certainly be glad to come over and talk to Kari."

"Thank you, thank you, Emily. I know you'll figure this out."

As Emily hung up the phone, she noticed Jack's bemused expression.

"And now you are officially on the case?" he asked.

"No, no. You heard me tell Sarah I couldn't possibly."

CHAPTER 22

Rain was falling in a soft mist, beading the windshield as Emily drove toward Brent and Sarah's house. She already regretted being swayed by Sarah's touching confidence that she could find out who had killed Amanda. Emily had been considering various possibilities, turning ideas over in her mind, but that was far different from actually trying to solve a baffling murder case.

Emily turned into the curved driveway and pulled up in front of the massive white stucco house. The sun was coming out behind a cloud and a rainbow arched over the ocean. Emily stepped out of the car and paused for a moment to admire the spectacular view, feel the warm sun on her face. No need to hurry. She dreaded trying to extract information from Kari. Every encounter she'd had with the girl had ended badly. But she'd promised Sarah, and she had to go through with it. Taking a deep breath, Emily went up to the door, and pressed the button.

Chimes rang, the door sprang open. Sarah must have been waiting for her, watching out the window.

"Thank goodness you're here," Sarah said. She lowered her voice. "I told Kari why you want to talk with her. She's willing to cooperate." Sarah looked pitifully grateful that Kari was allowing Emily to help save her neck.

Emily resolved that if she ever had a daughter, she would not tiptoe in fear of her moods, then quickly knocked on wood, lest this thought might invite Fate to send her a cross and broody child, doomed to become a suspected murderess.

"Would you like a cup of coffee? A Coke?" Sarah asked.

"No, no, I've just had breakfast."

"Kari feels terribly guilty because Matt's still in jail and she's out. Naturally, Brent wasn't willing to post bail for Matt. Why would he? For a while Kari thought she could force Brent to pay up by not talking to the police. I don't think she realized how awful it would be in jail. Kari blinked first. Brent can be very firm."

Sarah led the way to the patio and pool, then paused, her hand on the latch of the French door. "You're kind to help us, Emily."

"I'll do what I can. But don't expect too much." Emily, seeing hope gleam undimmed in her friend's eyes, wished she had not come.

The situation was ridiculous, Emily thought as she followed Sarah out onto the patio. Kari, wearing a black bikini, was leaning back in a lounge chair, her face turned toward the sun, eyes closed. She glistened with suntan oil. She did not appear wracked with guilt at not being confined next to Matt in a small jail cell.

"Emily's here to see you," Sarah said in the bright voice of an anxious hostess.

Kari's eyes snapped open. She raised her hand to shade her face. "Aloha," she muttered, then leaned back and closed her eyes again.

On closer inspection, Kari looked exhausted. Emily examined her face for traces of Brent's features, but found it hard to see the resemblance between the man and girl. But their different coloring might mask more subtle similarities.

"I'll leave you two alone to chat," Sarah said. "Just let me know if I can get you a cold drink or anything." She vanished back into the house.

Emily sat in an upright chair next to Kari. "You must be glad to be home." She'd almost said, "out of the slammer," the first phrase that leapt to mind.

"I've been put on indefinite leave from teaching," Kari said, opening her eyes and sitting up, gripping the arms of the lounge chair. "Can you believe that? Isn't the accused person presumed to be innocent?" She didn't wait for a reply. "Our principal says it's standard procedure. He has no choice. Bullshit. He's probably had calls from parents who think I'm going to corrupt their children. Conklin's a weak man. I have no patience with him."

Emily didn't find it too surprising that someone suspected of being involved in a murder should be suspended from teaching small children. "Perhaps you need time to help with your defense," she said, pointing out the bright spot.

"Mother thinks you can find out what happened to Amanda," Kari said in a tone that suggested it was about as likely that Emily would sprout wings and fly about the room oinking.

"She gives me far too much credit."

"I agree. You didn't do a very good job of persuading Lillian to give you my birth mother's papers. I had to take care of that myself. Did you read them? Did you find out anything?"

"Not so far," Emily hedged.

"As soon as I move out of here into Matt's apartment, I'll take them back and look through them myself. Dad wants me to stay here until Matt is cleared."

Relieved that Kari had not demanded the letters, Emily resolved to insist that Brent return them.

"The police have made up their minds that Matt and I conspired to murder Amanda," Kari said. "They aren't going to look any further. Did Mother tell you that?"

"You can hardly blame the police."

Kari looked shocked. Apparently she was not accustomed to being forced to face unpleasant realities. "Of course I blame them," she snapped. "I told the police what happened."

"The physical evidence gives the prosecution a good case."

"It fits exactly with my story."

Emily wondered if "story" was all too accurate a word for it. "You have to admit that moving a body is an odd thing to do. It's a crime in itself. You must know that."

"You sound just like Scanlon. I thought you were going to help me."

"I can't help if you don't level with me." Emily found herself sinking into the patois of detective fiction. She was beginning to relish her new role. Perhaps she could solve the case after all.

"I've explained why we did it," Kari said with weary patience as if speaking to one of her slower students. "I thought Amanda committed suicide. Just swam out to sea until she became exhausted, then relaxed, let the ocean waves take her, and later was washed back on the incoming tide. As it turned out, I was wrong. According to the so-called experts, Amanda was murdered. How was I to know? If she had committed suicide, it would have created a scandal."

"Suicides aren't buried at the crossroads the way they once were. There's more compassion for people who are so depressed they take their own lives."

"Suicide is still a scandal. Imagine the gossip, the news articles speculating about Amanda's motives and her relationships. I couldn't allow that to happen. Besides I wanted to say goodbye in my own way, the way my ancestors used to do."

Emily was surprised to hear that moving Amanda's body still made perfect sense to Kari. Regardless of later developments and disastrous consequences, she was not a prey to self-doubt. "Why did you think Amanda committed suicide? It seems out of character for her."

"How would you know? You haven't seen her in years."

"People don't change that much. Not fundamentally. The most important trait I remember is her resolve to do the right thing. Amanda was a strong-minded woman. I don't think she would have given up, no matter what disappointments she encountered."

"What about finding out that she had built her whole life on a mistake? What about betrayal? How can anyone go on then?" Kari looked fierce, tears shining in her dark eyes.

"Who betrayed her?"

"Who do you think? I don't have to spell it out."

"Todd?"

Kari didn't answer for a moment. "You're supposed to be the detective."

"No, that was your mother's idea." Emily resisted the urge to grab Kari and pitch her into the pool. "She just wants to help you. She's clutching at straws."

"So, are you going to help?"

"If I can. But you have to answer my questions. Why was Amanda so depressed? Was it because of Todd?"

"I don't know," Kari admitted, dropping her eyes. She twisted the silver ring on her finger round and round. "Maybe she found out about his girlfriend."

"Why did you say Amanda had been betrayed?" Emily persisted.

"That's what she told me."

"When? Come on. I don't want to drag every tiny fact out of you. Spit it out."

"All right." Kari heaved an ostentatious sigh as if Emily had demanded of her some extraordinary effort. "It was the last time I saw Amanda, about a week before she died. She wasn't expecting me. I was driving by the house and thought I'd stop by and say hello. When I rang the doorbell there was no answer, so I walked around the back of the house. Amanda was standing there, facing the ocean. I called out to her and she turned around. Right away I could see that she'd been crying." Kari lowered her eyes.

"What happened next?" Emily prodded her.

"I asked what was wrong and Amanda said, 'I've been betrayed.' Very dramatic. She didn't explain what she meant, just shook her head, and walked back up to the house. So I left. That's all there was to it."

Emily suspected there was a good deal Kari was leaving out. "What about the argument you had with Amanda? Did it happen the same day? Is that why she was so upset?"

"Who told you that?" Kari swung her legs off the lounge chair, and stood up, looking ready to bolt or attack.

"You're the one who's supposed to be answering questions," Emily snapped. She was beginning to enjoy the role of hardboiled detective. "Why were you furious at Amanda?"

"I wasn't 'furious.'" Kari paced up and down by the edge of the pool, running her fingers through her long dark hair. "I don't know where you got that idea. Or the police, for that matter. Amanda was losing interest in the Trust. Naturally, I minded. She was pulling the rug out from under us just when we needed her most."

"Why would she do that?"

"How should I know? Our minor disagreement has been exaggerated beyond belief. I didn't fight with Amanda. I loved her. Todd told you, didn't he? Why do you suppose he's trying to get me convicted for murder? Just think about it." Kari came over and towered over Emily, who remained seated, looking up into Kari's angry face.

"Was it after you quarreled with her that Amanda mentioned betrayal?" Emily asked.

"No!" Kari screamed. "Hell, no! If you think I was the one who betrayed her, the one who was responsible for Amanda's misery, you're wrong."

The girl certainly has a temper, Emily thought, and decided to switch gears. "I still wonder why Amanda wanted to talk to me. Do you think it was about the decision she was going to make about the Trust?"

"I have absolutely no idea." Kari turned away, rubbing her arms, as if she were cold.

Emily tried another tack. "Todd gave me some letters written many years ago by women in Amanda's family. Amanda wanted to show them to me. I think they had something to do with the decision she had to make. Do you know what I'm talking about? Have you read the letters?"

"Sure. The letters were a big deal to Amanda." Kari stood gazing at light glittering on the pool. "She let me read them a few years ago, expecting me to be thrilled by a story of the rape of our homeland by missionaries and other *haoles*. They came here determined to force their beliefs down the throats of the *kanaka maoli,* our native people, teaching them that our traditional ways were wrong and primitive, and then when the *haoles* had battered down our pride and destroyed our independence, they robbed our people of everything that was most important, our land, *Aina*. Amanda's great great grandmother had some insight into how wrong the missionaries were, but she was too weak to stand up to her husband or her son. She just wrote letters and moaned and did nothing. Women don't have to behave like that anymore, if they ever did. Amanda said she wanted to make amends. How could she have changed her mind?" Kari's face was contorted with rage.

Kari glared into space for a moment before continuing. "When Amanda read the letters, she felt she could hear the voices of women in her family who had lived years ago. It was almost as if she could step back in time and visit them. Amanda began to identify with Hannah and Eliza. She wanted to help them make amends, as if she could reach back into the past and rearrange things, right old wrongs. It was a little crazy. But when Amanda talked to me about my own heritage and the importance of keeping traditions alive, the meles and the hulas of my ancestors, I thought we totally agreed."

"If she felt that way, why would Amanda change her mind about the Trust?" Emily pressed her.

"Who knows? It didn't make any sense. Amanda wouldn't follow her reasoning to its logical conclusion. She wanted to make a gesture, one that would be easy to make with her huge fortune, but she didn't approve of the move to decolonize Hawaii or to give back the land, or even to make reparations. Amanda claimed not to care about wealth but that's because she always had it. She was very much the daughter of Benjamin and of Hiram as well as of the women who whined and moaned and wished they were back in Boston."

"So you quarreled?"

"It wasn't much of a quarrel. I disagreed with her."

Emily had noticed that Kari's disagreements were never couched in calm reasonable arguments. Amanda would have taken her angry words to heart and wilted under Kari's ferocious glare.

Emily let the silence lengthen, waiting for Kari to explain. "Okay, I was angry," Kari admitted, turning to her defiantly. "I wanted some answers. That was the least Amanda could do, tell me why."

"Was that the way you parted from her?" Emily asked, feeling some pity for the girl. "Or was there a chance to reconcile?"

Kari stood up. "You believe Todd and the police, don't you? Why should I bother talking to you? You aren't going to help." Kari turned away, opened the French doors leading into the house and paused to look back. "You're just humoring Mother. Well, don't. Don't patronize either one of us." Kari walked into the house, shutting the door so firmly the glass trembled in its frame.

Sarah quickly emerged into the hallway, her eyes alight with anxiety. "I won't even ask how it went," Sarah said, walking beside her toward the door. "Kari can be difficult." She stopped and put a hand on Emily's arm. "Can you stay? Do you want a cup of coffee?"

"No, I can't. I have to get back to my writing."

"Oh, Emily, I'm being so selfish. I keep forgetting that you're here on business."

"It's okay. Don't worry about it." Emily took the car keys out of her purse and jingled them meaningfully.

"Who are you going to question next?" Sarah asked, her hopeful tone revealing a touching confidence in Emily's detective abilities. "After you've done some more writing, of course."

"I don't know."

"Please don't give up on this, Emily," Sarah pleaded. "I have no one else to turn to."

Emily could not find it in her heart to refuse her.

CHAPTER 23

Driving back toward Waikiki, Emily wondered who could have been privy to Amanda's secrets. Not her husband. Not her best friend. Not her goddaughter. Emily remembered that Father Welch had seemed to know more than he was willing to reveal, but maybe that was just his way. Perhaps he managed to seem wise and all-knowing while being as mystified as everyone else.

Emily pulled over to the side of the road and rooted around in her purse until she found her phone where she had recorded the priest's phone number and dialed. "You probably don't remember me, but..." Emily began.

Father Welch remembered her right away, greeting her as warmly as if she were an active parishioner. He agreed to meet her at the school.

Emily walked through the school corridor, her nose pinching from the smell of disinfectant. Crayoned drawings were pinned to the walls and the muffled sound of children's voices drifted to her from the classrooms. It brought back vivid memories of St. Agnes Elementary that made her glad to be roaming free instead of sitting confined in a small desk. Emily pushed open the door that connected the school to the rectory. Father Welch walked toward her. He was wearing an Aloha shirt, shiny black slacks, and sandals.

"Thank you for agreeing to talk to me again, Father," Emily said, wrenching her eyes away from his unclerical footwear.

"Not at all, not at all. So glad you're here." He ushered Emily into the cozy room where they had met earlier. Sun streamed through the tall window, backlighting the priest's head. Emily was fascinated by strands of his red hair that had somehow formed into a small curl on top, creating a Kewpie doll effect. He was a homely man, but his wide grin made him look good humored and kind.

"Would you care for a cup of tea?"

"No thank you." Emily settled into an armchair. Resisting the comfort of its deep cushions, she leaned forward, eager to make the priest understand why he should tell her any tidbits of information or gossip that might help her solve the murder. "Last time we met, I told you I was curious about why Amanda wanted to talk to me. She wrote to me, saying she wanted my advice about a major decision. What I didn't tell you is that I suspect this decision might have some bearing on her murder. At the time, it seemed farfetched and I knew the police were the ones to solve the crime, not me."

"Have you lost confidence in the police?"

"I'm not sure. Maybe it's because I know Kari. It's hard to believe that someone I know is capable of murder. By all accounts, Kari loved Amanda. I don't believe she killed her. The police apparently are convinced otherwise."

"Poor Kari. She was devastated by Amanda's death."

"Do you know her well?"

"No. Mostly at secondhand. Amanda talked about her a good deal. I met Kari for the first time when she asked if she could bring the little children to sing at Amanda's funeral. The poor girl was terribly distraught, barely holding herself together. Also, I might add, quite defensive. Clearly, she expected me to say 'no' and was braced for a fight. When I said it was a lovely idea, she looked surprised." He chuckled. "I know this sounds crazy but for a minute I thought she was disappointed to miss out on an argument. I told Kari that she was right. It would have meant a great deal to Amanda to hear those children's voices. I suspected it was a way for Kari to be reconciled with Amanda and make amends for her past behavior. They had quarreled, you know. I didn't let on to Kari that Amanda had told me about it, but now it's been published in the newspapers."

"It has?" Emily asked in alarm.

"Sadly, yes." The priest moved a folder on his desk and lifted up the newspaper that was underneath. He shoved it toward her.

Emily gasped. There was a grainy photograph of Kari. "School Teacher Charged as Murder Accomplice," she read. This article hadn't been in the morning edition. "Do you mind if I just skim it?"

"Go ahead." The priest rearranged the papers on his desk, not looking at her, giving her time.

"Rift over funding for radical group was suggested as possible motive by an unnamed source," Emily read. Was it Todd? She quickly scanned the article.

"Once Kari was charged, the newspapers felt free to publish all they could find out," Father Welch said. "Somehow the reporter heard about the quarrel between Amanda and Kari. It sounds exaggerated to me." He paused, looking thoughtfully at Emily, apparently sizing her up before deciding whether to go on.

Emily assumed her most trustworthy expression and waited in silence.

Finally, the priest leaned back in his chair, formed a steeple with his fingers, and continued, "Amanda was hurt by Kari's outburst, but she understood it. The Trust had meant a great deal to both of them. Then Amanda developed other interests."

"Maybe that was the decision Amanda wanted to talk to me about," Emily said. "What to do about the Trust? Her letter was vague, which at the time didn't bother me because I expected Amanda to explain it all in a few days. Now I wish I had called her and asked what she meant."

"I'm sure Kari would have apologized to Amanda if she had known what the future held. As it was, her song at the funeral was an apology of sorts."

Emily felt a sudden impulse to confide in the priest. "Father, can I tell you something in absolute confidence?"

"Oh course," he said, concern darkening his eyes. "Unless secrecy would harm someone," he added in a quick afterthought. This was not a confession.

Emily described Kari's account of the ceremony on the mountain, all the while wondering if the priest was shocked by such a very non-traditional ceremony. She knew that Sister Perpetua, her eighth grade teacher, would have pursed her lips and muttered about 'pagan shenanigans.'

The priest seemed untroubled. "Amanda told me that Kari was becoming interested in the old gods, in Lono, the god of harvest, and Laka, goddess of the hula. Amanda regarded that with some concern. I told her not to worry, the girl was a seeker. Those who practice the old religion want to return to a reverence for the land and a sense of harmony among people. Nothing wrong with that. Kari wasn't rooted in any traditional religion so she sought meaning in a way that made sense to her and honored her ethnic heritage."

"So the return to the old religion doesn't seem dangerous to you?" Emily recalled the grim site where Amanda's body had been found.

"Any belief can be dangerous. As far as I know, nobody wants to resurrect the cult of the bloodthirsty war god Ku. Long ago Ku's followers got the idea that he demanded human sacrifices. Ku was a favorite of the ruling classes. The ordinary people were more loyal to their aumakua, a family symbol, usually an animal like a shark or owl."

"So this doesn't seem farfetched? The ritual burial?"

He laughed. "Farfetched is just what I'd call it, but not impossible."

"Even now Kari doesn't seem to regret putting Amanda in the heiau."

"Kari's apparently very firm in her opinions. Amanda was worried about her. That's why she kept going back and forth about the Trust. She didn't want to hurt her," the priest said.

"I still can't understand why Amanda would even consider cutting funding to the Trust. She had kindled Kari's interest in her Hawaiian heritage. Plus she wanted to make up for the actions of her family, who had bought up land from people who didn't understand the whole concept of property. Why pull the plug now? It doesn't make sense."

"Probably a combination of reasons. For one thing, Amanda thought Kari was going too far, getting involved with a group that wanted to secede from the United States and take back land they say was stolen. Amanda had meant to spark Kari's interest in her Hawaiian heritage, but Kari took it further than Amanda would ever have dreamed. Some people here believe Kari is right."

Emily recalled reading that President Cleveland had admitted in 1893 right after the United States had taken over Hawaii that he was ashamed of the whole affair and yet he had not reversed it.

"The sovereignty movement is split," Fr. Welch continued. "Some people believe reparations are in order, but they don't agree on how to do it. Amanda didn't want to get involved. She was more comfortable funding cultural activities where there was no controversy. The sovereignty movement seemed threatening to her."

Emily remembered how angry Kari had been that Amanda would not follow her beliefs to their natural conclusion. Matt must have shared her anger.

The priest continued. "Perhaps more importantly, Amanda had simply developed other interests. As I told you, she was deeply touched by the needs of the orphans suffering from AIDS, innocents who were born doomed into this world. It began to seem more important to ease their pain than to preserve the Hawaiian heritage. She was losing confidence in the Trust and the orphanage seemed simple and uncomplicated. Here, let me show you a picture." The priest reached into a drawer and pulled out a snapshot of two toddlers, sitting in a double stroller, eating sticky rice. Wide smiles lit up their faces.

"They're adorable! No wonder she wanted to help them. Still… it was a change." Emily waited for the priest to volunteer information, but he used the pause to peek at his watch.

"I've been thinking about something you mentioned last time, Father," Emily said. "You said that Amanda's unhappiness might have been caused by a discovery of some sort. I thought you were hinting at something."

"I didn't mean to hint. Perhaps I did, though." He sighed heavily and stood up, made his way to the window and pulled the shade half way down, dimming the sun's glare. "If it can help you make sense of this, I might as well tell you what Amanda said. I've been afraid it would just spur speculation, and I don't really know enough to be helpful."

"Any bit of information might help."

He thought for a moment, his fingers rapping on the table. "Amanda told me she had discovered something that deeply shocked her but she didn't tell me what it was. She didn't want to hurt anyone. She just wanted out."

Oh dear, the same old story. "Out of the Trust?"

"I thought that's what she meant. Now I wish I had pressed her to tell me more, but she was upset and I thought there would be other opportunities."

The school buzzer shrieked, and there was a clamor of school children let loose. "I hate to cut you short, but…"

"You've been most kind. Thank you for taking the time to talk to me, Father."

"I wish I could have been more helpful. Amanda often confided in me. But she kept at least one secret."

Would she be alive now if she had told what she knew? Emily wondered.

CHAPTER 24

Since Jack had a dinner meeting that night, Emily agreed to meet Sarah for dinner. She met her at a restaurant under a thatched roof trimmed with twinkle lights. Sarah was perched on a stool, a glass of white wine in hand, gazing at the stage where a young girl was plucking a ukulele and singing a plaintive Hawaiian love song.

"Hey, Sarah," Emily said, touching her shoulder.

Sarah was startled out of her reverie. She smiled and patted the empty barstool beside her. "Our table will be ready soon."

Emily ordered a Mai Tai, thinking she owed it to her readers to keep up her research.

"I'm not late, am I?"

"Oh no, right on time. I was a bit early. It feels good to be out of the house." Sarah took a gulp of wine, draining her glass. "What did you find out?"

"Not much. Amanda told both Kari and Father Walsh that she had been betrayed, but she didn't say by whom."

"I thought Amanda was my best friend, but apparently there was a lot she didn't tell me." Sarah's lips tightened.

"There must have been a reason," Emily hedged. She couldn't tell Sarah that Amanda might have found out that Brent was Kari's father and was trying to protect her.

"Hmm. I suppose. Apparently Amanda suspected Todd had a girlfriend, but was too loyal to him to tell me about it." Sarah chewed her carefully manicured fingernail. "Too bad. I would have told her the girl is just a fortune hunter."

"The Crumpet?"

"Absolutely. Dippy as she seems, Heather's a steely eyed accountant at the Trust. I think she expected Todd to get a fabulous divorce settlement and was already toting up the figures in her perky blonde head. Now nothing stands in her way."

"Their affair was certainly a betrayal. So you think the Crumpet and Todd..."

"No, no. Todd would never have hurt Amanda," Sarah said, backtracking quickly. "To tell you the truth, Emily, I think the killer was just a drifter, someone on the beach. I don't think there's any connection with Amanda's problems."

Emily wasn't going to argue, not with a woman whose daughter was out on bail. She seemed to have abandoned all thought of Matt's guilt now that Kari was implicated.

"It must be terribly stressful to have a murder investigation hanging over Kari."

Sarah nodded. "Not to mention the tension between Kari and Brent." She arched an eyebrow at the bartender as he brought Emily her fruit laden Mai Tai and pointed at her own empty glass. "Those two are so alike. The battleground is set. I try to mediate, but lately it's been exhausting."

"It was kind of you and Brent to adopt Kari after her mother died," Emily said

"It was the best thing we ever did."

"You must have been very close to Kari's mother."

"Not really. Julie worked in the office with Brent. At that time, when we were first starting out, there was a lot of socializing among the staff at the Trust. I was new to the island and wanted to be the gracious hostess, help my husband in his new career. So I had luaus out on the patio and cocktail parties. Julie was just one of the office crew."

"Sounds like a convivial group, everyone getting along, having fun together."

"It was. Amanda was excited about her new project and Brent was a little scared but awfully enthusiastic about managing the Trust." The waiter set another glass of wine in front of her and Sarah pounced on it like a lioness upon its prey.

"What did Julie do for the Trust?"

"Officially, she was the accountant, but it was a small staff so everyone did a bit more than their job. Julie also helped come up with ideas for worthy projects to fund."

"So you were friends?" Emily prompted.

Sarah smiled, remembering. "Julie had an outgoing, engaging personality. Very bubbly. It was impossible not to like her. She was popular with guys, lots of guys," she added meaningfully. "But she wasn't a close friend." Sarah looked behind her as if someone might be listening. "Emily, I'll tell you a secret, but promise me you won't repeat it to anyone."

"Of course not, Sarah," Emily said leaning forward.

"Just before Julie died, Brent and I found out we couldn't have children. We'd been trying for a couple of years." She lowered her voice. "It was his low sperm count. Damn few of the little suckers were swimming around and those few were slow and listless. I was disappointed, but Brent took it as a personal affront to his manhood. He was furious at the doctor, didn't believe him, and then sunk into a black depression. I still wanted kids, but I dreaded the thought of trying to convince Brent to adopt. He was so touchy that I couldn't say a word without crushing him."

Emily's surprise must have been evident.

Sarah went on, "Oh I know Brent seems confident and brash. But he's easily hurt and I knew how sad he was about disappointing me."

"No chance Brent could father a child?" Emily asked in disbelief.

"Almost none. Doctors don't like to say absolutely never, lest they be proven fallible, but they made it clear that it would require a miracle. So after the accident, I wanted to adopt Kari. She was an adorable little girl and, of course, we'd known her from day one. Right after she was born, I had a baby shower for Julie, bought a little pink dress and booties with bows. Sometimes if Julie couldn't find a babysitter, she would bring Kari to parties at our house. She'd bring her dolls and play in the bedroom."

"So Brent didn't want to adopt a baby he didn't know, but it was different with Kari."

"That was part of it. She was a darling little girl, and then he felt terrible about Julie's death. Brent's a good driver and there was nothing he could have done to avoid the crash. Still, a young girl was dead and her three-year-old child was left an orphan. It wasn't hard to persuade him to adopt Kari."

"And you never found out who Kari's father was?" Emily watched her closely, but Sarah seemed unfazed by the question.

"No idea. Julie had a lot of boyfriends. The day she found out she was pregnant, we were having a party. I was in the kitchen, putting canapés on a tray. Julie came in to help. She didn't say much, kept putting shrimp on the toast triangles, her head bent over as if it were the most exacting task in the world. Through the window we could hear everyone out on the patio, shrieks of laughter, loud music. Just as I began to wonder why Julie was helping me, instead of laughing and chatting out on the patio with everyone else, she told me she was going to have a baby. When I asked her who the father was she said it didn't matter, she was going to keep the baby and raise it on her own. I thought she was crazy, but didn't say so."

"Julie sounds like a plucky girl."

"Oh, she was. At that time, Brent and I were trying to get pregnant and not having any luck so I felt a little jealous. I probably would have felt worse if I had known then we'd never have any luck. It was all so easy for Julie. She didn't seem fazed by the difficulty of raising a child without a husband. I think she was counting on her sister Lillian to help her, but that didn't work out. Lillian had her own plans."

"So Lillian was part of your group?"

"Lillian's a school teacher. She used to work at the Trust in the summer helping Julie in the accounting office. Occasionally she'd show up at a party, but didn't stay long. I don't think she approved of Julie's "whoopee" approach to life. But even without her sister's help, Julie had no regrets about the baby. Or if she did, she brazened it out pretty well."

"Lucky for Kari she found a loving home with you. Brent seems devoted to her." Emily couldn't give up her conviction that Brent was Kari's father. Why would he confess to an infidelity he didn't commit? To get those letters? Again Emily cursed her restraint in not reading them.

"Brent is a wonderful father. Once Kari came to live with us, he adored her. He wanted to forget she was adopted, pretend she was our own child. It didn't surprise anyone but Brent that eventually she became interested in her Polynesian heritage. It is her family history after all. That caused some friction." Sarah sighed.

Emily noticed how tired Sarah looked. Her eyes were bloodshot and small lines showed around her mouth. Sarah's hand shook as she reached for her glass.

"We shouldn't be talking about Kari and Brent," Emily said, patting Sarah's arm. "Since I have no progress to report, I should be distracting you from your troubles with amusing chatter."

"Impossible, I'm afraid. I just hope to run through all my worries before bedtime so I'll have some chance of sleeping a good part of the night."

A waiter in an orange shirt emblazoned with red and yellow parrots told them their table was ready. Emily and Sarah followed him to a table under a canvas umbrella. Emily relaxed in the warm tropical night. It was soothing here in the dark, the only illumination coming from twinkle lights in the palms and candles on each table.

The atmosphere did not appear to be having the same calming influence on Sarah, who looked grim, strumming her fingers against her glass. Emily made futile efforts to amuse. Discouraged at last, she fell silent. The waiter brought their plates of mahi mahi garnished with a pink orchid.

After a few minutes of poking at her fish, Sarah picked up the thread of their previous conversation as if there had been no interruption. "Everything changed for us very quickly after Julie died. A month before the accident we were still hoping to have children. We were going to a fertility doctor and thought she could help us. Then everything fell apart all at once. We found out about the lackadaisical sperm, and, for some reason, Brent started to worry about the Trust. After three years it had grown to be a sizeable responsibility. I'm sure nobody but me ever guessed he had any doubts. Brent's the kind of guy who inspires confidence, partly because he's tall and has a deep, reassuring voice.

"It's really an unfair advantage some men have," Emily said. "How nice to be able to announce something perfectly obvious in a deep voice and have everyone take you seriously."

"Unfair," Sarah agreed, sipping her wine. "But quite nice for Brent. His father, the old devil, was still alive then, and he kept goading Brent, telling him he was out of his depth, he couldn't handle that much money. He even told Amanda she was ill advised to leave her money in the hands of someone as inexperienced as Brent. The Trust had grown too large for his abilities, he said. I was furious. How could the old goat undermine his son like that?"

"How did Brent react?"

"He pretended to brush it off, but I know it bothered him terribly."

"Still, Brent has done very well with the Trust, hasn't he? He proved his father wrong."

"He did and was damned proud of it. Of course, the old guy never admitted that he had misjudged Brent."

"You can only hope that the realization of his error dampened the pleasure of his last days," Emily consoled her. "What will happen to the Trust now? Is Brent worried?"

"No. His job is secure. I don't know what Amanda had in mind for the Trust, what changes, if any, she was considering, but Brent and Todd are the only trustees left and they'll make the decisions. I expect Kari will press them both to fund projects that Amanda wouldn't have approved. This will cause even more arguments." Sarah sighed. "But if that's the least of our troubles, I'll be satisfied. Anything short of long-term incarceration for Kari would be just fine."

As she finished her dinner, Emily wondered about Brent. Could mischievous Fate have allowed one of his few listless sperm to drift to just the wrong place? Or had Julie lied to Brent, tricking him into believing he was the father of her baby? Emily suddenly felt cold. Maybe Brent had another secret to protect.

"I know I've been taking up a lot of your time, Emily," Sarah said, folding her napkin, and placing it on the table.

Emily realized she had been silent too long, lost in her own thoughts.

"Not at all," she hastened to reassure Sarah. "I just don't want to raise false hopes. I'm baffled." She reached down for her purse.

"I'll make it up to you," Sarah said. "I have a great idea for your article." Suddenly she looked quite pleased with herself.

"Do you? What idea?" Emily asked warily.

"Visit an active volcano."

Emily paused, credit card in hand. "Hmmm. That does sound interesting." George had made a few disparaging comments about the lack of action and drama in her articles. His own taste ran to bungee jumping and other death defying sports.

"Hawaii Volcanoes National Park on Big Island. You'll love it."

A park! How safe and pleasant that sounded. Emily pictured herself lolling in a tram like the one at Sen. Fong's Garden or strolling along a path, viewing a volcano from afar.

"We can spend the night, make an expedition of it. There's fabulous snorkeling at the beach too."

Emily recalled her aborted snorkeling adventure at the famed Haunama Bay. She loved snorkeling, so relaxing. "That really does sound like a good idea."

"Leave it to me. I'll make the plane reservations." Sarah looked so pleased to be making arrangements that Emily let her do it.

They planned to go on Friday, two days later, and stay overnight.

After parting from Sarah, Emily hurried back to the hotel room. She wanted to look through the final, least promising file of papers. She found Jack carefully folding his slacks and putting them in a drawer.

"Jack, thank goodness you're here!"

"What a warm greeting! I don't think we're spending enough time together. We're going to have to correct that." He came over and kissed her. Then he took off his shirt and hung it in the closet.

Emily ran a lascivious eye over his scantily clad body. "How do you get so tan without even trying?" She stepped out of her sundress and hung it in the closet.

"I owe it all to concentration. You talk the whole time you're lying in the sun and it deflects the tanning rays."

"Your theory does not have the ring of pure science." Emily slipped her nightie on over her head.

"Observe the evidence." Wearing only his red boxers with blue palm trees and surfers, Jack bounced onto the bed.

It was true that Jack with little effort had turned a delectable shade of brown while Emily had achieved only the color of a well-scrubbed potato. She settled beside him on the enormous hotel bed and Jack leaned over to kiss her. "Wait, Jack. First I must tell you what I found out or I'll be distracted." She brushed back a lock of dark hair that had fallen over his forehead.

Jack sighed. "Okay, if you must. Tell your tale, but make it snappy." His blue eyes sparkled with amusement.

"Brent may have been lying when he told me he had an affair with Julie and that he was Kari's real father."

She explained all that Sarah had told her about the listless sperm.

"That is astonishing. Few men confess to faults they have committed, much less those of which they are innocent."

"Exactly. So why would Brent tell me something that was blatantly untrue?"

"I observe from the gleam in your eyes that you have a theory."

"Maybe Julie tricked him. Brent would be eager to believe that he could father a child. She might have been blackmailing him, threatening to tell Sarah."

"Possibly. But then who is Kari's father?"

"Maybe it's Todd. Julie could have been blackmailing both of them. There must be a clue in those papers."

"You've already looked through them."

"Most of them. But I must be missing something." Emily sat up. "Jack, where's your briefcase?"

"In the closet, a fine place for it, too. Tomorrow is another day, my love." He drew her into his arms.

CHAPTER 25

When the sun woke her, Emily smiled and stretched. Another lovely morning in Paradise. Then she remembered the documents in the briefcase and jumped to her feet. Jack's side of the bed was empty, the sheets already smoothed down. She was relieved to hear the shower come on and Jack's baritone voice belt out, "Oh what a beautiful morning." Good. He had not left with briefcase in hand.

The phone rang. "George, how nice to hear your voice," Emily lied, slipping into her short silk robe. How could she make up a plausible excuse for not filing her article? She didn't have a single cup of coffee under her belt.

"Dammit, Emily, another article is due in two days. How are you coming?"

"Practically done."

"So tell me about it." He sounded somewhat mollified.

"The wonders of the Foster Botanical Garden right here in Honolulu," Emily improvised quickly. "Anything grows in this tropical Paradise. It's spectacular. I've taken fabulous pictures. You'll love them, George. I'm just going to make a few final edits before I email it to you."

After a few minutes of describing her non-existent article in reassuring detail, Emily said aloha to George, hung up the phone, padded over to the table and poured a cup of coffee from the automatic four-cup carafe. Thoughtfully, the hotel had provided its guests enough caffeine to allow them to make their way down to breakfast.

"Sheep and ducks and geese better scurry…"

Good lord. How could anyone awake in such a robust, hearty mood? Emily wondered. She shook powdered cream substitute into her coffee, stirred it with a swizzle stick until the lumps melted, and took a swig. She knew Jack loved to reprise his role as Curly in a college musical.

Then she went to the closet and pulled out Jack's briefcase. She opened it and rummaged about among meeting handouts until she found the last and least interesting of the three files she had organized from Lillian's box of papers. Emily shook out what appeared to be spreadsheets and budgets. Dull rows of figures. Or perhaps not so dull. Perhaps the secret Amanda had discovered, the secret that Julie was using to blackmail someone had nothing to do with the identity of Kari's father. Emily resolved to bring the papers along to the Botanical Garden so she could multi-task.

Emily drove down Ala Moana Boulevard past the Honolulu Harbor where she and Jack had admired the sailboats and past the entrance to Chinatown, guarded by a pair of intimidating stone dragons. The narrow street looked slightly seedy but inviting with its green clapboard storefronts and crowds of people. In a few blocks, she saw the Kuan Yin Buddhist Temple and beside it the entrance to the botanical garden. Emily parked and went to buy her ticket.

The minute she stepped into the forest Emily felt as if she were in another world far from the bustling city of Honolulu. With her knapsack over her shoulder and her reporter's notebook in hand, she strode down the path in the manner of a tropical explorer going where no woman had gone before. Royal Palms towered forty feet above her head. Birds of Paradise, thrust their orange and purple beaks above mounds of deep green leaves. She paused to touch the smooth bark of a tree so colorful it looked as if it had been crayoned in many different colors, then smudged and streaked with a tissue. Overhead its lacy fronds swirled out in a circle palm-tree fashion. Brilliant orchids hid in low lying foliage and hung from trees. She heard birds cry and looked up to see a flock swoop down and settle in a Banyan tree whose dangling roots made it appear to be standing on tiptoe.

Traveler's Tip: Take a mini-break from bustling Honolulu and lose yourself in a tropical forest. Wander down the path of the Foster Botanical Garden where unusual trees and plants from around the world will delight and astound you. Sit at the foot of the sacred Bo Tree under whose broad leaves the Gautama Buddha achieved enlightenment. You'll be all the better for it.

Every now and then Emily paused to take a picture and jot down notes. She had no confidence in her ability to remember names and match them to the brief descriptions of trees in her brochure. Fortunately Emily had an excellent camera.

She didn't meet a soul as she strolled down the path. Where were all the tourists? Lounging at the beach? Buying souvenirs at Honolulu Hattie's? Emily resolved to tell her readers about this marvelous sanctuary. Of course, once they came flocking to the garden, its character as a peaceful, quiet oasis would be pretty much shattered. She thought of what Kari had said about tourists destroying the land they came to admire and quickly appended another message to her traveler's tip: *Be careful to leave as little mark on this fragile island as you can. Pick up your trash, leave a donation, stay on the path, don't pick the flowers, or God forbid, dig up a plant.*

Now she felt better.

Emily looked for a place to settle down and look through the documents in her knapsack. Soon she came to the perfect spot to seek further knowledge. The immense bronze statue of the Great Buddha of Kamakura sat in the lotus position on a tall granite pedestal. Flourishing above him was an orchid tree, forming a cloud of pink blossoms about his head and shoulders. She sighed with contentment and sat down at the base of the statue, leaning against the sun-warmed stone. Bird song was the only sound in the garden.

Emily reached into her knapsack and extracted the file, then shook the documents out on the grass. Rows of numbers and abbreviations were spread out before her. Hmm. Deciphering this would be no easy job for an English major.

Emily picked one up one page with the header Hawaiian Cultural Trust and read down the columns: grants, HR, consulting and contracting, supplies, office rental. She frowned and applied her mind. Expenses apparently. The abbreviations under "grants" were incomprehensible. They were organized by date. Why would Julie have taken monthly lists of expenses home and squirreled them away?

The figures must be significant, but the more Emily examined them the more their meaning eluded her. She reached again into the envelope and pulled out a sheet of plain ruled notepaper. Under "Grants" she saw listed "Cultural Revival Coalition" and the "Maritime Reconstruction Group," followed by sizeable dollar amounts. She looked back at the spreadsheets and identified them as CultRevCo and MarRecGrp in the list of organizations that had received grants. What was significant about these two?

Emily sighed and glanced up at the Buddha who sat on his lily with downcast eye. The pink flowers stirred in the slight breeze. Julie was the accountant. Perhaps she had found something irregular and noted it. And yet surely auditors appeared each year to invade the office and sort through all the books. They would have noticed if there were discrepancies in the books.

Emily looked again at the handwritten note and saw dollar amounts listed in a column under each of the two organizations with a date by each. Finally, at the end of the column was scrawled: Accurate Total. Hmm. Her suspicion piqued by the unnecessary word, "accurate," Emily compared the handwritten numbers with the ones on the typed spreadsheet. The numbers were identical.

Emily wished she knew more about the world of accounting, at least at this moment; most of the time it held no interest for her. She bent her mind to the task of unraveling the mystery.

If these numbers were accurate, there must be others somewhere that were inaccurate. Unless Julie was in the habit of using redundant words. Emily wondered if these totals matched the information the Trust had presented to the auditors and kept in their files. Maybe Julie was embezzling and wanted to keep an accurate tally. Or maybe she suspected that someone else was skimming off the top and she was conducting her own personal audit. What then? Would Julie have turned them in to the police or blackmailed them?

Emily did not want to sully the name of a dead woman to no purpose. If Julie had been embezzling, she was doing so no longer. Nor did Emily want to alert the police if this was just some minor irregularity in bookkeeping, a pursuit whose intricacies were a closed book to her.

But if Julie had been planning to go to the police or if she was blackmailing someone, then it was horribly significant that Julie didn't live long enough to do anything about it. Emily felt the hair on the back of her neck stand on end. Maybe she should take these papers to the police and let them figure it out. But how would she explain exactly why she was showing up at the station with twenty-year-old accounting information of dubious significance? The police would laugh at her.

Emily realized she needed help. Lillian was the logical person. She had worked in the Trust part-time in the summer and might be able to explain the significance, if any, of these numbers. Plus, she would know whether or not the accounts were in Julie's handwriting.

Emily groaned. She did not want to face Lillian and hear another tirade about how she had been in league with Kari to steal the papers. There must be another option. Emily glanced up at the inscrutable Buddha, closed her eyes and waited for inspiration. Nothing. On to Lillian's house then. Sighing, she packed up the papers. Best to surprise her. A phone call would only give her an opportunity to think of an excuse not to open the door.

On the way back to Ala Moana Boulevard, Emily looked for a Kinkos. She would have to make copies of the accounts as a precaution. She saw the familiar sign, parked, dashed in, and copied the accounts. This was where she should be making a hard copy of her article as backup, Emily realized. Oh well. Later this afternoon.

Emily put the originals in the trunk and drove to Lillian's house. Lillian, wearing blue jean shorts and a polo shirt, was out by the front steps. Pruning shears in hand, she was hacking away at the bougainvillea vine above the porch, sending down a shower of hot pink petals.

Emily called out, "Hello there."

"What the hell. You have a nerve coming here again." Lillian held the shears menacingly before her.

Probably she was unaware how fierce they made her appear.

"Honestly, I had no idea what Kari planned."

"Hah. I'd bet anything you have those papers."

Emily sighed. "Well, I admit I have them now. But I didn't know ahead of time that Kari planned to take them. She just dumped them on me."

"And you've come to give them back?"

"Lillian, can we go inside? I have something important to talk to you about."

"I need to do my yard work. The vegetation gets away from you if you don't keep at it. We're living in a jungle." Lillian turned her attention to the vine.

"Lillian, I found accounting papers that might be significant."

"Not likely. All that's stuff's old." She pulled down a perfectly good strand of blossoms and threw it in a black plastic bag.

"You're the only one who would know what they mean."

Lillian looked at her with disfavor. "Let me get this straight. You and Kari conspired to steal these papers from my house and now you want me to help you figure out what they mean?"

Emily groaned. This was going as badly as she had feared. "Lillian, someone wanted these papers badly enough to break into our hotel room and tear it apart looking for them."

"You don't know that. More likely you were the victim of an ordinary garden-variety robbery."

Emily knew this was another possibility but she did not intend to be sidetracked into admitting it. "Just take a quick look. The papers might mean something to you."

"They're twenty years old. No reason to rake up trouble now."

"Your sister must have taken them out of the office for a reason. Maybe she found some irregularities in the bookkeeping. Aren't you curious?"

"Julie wouldn't do anything wrong."

"That's what I'm saying. Julie may have been planning to go to the police." Emily switched from her embezzling and blackmailing theories with ease. "Then she was in the accident." Emily paused to let that sink in.

Lillian looked alarmed now, thinking of the possible implications. "Let's go inside." She climbed onto the porch and held open the screen door.

Emily walked into the cool dark room. The drapes were drawn against the sun. She turned to Lillian. "Did Julie ever say anything to you about irregularities in the bookkeeping at the Trust?"

"No." Lillian looked distracted, perhaps searching through her memories. She watched as if hypnotized as Emily took out the spreadsheets, walked over to the coffee table and laid them down.

"She would have told me if she suspected anything," Lillian said. But she didn't sound convinced. Lillian leaned over, picked up a spreadsheet and started to scan down the rows of figures. She didn't speak. Emily watched in silence. Lillian took up the extra sheet with the short list and compared the two as Emily had done. With difficulty, Emily did not advance her own theories.

"Is it Julie's handwriting?"

Lillian nodded grimly. "Looks like she was conducting her own audit. Lillian took her time, studying each sheet. Finally, she laid them down again on the table. "Maybe someone was skimming money out of these two accounts," she said slowly.

"But the numbers match."

"They do. But we don't know if they match the spreadsheets on file in the office. It's possible that these are duplicate books."

"So what we have here are accurate totals as opposed to fiddled, tampered, trumped up totals?"

"That's a possibility. I couldn't tell you without examining the accounts on file in the Trust office."

Hmmm. How could she manage to examine those files? Emily recalled that most modern offices were secured by locked doors, offices and file drawers, security systems of all sorts. It would be impossible to wander in off the street and look in the Trust's files. She would need an accomplice. She smiled at Lillian.

"That's a very good idea," Emily said. "Perhaps we should check out the accounts together."

"Absolutely not."

"Aren't you curious? Don't you want to know what your sister was trying to find out when she was killed?"

"Died. Died in an accident."

"Julie saved these papers because they were important. Maybe she even died because of them. You can't just ignore it. We have to get into the Trust's office."

"Nobody's going to let you come waltzing into the office and paw through the files."

"I don't want to go to the police and stir up trouble for no reason."

"No, of course, not." Lillian said quickly. Emily wondered if the blackmailing and embezzling scenarios were running through her head. Why else would Julie not tell her sister?

"If I can get into the office and look around, maybe we'll be able to figure out if this information is really important. If Julie planned to go to the police with it, we want to know what she would have told them. You can do that for her."

Lillian didn't answer. She was looking at the supplemental sheet in her sister's handwriting.

"If we got in, what would we look for?" Emily asked.

"Accounts that look just like the ones you have here. They're all filed in the accountant's locked office."

"You don't still have a key to the office, do you?" Emily asked.

"After twenty years? Of course, not. I turned my key in when I left the Trust the end of that last summer. H.R. is careful about that sort of thing."

"What about Julie's key? Did they come to reclaim it after she died?"

"No," Lillian said softly. "Nobody would have thought to do that. We were devastated. The police brought back her things after her death. Her purse, her keys. I suppose they must be here somewhere."

"Could you look?" Emily prompted.

Lillian went over to a secretary in the corner and pulled it open. "We've always kept our keys in these drawers. I might have put it there out of habit. If I did, her key's probably still there." Lillian rummaged in the drawer for a moment and then pulled out a handful of keys. She picked them up one by one and scrutinized them. Finally, she held a set of keys dangling from a spangled heart-shaped fob.

"Is that it?" Emily asked eagerly.

"Yeah."

Emily held out her hand, but Lillian apparently didn't see it. She turned away, put the keys in her pocket.

"You'd better give me those documents. They were Julie's." She was jingling the keys in her pocket, looking out the window, away from Emily.

"Okay," Emily agreed quickly. She scooped the spreadsheets off the coffee table and held them out.

Lillian turned and looked in surprise at the documents Emily held out to her, then accepted them, holding the papers flat on her hand, as if testing their weight. "You made copies," she said finally.

"I did," Emily admitted. "These papers could be important. Maybe your sister was going to show them to the police. We have to figure it out."

Lillian drew in a deep breath and pursed her lip. "It won't be easy to get in," she said. "You need a security card to get into the office itself. This key only unlocks the accountant's office where the files are kept."

"Oh," Emily felt deflated. "Is there a security card in the drawer?"

"No. It wouldn't work anyway after all this time. They erase them electronically from time to time and start over."

"So it's impossible then."

"Maybe not," Lillian said slowly. "If you get into the office before they close up, you could hide in the library, wait until everyone's gone home and then look around. It's risky though."

Emily reached for the key. "Want to come with me?"

Lillian gave a mirthless chuckle. "I'll visit you on Sundays."

CHAPTER 26

Emily spent the afternoon working on the article she had assured George was already written. It was hard to force herself to concentrate, but virtue was rewarded. At four o'clock, when Jack came back from a meeting Emily was putting her laptop back in its case.

"I have been so diligent, you have no idea. I've been cloistered here, far from the sunny beach, pounding my fingers raw all afternoon. But the article is written. I have already pressed "Send" and my article is on its way to George. He will be pleased."

"I noticed your virtuous aura. You seem to glow." He put his arms around her. "I wish we could be alone for dinner tonight but unfortunately I have to meet with a few of my colleagues to hash out what we're going to say tomorrow. Would you like to join us?"

Uh oh. Emily fumbled for an excuse. "Will you talk about diseases?"

"Maybe."

"Will you dwell on horrible symptoms, giving the impression we are all in danger every moment?"

"I must admit it's possible."

"Then unless you really want me to come, I'll pass. I want to stop by Brent's office before it closes," she added innocently.

"What an extraordinary thing to do."

"I've heard so much about the Trust."

"I imagine it will look very much like other office buildings. Be sure to notice the glass walls, potted industrial-sized plants and file cabinets." Jack narrowed his eyes, viewing her with deep suspicion.

Emily gave a guilty start. If she told him about her plan to invade the trust's office and paw through the file cabinet looking for accounts that matched or didn't quite match the ones locked in her car trunk, Jack would surely advise against it. He would be much happier not knowing. It would hardly be fair to make him an accomplice before the fact in this slightly illegal venture.

"I want to see the office where Amanda worked or, at least, where she stopped in at times to approve grants." Emily didn't imagine that Amanda set her shoulder to the wheel on a daily basis. She hoped this excuse sounded plausible to Jack.

"You are becoming obsessed with your former classmate," Jack said.

He bought it! Emily quickly changed the subject. "Did I tell you that Sarah and I are going to Big Island to snorkel and see an active volcano tomorrow?" she asked. "I wish you could come, but I know you have to work. Do you mind that I'm going off without you?"

"Not at all. You'll be taking notes for your article most of the time anyway."

"Right, right."

Emily changed into a dress that she hoped made her look as if she had some reason to go into an office building, kissed Jack good bye, and drove to the center of the city. The Trust offices were steel and glass as Jack had foretold. Once inside the lobby, Emily found marble floors, gray walls, and exposed pipes. She might as well have been in downtown Minneapolis. Hawaii had vanished.

Emily rode the elevator to the third floor and tried to open the double glass doors labeled Blake Hawaiian

Cultural Trust. They were locked. Through the glass, Emily could see the receptionist, a middle aged woman with close-cropped black hair and dangling pearl earrings, working at the computer. She seemed completely absorbed in her task. Emily tried in vain to catch her eye, then finally tapped on the glass. The receptionist smiled an apology and quickly buzzed her in.

"Aloha. Is Brent Gardner in?" Emily asked.

"Is he expecting you?"

"No, I just dropped by. I'm a friend from out of town. Emily Swift."

"Just a moment. I'll see if he's free. Please sign our visitor's log."

Emily wrote her name. Apparently the receptionist was supposed to keep track of everyone who was in the building. Emily would have to remember to sign out before she went into hiding. She sat in a straight-backed chair beside a table strewn with glossy four-color brochures describing the Trust's activities. She admired photographs of smiling children in grass skirts learning to dance, a close-up of a beautiful boy licking poi from his finger. Emily heard rapid footsteps and looked up to see Brent hurrying down the corridor.

"Emily, what a surprise. What brings you here?" His brown eyes were warm with welcome.

"Hi, Brent. I don't want to disturb your work; I'll just stay a minute, but I've heard so much about the Trust. I was passing by so I just thought I'd stop in. I'd like to learn more about the Trust's contributions to the revival of Hawaiian culture. It could be a great sidebar for my article. I'd like to showcase all your good work." She was babbling. Surely Brent would see guilt written all over her face.

"I'm so glad you came. Come on back to my office."

Brent was much more cordial than she had expected. Emily began to relax. Perhaps she would not end the day in jail. She followed him down the corridor to his corner office where Hawaii reappeared in all its splendor. Windows on three sides looked out on the mountains. An enormous hibiscus tree with yellow blossoms bloomed in one corner.

"We have some rather interesting photographs of projects we've done through the years," Brent said, gesturing toward the cream-colored wall decorated with photographs: an ancient Polynesian canoe out at sea, a close-up of an orchid, an elderly woman and a child doing the hula, their faces alight with joy.

"The Polynesian culture had all but died out, but now it's a source of pride to all Hawaiians," Brent said. "Amanda made a real difference. Of course, there were lots of other people involved but she was part of it."

"Is that the Hokulea?" Emily asked pointing to the Polynesian canoe.

"Yes, have you seen it in the harbor?" His face lit up. "The Hokulea was on its way to Easter Island in that picture. Now it has sailed around the world." Brent wandered along the wall, his pride evident as he pointed out his favorites.

The door swung open and Heather strode in, talking briskly, "Brent, I need you to initial these vouchers." She stopped and shifted her minuscule weight, her gray skirt edged with hot pink showing off long tan legs. "Oh, excuse me. Hello, Emily." Her brow furrowed as she turned to Brent. "Sorry. I checked your calendar and saw this time was free. Otherwise I wouldn't have barged in."

"Emily is going to include the Trust in her travel article," Brent explained.

"Oh, well then." Heather relaxed. She turned to Emily. "Good choice. I'll just be a minute." She turned her attention to Brent, setting the vouchers before him.

"Here, I need your approval so we can send a manual check. We're a little late with this one and I've had a phone call." Her girlish voice was apparently reserved for beach days. In the office, the Crumpet's tone was crisp, and her manner all-business despite the touch of pink in her gray outfit. She whipped the signed papers off Brent's desk and strode out with a quick nod to Emily.

"Maybe I should go. I can see you're busy," Emily said.

"Not at all. Let me show you more of these photos." Brent moved along the wall and stopped, grinning. "Look at this. Here's Kari. She was just starting to teach the kids the hula."

Emily bent closer to the photo and noticed Kari's wide grin, clear untroubled eyes. Little children crowded around her. "What a pretty girl," Emily said.

Eager though she was to move to the second stage of her plan and conceal herself in the library, Emily forced herself to take her time. She admired the photos, asked questions, took notes, and smiled a lot. She asked if she could keep one of the brochures she had picked up in the lobby. This was going pretty well.

The phone rang. Brent glanced at it. "Just a moment. I've got to take this call, sorry, won't take long." Brent began grabbing at papers, punching up his computer screen, talking a mile a minute.

Emily stood up and whispered her thanks. "That's okay. I'll show myself out. You're busy. I've taken enough of your time. So kind."

Brent, his phone cradled to his ear, nodded smiled and waved good bye.

Emily backed out of the office and walked down the corridor as if she had every right to be there. At the front desk, the receptionist was talking to two young women. They were giggling, looking at photographs that were on their phones. They seemed entirely absorbed in their conversation.

Emily signed out on the visitor sheet, then faded back to the women's restroom which was right behind the reception desk. The receptionist didn't look up. Emily took her time. It was just about 5 p.m. When Emily came out the reception desk was deserted. She headed quickly for the third door on the left, where Lillian had told her she would find the library. The unmarked door was closed. Emily paused, hoping the office had not been rearranged since Lillian had last been here. She did not wish to burst in on some employee working away in an office that had once been the library.

Emily slowly opened the door and peeked inside. Fortunately, Lillian's information was still correct. There were book shelves along all four walls, a round table and six chairs in the middle of the room. If the cleaning staff looked in, Emily would appear to be an office worker doing research. Even if Brent looked in she could make up some story about the lure of historical books. Now she had only to wait until the office was deserted. She pulled a book off the shelf, sat down, placed the book in front of her on the table, and opened it at random. She was too nervous to even glance at the page. In the knapsack at her feet were Julie's accounts and her phone with its excellent camera.

Emily heard voices outside the door, the sound of footsteps passing by. Then Brent's muffled voice. The Crumpet answered. A chill ran up Emily's arms. What would she say if they came in? Finally the office was quiet. The hum of the air conditioner switched off. It was warm in the windowless room, the air felt stale.

After an hour, Emily felt it was safe to emerge. The office was dark now. Without turning on the lights, she walked down the corridor to the fourth office on the left where Lillian had told her she would find the accountant's office, the one that had once belonged to Julie. Now it must belong to the Crumpet.

Emily stopped outside, listening. She placed her ear against the door. No sounds of activity. She turned the key and slipped inside. Metal file cabinets lined the walls. She switched on the light and went quickly to work. A small label on the front of each file drawer listed a range of years. Emily found the matching years and pulled it open. No time to examine the accounts here. She would have to make copies. She pulled out the file for January, and found the spreadsheet. A copy machine was right outside the door. Emily placed the spreadsheet in position and pressed "Go." A small box on top flashed a red neon message: "Error. Submit Project Code." Rats. Maybe she would have to use the camera. Then Emily noticed a helpful list of project codes posted on the wall for forgetful employees. Obviously they didn't expect criminal copiers to sneak in. She tapped in the top code. Sure enough, the machine sprang into action, its green light flashing, making an all-too audible humming noise. Working rapidly Emily continued to make copies until she had recorded six months of accounts. Her panic was beginning to fade. Clearly, the office was empty.

Perhaps she should compare the first set of accounts with Julie's. If they were identical, why continue? Emily reached into her knapsack and pulled out Julie's accounts for January and laid them beside the version in the file. Staring hard at the numbers, Emily blinked. Her right eye was beginning to feel scratchy and raw. It must be her contact lens. She wished she had brought her glasses or at least some eye drops. Emily decided to ignore the discomfort, close one eye, and press on. She looked down the row of figures and saw the differences in the totals. The "Accurate Totals" in Julie's version were considerably larger than those in the file versions.

Suddenly, she heard the door open. Her heart pounding, Emily jumped to her feet and bent over the desk, trying to shield the pile of papers on the desk.

"Sorry, miss. I didn't know anyone was still here." A young woman with a huge plastic sack of trash in hand stood in the door, staring at her, wide-eyed.

Before Emily could concoct an answer, the woman grabbed the wastebasket and closed the door.

Trembling, Emily slumped down in the chair. I've got to get out of here. I don't have to look at every single year. She scooped up the papers and stuffed them into her knapsack. She already knew the answer. Someone had been skimming money. The books were rigged.

Emily forced herself to walk slowly down the corridor like an employee or maybe a consultant, working late, someone who was very diligent and had no reason to hurry. The young woman was vacuuming the hall. She did not look up as Emily passed her.

Emily let herself out of the office. She had to call Lillian, then tell Jack. He would be critical of her methods, but surely he would admire her enterprise in gathering what could turn out to be evidence. Now she could turn the spreadsheets over to the police.

When Emily returned home, Jack was still at his meeting. She dialed Lillian's number. No answer. Emily didn't want to leave a "detailed" message as the answering machine requested.

"Hi, it's me Emily. I found what we were looking for. Talk to you later." She hung up.

Emily glanced at the phone, saw the red light blinking, and quickly dialed to pick up her messages. She heard Sarah's familiar anxious voice. "Emily, it's all set for tomorrow."

Emily groaned. She'd forgotten their trip to Big Island to see the volcano was scheduled for tomorrow. Her discovery at the Trust office had knocked it out of her mind. Maybe she should cancel. She couldn't spend a whole day with Sarah, not now.

Emily decided to go down to the pool and get something quick to eat while she figured out how to get out of this. No reason to stay in the hotel room. She felt too restless, the adrenalin left over from her breaking-and-entering adventure still coursing through her veins. Maybe a drink was in order. Emily grabbed her purse and headed out the door.

As soon as Emily stepped into the elevator, her cell phone rang. She delved into her purse and answered on the third ring.

It was George. "I got your email."

"So how did you like it?" Emily waited for the torrent of praise that should be forthcoming if he had any taste at all.

There was a pause.

"Good, huh?" she prodded him as she stepped out into the lobby.

"Yeah, sure, it's fine."

"I sense a lack of enthusiasm," Emily said.

"Well, for God's sake, Em, it's good stuff, but your Hawaii articles have a girly tone to them."

"Yeah. So? What's wrong with that? My readers like that tone."

"Sure, I know they do. All I'm saying is that you might give us a boffo finish. A little adventure. Why don't you get off the beaten track. Hike, at least, for God's sake. Stir your stumps, Em."

Grrrr. "Thanks for the excellent suggestion, George. As a matter of fact, I'm planning a trip to see an active volcano tomorrow. I was setting it up when you called."

"There you go! That's more like it."

Emily hung up the phone with a sense that she had just been taunted into doing something extremely foolhardy. She definitely did not want to spend an entire day with Sarah.

At the pool, she ordered a martini and a club sandwich for dinner.

Emily knew she would have to tell Sarah about what she'd found. She couldn't go to the police with evidence that there had been tampering with the Trust's accounts without warning her friend. She would feel too much like a Benedict Arnold, backstabbing sort of person.

The waiter set a shimmering silver martini in front of her. Not a tropical drink to be sure, but she needed something medicinal after such a hard day. No wonder there was so much drinking among the criminal classes. Emily took a swig.

Who cooked the books? Emily wondered. Was it Julie? Brent? Todd? Or someone else who worked in the office? Emily had no idea how seriously such finagling would be regarded now, almost twenty years later. Unless the skimming was still going on.

The waiter set down her sandwich and potato chips. Emily began to munch. Food would help her think better. Maybe she would need dessert too. She took another sip of her drink. It was surprising how well a club sandwich went with a martini.

The fact that Julie had been killed in a car accident was looking more and more suspicious. But maybe it was just a coincidence. Everyone, including Lillian, had assured her Julie's death was an accident; there was nothing Brent could have done to prevent it.

Emily remembered how warmly Brent had greeted her that afternoon. Could he be a killer? He seemed too normal.

Emily finished the last of the chips and still felt hungry. She was definitely going to need ice cream. She signaled the waiter and ordered Macadamia Fudge Nut.

Maybe when Amanda had found Julie's spreadsheet she suspected what had been going on, Emily theorized. She could easily have compared them with their counterparts on file at the Trust. Maybe this was the betrayal, the secret that she had hinted about. Her decision would have been what to do next. Turn in the guilty party even though twenty years had passed? Or stop funding the Trust and fire him? Emily felt a chill run up her arms. She was closing in on Amanda's secret.

No wonder Amanda couldn't confide in Sarah. Even if Brent hadn't cooked the books, the fact that it happened on his watch would look bad. Amanda would have found it easier to tell Emily and ask her advice.

Had Amanda figured out who had been skimming? Maybe she confronted the perpetrator and that's why she was killed.

Emily knew she had to go to the police. But first she would let Sarah know what she was going to do. Sometime tomorrow while they were on Big Island, she would tell her. Maybe Sarah would say, "Oh that was all cleared up years ago." Or maybe not.

CHAPTER 27

When Emily came back to her room, she felt exhausted. She glanced at the clock. It was too early to go to bed. Besides, she wanted to stay up until Jack came in so she could talk to him about her plans for tomorrow. She would just rest for a minute. Emily changed into her nightie, brushed her teeth and settled down in bed with a travel book about Hawaii Volcanoes National Park.

Her eye started to hurt again. Fumbling in the drawer, Emily found her eye drops. She popped the contact out of her painful right eye and squinted at it. Damn. It had torn. She threw the damaged contact away, put soothing drops in her sore eye, closed it and let the artificial tears stream down her cheek, and dribble onto her nightie. She kept her right eye closed and turned once more to her article. She could read with her left eye. No problem. That would be fine. It was easier than walking all the way over to her suitcase and plowing through it, looking for her owl-like glasses. Emily started to read about the volcano. How fascinating, *I really should be making notes,* Emily thought. But the pen is so far away, all the way across the room on the desk. I'll probably remember what I've read. I'll just close my eyes and let the facts sink in. The book slid from her hands.

When she awoke, it was morning. Jack's side of the bed was rumpled but empty. Damn.

Emily scribbled a note to Jack: "Someone was fudging the books for the Trust. Was it Brent? Todd?

Julie herself? Is this serious enough to be a motive for murder? As you know, Sarah and I are going to Big Island to see Volcanoes National Park. Back tomorrow night. Hugs and kisses, E."

Emily was pleased that her brief note managed to suggest intrigue and drama. Emily did not wish to fall into a habit of leaving her loved one dreary notes solely about the laundry or dinner arrangements.

She called Lillian again, but there was no answer. This time Emily didn't leave a message. She headed for the Honolulu airport.

Traveler' Tip: Delightful as Oahu is, you may wish to check out Big Island, the only one of the Hawaiian Islands where the volcanoes are still active. You'll find less big city bustle and night life than in Honolulu, but plenty of sandy beaches and beautiful rainforests.

Sarah was waiting at the airport, ticket in hand. "This will be a wonderful adventure. See how lightly I've packed," she said, holding up her knapsack. "Only my bathing suit, a towel, a night gown, and an outfit for tomorrow. Most unlike me." Sarah was wearing camp shorts, a polo shirt, and hiking boots. It suited her strong, athletic body, making her look like a serious explorer.

Seeing Sarah more relaxed than she'd been since Kari's arrest, Emily decided to delay telling her about her discovery. Let Sarah enjoy the day.

"George was right about the volcano being a good idea for a story," Emily said, when they were aloft. She had brought along a stack of books and brochures for research purposes. "Listen to this. 'A fiery display of lava could reward visitors to this 344-square mile park.' I do hope so. I want to slake George's thirst for adventure."

"There's a lot to see. Maybe we should go to the beach today and spend all day tomorrow in the volcano field," Sarah suggested. "Snorkeling at Cook State Park is wonderful. Crystal clear water."

"A sound plan. That will give me time to read up on the volcano when we're at the motel tonight." Emily closed one eye to read.

"Why are you squinting like a pirate?" Sarah asked.

Emily explained that her contact had torn. "I could wear my glasses, I suppose. But they are not very flattering."

"Neither is the squint."

Emily sighed, took out her one good contact, and reached into her satchel for the glasses that made her look like a large owl. She read for a while, then paused to share her new knowledge with Sarah.

"Listen to this. The crater of Kailauea—that's where we're going—was sacred to Pele, the volcano goddess. When the native people approached, they would do so fearfully, holding out clusters of the sacred ohelo berries. Then they would face Pele's volcano, break a branch in two, throw half of it down over the precipice and say, 'Pele, here are your ohelos: I offer some to you, some I also eat.'

"Everyone was very careful not to dig in the sand or even scratch it. Apparently, Pele was touchy. When she was annoyed for one reason or another, Pele rained down hot molten lava. So you can see how everyone would want to avoid that.

"Then foreigners came barging in, paying no attention to all the rules, munching on the sacred ohelos, overturning stones, digging up sand, disrupting everything. Pele's priestesses were terrified. They begged the chiefs to banish the *haoles* before Pele went into a fury and made the volcano erupt, killing everyone. The chiefs ignored them."

"Kari thought those chiefs made a big mistake," Sarah said.

"Of course, you would know all about Pele."

"Only because of Kari." Sarah sighed. "So many religions to choose from and my daughter would have to find one …so...so out of the mainstream."

Emily knew she had to tell Sarah about the information she was going to reveal to the police, but she stalled, putting off the unpleasant task. "You probably know that Pele shifted shape, sometimes appearing as a lovely young woman, sometimes as a crone, sometimes as molten lava. If someone was kind to her in her human form, they might be saved when she appeared as fiery lava."

Emily continued sharing stories about the volcano until she noticed Sarah's eyes had closed.

After an hour-long flight, Emily and Sarah landed at Hilo International Airport. Backpacks in place, they were striding down the terminal corridor toward the rental cars, when Emily heard footsteps coming up rapidly behind her. She turned to see Brent's flushed face.

"Surprise!" he cried, sliding one arm around her waist and the other around Sarah's.

Emily barely stifled a scream. She didn't want Brent to see how startled she was. Probably she was overreacting. Brent didn't know about the break-in. And he might not have had anything to do with the tampered books. Probably he would be as surprised as she was when he found out.

"What are you doing here?" Sarah asked. "You told me you had a busy day scheduled."

"True. But then I began to think I hadn't done enough to show Emily around Hawaii. She'll be going home in a day or two. Right, Em?" He squeezed her waist.

Emily nodded. She would have no chance to talk to Sarah alone now. She should have told her about the accounts on the plane even if it did cast a shadow on their day.

"Where did you come from?" Emily asked Brent.

"I was on the plane all along, sitting right behind you. I got on first, but I didn't want to spoil the surprise by letting you know so I pretended to be asleep under a newspaper."

What a creepy thing to do. Emily stuck her hands in her pockets to keep Brent from seeing how they trembled. She was glad she hadn't told Sarah how she had broken into his office while Brent was sitting right behind them.

Brent grinned like a schoolboy. "You look a little jumpy today, Emily."

"You startled me."

"Sorry, I meant this to be a nice surprise." He smiled at her, friendliness kindling his soft brown eyes. "Do you have all your bags? If so, let's get going. I called ahead for a rental car."

"Brent, I think I'm going to let you and Sarah go off on your own. This really is a working trip for me," Emily said firmly.

"Oh Emily, please," Sarah cried. For some reason she looked extremely upset, on the verge of tears. The strain of the last few days must be taking its toll.

"Hey, Emily, I didn't mean to barge in and spoil your plans," Brent said. "I thought you'd be glad to see me." He looked as hurt as a small child, left behind while the rest of the family drives off to the zoo.

Sarah looked in anguished appeal at Emily, waiting for her kinder self to reassert itself.

"If you want me to go right back to Honolulu, just say the word. I'll go." Brent's sad eyes were downcast now and he scuffed his hiking shoe against the ground.

How Emily wanted to say that word! But before she could speak, Sarah jumped in, "Brent, of course, you're not going back. Don't even think of such a thing! We're delighted you're here, aren't we, Emily?" Sarah nudged her, trying to awaken a social conscience that seemed to be dozing.

"Sure," Emily said without enthusiasm. Brent was smiling at her now, his good mood restored. Sarah looked relieved and grateful. Everything seemed too normal to be threatening. Emily took a deep breath. "Okay, but I will have to go off by myself and write from time to time."

"No problem," Brent said. "Here let me take your backpacks. They look heavy."

In a few minutes they were driving along Kanoelehua Avenue.

"This road leads directly to Volcano National Park, it's about thirty-five miles away. We'll be there in no time," Brent said.

"We were going to save the volcano for tomorrow," Sarah said, "There's just time enough to check into our motel and go to the beach today."

"Nonsense. Volcanoes are what Emily came to see, right?"

"It's quite a drive. We could go there tomorrow."

"Sarah, you know it takes more than one day to see the volcanoes properly. You can go to the beach anytime."

Emily didn't say a word. She let them duke it out.

They argued for a bit. Brent kept driving toward the volcano. He shifted into his tour guide mode. "Now, Emily don't expect these volcanoes to look like the classic cone-shaped mountain with lava shooting out of the crater. These are shield volcanoes. Lava oozes out of fissures, adding layers slowly. That's how these islands were built." He sought eye contact in the rear view mirror.

"Why are they called 'shield volcanoes'?" Emily asked.

"The lava oozes out into a long low shape that looked to the ancient Hawaiians like a warrior's shield."

"It can be dangerous," Sarah said, shooting Brent a reproachful look. "The volcanoes are extremely unpredictable."

"The danger's half the fun. That's why tourists love it. Isn't that right, Emily?"

"My editor would agree." Emily pictured George grinning with glee at the prospect of her reporting from a treacherous volcanic area.

Emily pulled out her cell phone and called her hotel room, hoping to catch Jack. No answer. She dialed the front desk and picked up her phone messages. There was one from Lillian, "I'm leaving the island this afternoon. Urgent business. There's no significance at all to what you found. If I were you, I'd go home to Alaska or wherever you came from. Don't bother to contact me again. Everything's fine."

What the heck? Emily felt an icy chill.

Someone must have gotten to Lillian. Why else would she bolt? It couldn't be Brent. He was right here beside them. He wouldn't have had time to terrorize Lillian. Besides why would he? He didn't know about the break-in. Emily thought back, trying to remember if she'd left anything behind, any clue at all. No. She was sure not.

Brent was chatting away about volcanoes, a font of information, not at all sinister.

It was already late in the day when they reached the Kilauea Visitor Center. A park ranger, who was tall, blonde, tan and fit, leaned into the van, bracing his thick arms on the side of the window. His eyes were blue, his lashes white.

"You folks are coming in here pretty late. The Park closes at sunset, you know."

"No problem. We'll just take a quick look around, maybe come back tomorrow," Brent said.

"Do you have a flashlight? Can't come in unless you've got one. It's dangerous in the park once it gets dark."

Brent looked at Sarah. "You came prepared, right?"

Emily and Sarah both began rustling though their purses. Emily recalled that the new flashlight she had purchased at the ABC Store was back in her room at the Sheraton.

Finally Sarah cried, "Found it. We're all set."

Traveler's Tip: Always keep your flashlight in your purse in case you unexpectedly need it. Also a chocolate bar.

Sarah leaned over the back seat and whispered to Emily, "It's really just a penlight, but I'm sure we'll be fine."

"Okay, folks, you've got your flashlights. Just one other thing. When you park? Be sure you park your vehicle on the shoulder of the road, pointing out, away from the lava field. That's in case you have to make a quick getaway. You never know when there's going to be a new lava flow and rocks can come shooting up out of the volcano."

Emily's misgivings about this expedition were mounting.

Brent drove down the Chain of Craters Road. He seemed at ease, the man in charge, eager to share his knowledge.

"On the *makai* side you can see where the visitor center was destroyed by lava," Brent said. Emily knew that it was next to the site of Waha'ula Heiau, a thirteenth century sacrificial temple now also covered with lava.

It took an hour to drive the switchback road down the side of the mountain heading for the shore. Black lava flows ran two feet above the level of the asphalt road stretching hundreds of yards ahead of them and finally out to sea. Its black surface rippled as if it were an ocean. The sky was overcast now.

Brent parked the van, facing away from the lava field as instructed. Another ranger walked toward the car. He looked almost identical to his companion. They must turn them out in molds like action figures, Emily thought.

"Sorry folks, you'd better turn back. We might get some rain." He looked up at the sky, which was slightly overcast now.

"Hell, it's only water. We've come this far, right?" Brent turned back to Emily and Sarah, but didn't wait for their reply. "We came all the way from Oahu."

"Okay, it's your decision. But be careful. And remember this part of the Park closes at sunset. You've got to be out by then. Nobody sticks around after that. I'm heading out now myself."

"No problem."

CHAPTER 28

Emily climbed out of the car and followed Brent and Sarah onto the lava field. White flags, fluttering from wooden poles, marked the path.

"We can walk on the upper surface where the lava is cold," Sarah said, leading the way down a path. "Look out, Emily. Watch your feet; there are cracks where you can see molten lava underneath."

"I hope George appreciates my risking life and limb for this story." Emily saw the flashes of red running like threads across the black field. She was glad she had thrown vanity to the winds and worn her round owl-style glasses. She looked up to see gray clouds race across the sky. It was alarmingly overcast all of a sudden.

Emily glanced at her watch. "This is going to be a quick walk, right?" She did not want to be out here in the rain with night falling. Why had she let Brent persuade her to come today instead of waiting until morning? He certainly managed to get a lot of mileage out of hurt feelings alternating with his macho, take-charge style.

Emily resolved to be firmer with Brent in the future, and not be so afraid of hurting his feelings or provoking a confrontation.

Brent walked ahead of them across the lava field. "We can spread out now," he said. "It's safe enough. We don't have to stay on the path if we pay attention."

Emily intended to stick like Velcro to Sarah. She moved gingerly forward. In front of her was a crack in the black surface, revealing the bubbling red lava below. She bent over to peer into it. The fissure was wider than a foot across.

"It's 1,800 to 2,000 degrees down there," Brent called back. His voice, borne on the rising wind, sounded gleeful.

Emily felt a cold drop of rain and looked up to see black clouds swirl overhead. She heard the rumble of thunder.

"No rain was forecast for today. It must be Pele threatening us," Sarah said, walking forward. Emily followed.

"Don't get your foot caught in one of the faults," Brent shouted. "We'll never get you out. The lava has sharp little needles like sharks' teeth."

Emily realized he was enjoying this, reveling in the danger.

"Stay close to me, Sarah," Brent commanded, sounding almost angry. He must be more worried than he wanted them to know.

Brent and Sarah were just ahead of Emily.

Suddenly there was a loud clap of thunder and rain poured down in sheets, drenching them in cold water. A wall of steam rose up as the rain hit the molten lava, hissing, enveloping Emily in whiteness. The air was thick and hot. Her glasses steamed up, blinding her. She took them off and rubbed them clean against her shirt, then put them on again. They fogged up in a moment. Emily stood motionless, stunned. She couldn't see Sarah or Brent.

"Sarah!" she called out. "Sarah, where are you?" Emily couldn't see her own hand. She dared not move for fear of stepping in a crack of hot lava.

Steam hissed, rising all around her, fog was closing in. "Sarah!" Emily called out. She stretched her arms out and swept them in all directions. Nothing. Where could Sarah and Brent have gone? They were here a minute ago. Emily started to panic. Why would they leave her alone in this awful place? Then she realized they had no way of knowing she couldn't see. Sarah and Brent probably had made their way out, expecting her to follow. The sound of steam would have masked their footfalls, and possibly drowned out Emily's calls for help. The impenetrable mist was terrifying. Waiting in silent isolation, she felt time stretch out. How long had she been standing there? Emily knew it could only have been a few minutes, but it seemed like hours.

Finally, Emily realized nobody was coming back for her. Or perhaps they couldn't find her. She knelt down and began to crawl on her hands and knees, reaching carefully for the edge of a crack with one hand, picking her way slowly through the lava field. With her glasses fogged she was blind. If only she would bump into one of the flags marking the path, she would know where she was. Then she could make her way from flag to flag, hoping she wouldn't go in the wrong direction, deeper into the volcano field.

After inching along for about ten feet, her head struck something. She reached out and felt a leg. A hand descended on her head like a blessing.

"Well, well, the lost lamb is found."

It was Brent. Right now, Emily wasn't feeling picky about her rescuer. "Thank God. I was so frightened. This is horrible. Where's Sarah?" She struggled to get up.

"Sarah's on her way out to the car. She'll be fine. Here, let me help you up." Brent took her elbow and helped Emily to her feet.

Why had she ever suspected that this kind, resourceful man could be capable of a crime? Clearly he was a prince of a guy. "Can you see anything?"

Emily asked, rubbing her glasses once more. Again they steamed right up.

"Yes, it's foggy, but fortunately I have excellent vision."

"Thank goodness. I'm hopelessly nearsighted. Let's get out of here."

"Don't rush through this little adventure, Emily. I want to ask you some questions."

"What? Now?"

"I was reviewing our videotapes from the office. There was a prowler last night."

Icy fear plunged into her heart. "Was there?" Emily croaked.

"You know there was. You broke in, unlocked the file cabinet and were nosing around in our accounts. Who gave you the keys? Kari?"

"No, it wasn't Kari."

"Thank God for that. Lillian. She must have kept a key, or found Julie's. I thought she must be the one. I talked to her this morning. She didn't really admit anything but she sounded guilty as hell."

"Okay, Brent. You're right. I was curious about those spreadsheets. I wondered why you wanted Lillian's documents back so badly and what you were trying to hide. I even wondered if you had hired someone to break into our hotel room. But I didn't want to set the police on you if it wasn't really important. So I decided to do a little investigating on my own."

"And what did you find out?"

"Nothing. Otherwise I wouldn't be here with you and Sarah."

"You didn't expect me to be here. It was going to be just you girls. And you would have told Sarah."

"I didn't have anything to tell her."

"I know you made copies of the documents in the file. It's all there on tape."

"I didn't see a surveillance camera."

"Of course not. You weren't meant to. It's very small, state-of-the-art."

"If you want the copies, I'll give them to you. I couldn't figure them out anyway. It must be old news, out-of-date financial information. I'm an English major, for God's sake. I don't know the meaning of that accounting stuff."

"You're not a very convincing liar, Emily."

"Let's talk about this back at the hotel. I want to get out of here. I'm cold and I'm wet and I can't see."

"No, no, I want to show you something." Brent held her arm firmly and walked her forward into whiteness.

"I can't see a damn thing." Emily was trembling from head to foot. She didn't like the idea of being propelled by Brent, but there was no alternative. She couldn't break free and run across the lava field where there were sharp little teeth and boiling lava.

"You don't have to see. Just keep walking."

Emily edged her feet along, not trusting him. What would he do? Wedge her into a crater and leave her?

"You know that I took money from the Trust. And you would never keep quiet about it. You plan to go to the police."

"Not necessarily. White collar crime just gets a slap on the wrist. Why bother after all these years?"

"You know it was more than that. Don't pretend to be dumber than you are."

Stung, Emily blurted out, "What do you mean? That you killed Julie? Is that what you're saying?" As soon as the words were out of her mouth, she regretted them.

She heard Brent breathing close to her ear. He shoved her forward. "No. I didn't kill Julie. It was an accident."

"So Julie found out you were fiddling around with the numbers. Big deal. That's not so bad. Who cares? It was a long time ago. If you didn't kill her, you have nothing to worry about."

Emily knew that Brent must have killed Amanda. She should never have challenged him about Julie. She didn't want to make him angry, didn't want him to know what she suspected. Accounting irregularities weren't so bad. She had to convince him of that. He had killed twice to conceal them.

"I didn't kill Julie. Hell, no."

"So what happened?" Emily asked, trying to keep him talking.

"Julie confronted me," Brent said. "Everyone else in the office had gone home. It was Friday night. I wondered why Julie was hanging around. She usually had a date. She came into my office and stood there, her hand on her hip, glaring at me. The bitch accused me of cooking the books, betraying Amanda."

"Weren't you?"

"Of course not. Julie was so damn righteous, she put the worst interpretation on everything. No wonder Kari turned out the way she did. I told Julie I was diverting her money to a place where it could do us all some good. It wouldn't hurt Amanda or the Trust, not in the long run. I said, 'You can benefit too. It can't be easy raising that little girl all by yourself.'"

"I wasn't trying to bribe her but that was the way Julie took it. I was just offering to help her out. You'd think she'd show a little gratitude, wouldn't you? Instead, she stalked out. Refused to even listen to me. I had to make her understand. I wasn't doing anything wrong, just borrowing money for a little while. I was going to pay it back. So I followed her out to the parking lot. It was pouring rain.

"Julie ignored me. She got in her car, a little convertible. It wouldn't start so she gunned the engine a few times and managed to flood it.

"'Come on, Julie, let me give you a ride,' I said. I had to talk her out of turning me in. It would be misinterpreted, blown out of proportion. I could see the headlines in the paper. 'Embezzler Faces 20 Years in Prison.'

"I would lose everything. My father would be dancing with glee. Sympathetic on the surface, of course, but pleased as punch that I had fulfilled his prophecy of failure. The old guy hated to be wrong and up till then I'd managed to prove that he *was* wrong about me.

"At first Julie refused my offer of a ride home. But what else could she do? The office was locked. Nobody else was there. It was raining hard. Finally she accepted.

"We continued arguing in the car. I was looking at Julie, not at the road. It was slippery, rain pouring down.

"Julie taunted me. 'You deserve to be in jail. You're just a common thief.'

"I was so angry I wanted to punch her. Just then the car started to skid and I turned the wheel hard, smashing her side of the car into a tree. She died instantly. I didn't kill her. It was an accident. But I blamed myself because I turned the wheel in a flash of anger. I've always been too hard on myself. Later when a car stopped and the driver asked what happened, I said I swerved to avoid another car. The police never were able to find that other car."

Guilty, guilty, guilty, Emily thought with horror. They had been standing still a long time. Emily prayed for the mist to lift, but rain continued to fall and now it was getting dark. The whiteness was turning to gray. If only she could keep him talking, anything could happen, the fog could lift, the rain stop, the ranger return. Where the hell was Sarah?

"Of course, it was an accident," Emily reassured him. "Brent, you've made tons of money. You've been incredibly successful. Why did you take money from the Trust?"

"Sure, now I have plenty. But at first I tried too hard. I was doing okay with the Trust's investments, being very careful, but I took too many risks with my own. I wanted to make money fast. I wasn't doing too well and my Dad was just waiting for me to slip up. When my stocks tanked, I had no choice. I had to siphon some money from the Trust to pay off my losses. It was surprisingly easy. I meant it to be a one-shot deal, but then when Sarah wanted to build that swimming pool, I thought, hell, why not? I can pay it back later."

"So you just skimmed a little off the top of two of the groups' funds? Did they know what you were doing?"

"I told them there was a fee for helping them secure the grants. They didn't have a problem with that. I didn't do it often, only when I really needed the money. It didn't seem like a big deal."

"Until Julie found out."

"Unfortunately, yes. But I've told you, there was the accident. I thought that was the end of it."

"What about Amanda?" Emily asked. "She figured it out, didn't she?"

"She went over to Lillian's house and looked at those old papers because she thought Kari would be interested. And she found the spreadsheets."

"So you killed her." Emily just stopped herself from saying "too." Brent seemed determined to deny even to himself that he was responsible for Julie's death.

"Amanda said she hadn't quite decided what she was going to do. She said she probably wouldn't tell anyone, just phase out the Trust as much as possible. It would be very quiet and orderly. I didn't believe her.

Eventually she would have told Sarah. They were best friends. That last night at the Charity Ball, Amanda snapped. She was yelling at Todd. Our quiet, perfect little Amanda raising her voice. It was so unlike her. That frightened me. What else would she do? Go to the police? Say to hell with the whole lot of us? And then there was the matter of the will. Amanda could have fixed it so that no more money came into the Trust. I'd already made commitments."

"Sounds like you were pretty much backed into a corner," Emily said, trying to make her voice sound sympathetic, keep his torrent of reminiscences coming. When Brent ran out of stories, Emily would run out of luck.

"I didn't have much choice. I couldn't let Amanda live and still keep my family and my livelihood. I would have been arrested. Sarah would have felt the same contempt for me that Amanda did. Amanda didn't yell at me the way she yelled at Todd. She was very quiet, tight lipped. She looked at me with utter contempt, as if I was something slimy she'd found under a rock. In that soft little voice of hers, she called me a thief and a traitor. Can you believe it? After all I'd done for that woman."

"Everyone says you do a great job managing the Trust, Brent." He was still holding Emily motionless in the unending whiteness. She looked up at the dark sky, praying that the weather would clear and give her a chance to bolt.

"I couldn't face failure," Brent said. "I've worked too hard. So I followed Amanda out to the beach."

Emily couldn't stifle her cry of dismay. She felt Brent's arms tighten around her, holding her from behind.

"Amanda was a very unhappy woman, Emily. It was really a mercy killing. Amanda felt betrayed by Todd, betrayed by me. She wanted to kill herself, but her religious scruples held her back. I set her free. I did what she wouldn't dare."

"How are you going to justify killing me? How are you going to explain that to Sarah?"

"Don't worry about that, Emily; we're going together. I won't have to explain a thing. No one will know. Right now, we're standing at the edge of a large crater. Most of the cracks in this lava field are not much bigger than my hand, but this one is wide enough for us both." She felt him trembling. This time Brent wasn't so eager to kill, not when he was coming along on the fatal expedition. No wonder he was so chatty. He didn't want to end the conversation any more than she did.

Emily had to keep him talking and wait for a chance to escape. He didn't really want to kill himself. Throwing her in, however, would be another matter. She definitely didn't want to make him mad.

"How did you manage it, Brent? How did you slip away from the party and kill Amanda without getting wet and sandy? The police found out she was killed on the beach."

He started to answer then paused as the mist faded away to reveal the crater at their feet. Emily looked down at the hot molten lava bubbling in the pit. Then she screamed, an earth-shattering, heartfelt scream of terror that came from her toes. Startled, Brent took a step back from the chasm, still holding her tight. Emily screamed again.

Then she heard Sarah's voice rising on the wild wind.

CHAPTER 29

"Sarah, here we are!" Emily yelled.

As Brent turned, looking for Sarah, his grip loosened. Emily brought her foot up sharply behind her in a hamstring curl, kicking him in the groin as hard as she could.

Crying out in pain, Brent stumbled backward.

Emily ran blindly across the lava field, away from the crater, praying she wouldn't catch her foot in a crack. She heard Brent behind her, panting, coming closer. Thank goodness she ran around Lake Harriet every day to keep in shape. He wouldn't catch her easily. Emily reached into her pocket for her keys and held one pointed forward between her knuckles, the only weapon she had.

"Emily! Brent!" she heard Sarah's voice, louder now, calling their names over and over.

Emily headed toward the sound of her voice. She was gasping for breath, her steps were slowing. She forced herself forward. He was closing the distance. She could hear his breathing. Suddenly Brent caught her by the collar, pulling her backward, and whipped her around. Emily flailed at his face, jabbing hard with the key. She couldn't see well enough to aim.

"Ow, dammit, you bitch." He let her go." My eye. Hell. My eye." He was doubled over, holding his face with both hands. Emily ran.

"What's going on?" Sarah cried. "Where are you?"

Emily sped toward the sound of her voice, stumbling now, wheezing, completely out of breath.

"Sarah," she gasped and bashed right into her.

Sarah staggered at the impact, then recovered and hugged her. "Emily, thank God, I found you." Emily could see the pale frightened look on Sarah's face. She turned to see Brent standing ghostlike in the mist, close enough to touch her.

Emily gasped, too weak to scream again.

"Brent, what's wrong? What are you doing?" Sarah turned her penlight toward him. Brent looked ghastly, his face drained of color, blood streaming from his eye, steam swirling around him. He stood there for a moment, then turned away. The mist closed over him.

"Brent!" Sarah screeched and started after him. Emily grabbed her arm, held her firmly.

"You won't find him unless he calls out. It's too dangerous to try. Wait here, Sarah."

Calling Brent's name over and over, Sarah tried again to break free, but Emily held on. She was surprised that desperation gave her enough strength to hold back this athletic woman.

At last, Sarah gave up, tears streaming down her cheeks. "What's going on? What happened?"

"We have to go for help. That's his only chance. Brent is desperate now. He's not going to let anyone catch him, not even you."

"Oh my God. Why? Why?" Sarah wailed. "What has he done?"

"Come on. Let's get out of here. I can't see a damn thing and it's getting dark. You'll have to lead us to the car."

"I can't leave him, Emily. No matter what he's done. He'll die out here."

Emily heard the terror in her voice.

"We have to find the park ranger and get help out here fast. It's Brent's only hope. The police will find him. They'll bring in high-beam lights and shine them around until they do. We have to hurry before Brent gets his foot caught in a lava crack." Emily did not add, "or finds a crack large enough to swallow a man."

Sarah led the way to the car. Emily clung to her. The darkness deepened. The rain was abating, but no stars or moon came out to light their way.

"There's the van," Sarah said.

A horrible thought occurred to Emily. "Does Brent have the keys?"

"No," Sarah said. "He gave them to me. It seemed odd. He kissed me and said, 'Here. You'll need these, sweetheart.' He never calls me sweetheart." She sobbed. "I laughed and said, 'Are you kidding? I'm not driving in these mountains.'" Sarah started to cry.

Emily was soaking wet, shivering. "Come on. We have to find the ranger." She climbed into the van and leaned back against the seat.

The rain had stopped now, and the mist was thinning, but there were no lights. It was darker than any place Emily had ever seen. They drove down the mountain road in pitch dark. Sarah was crying as she drove. She didn't ask what had happened. Emily wondered how much she knew. It had taken her a hell of a long time to come to her rescue.

As their van approached the entrance to the park, Emily could see red lights flashing. Three police cars were parked in front of the ranger station.

"Thank God," Sarah said. "The police will find him." She stopped the car and leaned her head on the steering wheel.

"Of course, they will," Emily said without conviction, as she stepped out of the van.

Jack rushed forward and pulled her into his arms. "Thank God, you're all right," he said hugging her fiercely.

Emily nestled against his warm, dry body. "What are you doing here?" she cried out in joy and amazement.

"When I read your note I began to worry. I called Brent's office and some woman very kindly told me that he was taking the day off to go sightseeing on Big Island. Such a helpful young person. She also shared the exciting office news that there had been a break-in the night before, all captured on videotape. Naturally, I thought of you, my felonious darling."

"You were quite clever." Emily didn't mention that he was not fast enough off the mark to have saved her. By this time, she and Brent could have been boiling in hot lava. Now the reality hit her and she began to shiver.

"You have to get out of those wet clothes. You'll catch your death."

"Please don't say that word."

Emily turned to see Sarah sitting in a sodden heap on a wooden bench outside the tourist building. She was weeping. An officer was beside her, asking questions, taking notes.

Another officer appeared at Emily's shoulder. "Can we ask you a few questions, ma'am?"

"Yes, of course." Emily did not wait for his questions. "There's a man out in the lava field. Brent Gardner. He's desperate. He's killed two people and he may try to kill himself."

"His wife told us he was missing. A couple of officers are heading out to search for him. So what happened out there?"

Emily told him all that she knew. She heard the sound of a chopper droning overhead and looked up.

"And you'll stick around for a while, right? No plans to leave the island?"

Emily groaned. Her plans were shaky at the moment. Pneumonia probably figured in her future. She was shivering from the cold, her teeth chattering.

"I suppose the police would have radioed back if they'd found him," Sarah said. Her voice was dull, her eyes hopeless. She wrapped herself in the towel, pulling it up like a cowl around her face.

"He'll be all right." The lie was an automatic reflex. Emily put her hand on Sarah's arm. "It's an awfully large area to search." It wouldn't make it any easier that he didn't want to be found, Emily thought but didn't say.

Sarah looked at her accusingly.

Emily wondered how much Sarah suspected. She hadn't asked any questions and since they were interrogated separately she hadn't heard what Emily had told the police.

"Do you want to go to the motel?" Jack asked them both.

"Of course not," Sarah snapped.

"Emily, we could go in my car. You're shivering," Jack said.

Emily was tempted, but she couldn't leave Sarah here alone to wait.

"I'll stay a bit. You go if you want."

"I wouldn't leave you."

Emily gave Jack a meaningful look, indicating he should go off for a walk or chat with the police while she sat with Sarah. Only a few subtle grimaces accomplished her purpose. Jack was getting much better at picking up unspoken cues.

Sarah did not look at her or speak. Emily had never seen anyone actually wringing her hands, but Sarah's fingers were twisting anxiously, the one huge diamond set with emeralds gleaming in the dim light cast by the police car's headlights.

After a time, Sarah broke the silence. "What happened out there? What did Brent say to you?"

Emily could see how hard it was for her to ask the question. She certainly didn't want to hear the answer.

"Brent wanted to protect you. You and Kari." Would that make the truth easier to take? Emily had no idea.

Sarah was grimly waiting for her to elaborate.

"I found out that Brent had skimmed money from the Trust," Emily said. "I wasn't the first person to stumble on that knowledge. Julie had found out. So had Amanda."

Sarah's face contorted in pain as she realized what Emily meant. "He couldn't have killed Amanda. Brent loved her like a sister. She gave him his chance at success."

"He couldn't bear *not* to be a success. He didn't want to let you down, Sarah."

"I don't believe it."

"He admitted killing Amanda. I was terrified out there. I'm still shaking from fear. If you hadn't come back, I'd be dead. Brent was holding me at the edge of a wide lava crack. He said he was going to push me in …"

"But he didn't do it," Sarah said quickly.

"That's because when I heard your voice, I broke away from him and started to run. Thank God I found you."

"When I heard you scream, I wanted to close out the sound, pretend to myself it was the wind. If I hadn't answered, Brent would still be alive." Sarah started to cry again.

"No, he wouldn't," Emily said firmly. "Brent said he was going to push me into the crater with him when he jumped."

"He would never have gone through with it. He would never kill himself."

"Maybe not. But he certainly would have killed me. You couldn't have let him do that. You're not that kind of person, Sarah. You wouldn't be an accessory to a murder."

Sarah flinched at the word. "When the steam rose up, I couldn't see you, I didn't know where you'd gone. Brent found me and guided me quickly to the car. He seemed so agitated, trembling a little. I wondered why because we weren't in any real danger. He told me to wait, not to move a muscle. I waited for a long time. Then I started to think about the way he had said goodbye and my flesh began to crawl. I didn't really suspect him, how could I? But I knew he was up to something and I didn't really want to know what it was. Horrible thoughts ran through my mind. I'd heard him on the phone this morning talking to Lillian. It didn't really make sense. It almost sounded as if he were threatening her. I was afraid to ask him about it. It sounded like a business problem of some sort, nothing to worry about, I told myself, but sitting in the car, I wondered what was going on. When I heard you scream, the terror in your voice….and then when I saw Brent's face." She buried her face in her hands.

Emily heard the police radio crackle and turned to see the officer climb in the squad car and shut the door.

She put her hand on Sarah's shoulder as they waited for the news.

CHAPTER 30

Brent's charred body was found face down, wedged in the lava crack. The next morning's headlines screamed of the danger to tourists and called for strict security measures. After the full story emerged, new headlines trumpeted Brent's guilt.

"Too bad Brent's not around to see his worst fear realized, public scandal and shame," Emily said, dropping the newspaper down on the table. She took a reviving swig of Kona coffee.

"Perhaps his soul is suffering," Jack said. "He certainly left a trail of misery, the greedy bastard."

"Poor Sarah. She loved Brent. She couldn't believe he was capable of murder. She'll always think of me as the woman who drove her husband to a ghastly death." Emily foresaw some tense moments at the next reunion.

"Perhaps in time she'll realize that you're also the woman who freed an innocent man from prison and lifted the shadow of suspicion from her daughter."

"True. I should feel better about all this than I do." Emily wished she liked Kari a bit more so she could better enjoy clearing her from suspicion.

Later that morning, Emily was sitting by the pool, composing a lengthy article about the murder when Kari came up to her.

"Mom wanted me to give you this, she said," thrusting a large envelope at her.

Emily glanced at it with misgivings, hoping Sarah had not poured out several pages of recriminations and stuffed them inside.

Kari sat down on a lounge chair, her shoulders slumped, one strap of her tank top slipping down over her arm.

"Congratulations," she said flatly, her eyes on the toe of her sandal. "Frankly, I'm surprised. I didn't think you'd figure out who killed Amanda."

"I wish the killer had been a complete stranger," Emily said, ignoring the vote of no-confidence.

Kari sighed. "I didn't want to believe it was Dad. How could he do it? He loved Amanda. We all did."

Emily had no answer.

"When my Mom told me what Dad had done, suddenly an image flashed into my mind. I remembered seeing my father's bare feet walking by us the night Amanda died. Matt and I were lying under the tree on the beach and I just caught a flash out of the corner of my eye. The image was stored in my mind all along. But I never remembered. It didn't fit with anything else I believed." Kari stifled a sob, bit her lower lip. "I wonder if my Dad would have let me and Matt go to jail."

"He probably would have come forward at last," Emily said, not believing it for a moment.

"For me maybe. But more likely he would have hired some slick lawyers to get me off, make some sort of plea bargain. It would have been a different story for Matt."

"Brent turned back into the volcano field to spare you and your mother," Emily said, trying to leave Kari with a crumb of comfort. "He didn't want to put you through a trial, months of publicity."

"It was a terrible death," Kari said, tears filling her dark eyes."

"We can only hope it happened quickly."

"Pele has no mercy," Kari said. "The poor goddess was harried from place to place by her jealous sister, the goddess of the sea, until she found refuge in the volcano. Pele's wrath is terrible when she's disturbed."

Emily shuddered. "I was lucky to be spared. It was a close call, running blind through the lava field."

"Pele often spares those who do her a kindness when they meet her in her human form."

Emily smiled. She hadn't had the pleasure of meeting Pele much less doing her a kindness.

"Many *kanakai maoli* are descendants of Pele," Kari said as if reading her thoughts. "You saved me and Matt. It was kind of you." She gulped out unfamiliar words, "Thank you." Kari looked up with tears in her eyes and held out her hand. Emily took it and squeezed it quickly.

As soon as Emily left, Emily opened the envelope and found the Blake family letters along with a note in blue ink on formal note paper.

"Dear Emily,

I'm not feeling quite up to talking with you in person right now, but please don't think I hold it against you that everything turned out so badly. I know you did just what I asked you to do—find out the truth. It's not your fault the truth turned out to be such a bitch.

I know Amanda would be pleased. She was always a stickler for the rules.

Her family letters were in Brent's briefcase. I suppose the revelation that my husband had your room ransacked does not come as a complete surprise. But, believe me, Brent was a good man who loved his family and tried hard to do what was right. Somehow it all got out of hand.

Fondly, Sarah.

Emily sighed. She supposed it must be a comfort to Sarah to believe Brent was a good man. But really!

Later that day, Todd asked Emily to meet him for a drink down by the pool of the Sheraton. She found him standing by a table, jingling the coins in the pocket of his white slacks, rocking back on his heels.

He turned and grinned at her. "Nice place you have here," he said, nodding at the pool where sunlight rippled on the water.

"I'll miss it," Emily said, sitting down at the table.

Todd sat beside her, reached out to cover her hand with his and gazed into her eyes. "Thank you, Emily. You spared me a lifetime of suspicion. I've been afraid to go to the club and see the way people cut their eyes away from me, whisper to one another. Nobody would ever have been quite sure about me."

"Oh well," Emily said, looking away, embarrassed by his intensity. "It must have been hard for you to lose such a good friend."

Todd shrugged and grinned. "Not as hard as all that. Not once I found out what a bastard Brent really was."

Todd sounded so excessively pleased at being washed clean of all sin that Emily was tempted to tell him that if he had never had an affair with the Crumpet then Amanda would never have yelled at him in public, and Brent might not have panicked and killed her. It probably wasn't true anyway, she reflected. Brent would never have trusted Amanda to keep his secret. Not for long anyway.

"I feel sorry for Sarah," Emily said. "She's the one who is suffering." Emily reached into her beach bag and pulled out an envelope. "Sarah sent me the Blake family letters. She found them in Brent's briefcase."

"Damn. So Brent really did steal them."

"He or his henchman must have grabbed all the papers he could see, expecting to find the spreadsheets and, of course, was sadly disappointed." Emily held out the envelope to Todd.

"Oh hell, Emily. You keep them. I don't have any use for a bunch of old letters."

Emily's fingers closed on the envelope for a moment, then she had an inspiration and shoved it back at him. "You know what would have really pleased Amanda?"

"No." Todd looked baffled.

"If you donated her family letters to the Bishop Museum. It's all part of Hawaii's history."

"If you think Amanda would have wanted it that way, yeah, okay."

"So you'll do it?"

"Sure, sure." He turned the envelope over in his hands and frowned for a moment, then his eyes brightened. "I'll send you copies of the letters and copy you on the gracious note to the Museum that will accompany them." He grinned. "Otherwise, you'll never believe I followed through."

Emily heard a sharp clicking of heels and looked up to see the Crumpet, dressed in a short black dress. Her hand descended on Todd's shoulder, one long red nail tapping impatiently.

"We're late."

Todd hunched his shoulders. "Late for what?" he asked warily.

"The Heart Disease Fundraiser."

He groaned.

The Crumpet turned to Emily. "I suppose you're on your way back to Alaska."

"Minnesota," Emily corrected her.

"Whatever." The Crumpet grinned.

Emily's good manners triumphed over her dislike of Amanda's would-be successor. "Thank you for telling Jack that Brent knew who had broken into the office and was headed to Big Island. Otherwise it all could have turned out very differently." Emily shuddered away from mentioning the specifics of a fiery grave.

Heather shrugged. "I suspected something weird was going on." She tightened her grip on Todd's shoulder. "I didn't want Todd blamed for it, did I, Love?" She leaned over to give him a kiss.

"I don't know if I imagined it or not," Emily said to Jack as they dressed to go to dinner that evening, "but Todd seemed to flinch when the Crumpet touched him."

"He apparently has a very short attention span."

"The Crumpet is a determined woman."

"I will await the outcome of their courtship with interest. I suppose we can count on Sarah to keep you informed."

"Possibly," Emily said, remembering Sarah's letter.

The closer she came to leaving Hawaii, the more Emily found herself thinking about Amanda. "No wonder Amanda was torn, trying to decide what to do," Emily said as she pulled her dress over her head. "She was too kind hearted to go to the police right away with evidence about Brent's nefarious activities at the Trust but, at the same time, she couldn't tolerate injustice or allow infractions to go unpunished."

"Sadly, her hesitation led to her death."

"She would have been horrified to know that, after her murder, an innocent man was in jail, Kari charged as an accomplice, and Todd under a persistent shadow of suspicion."

"Thanks to you, justice was done."

Emily smiled. Amanda would have approved of her detective work. Emily could imagine Amanda, former chair of the Judiciary Committee, giving her a thumbs-up.

After dinner, Emily sighed as she started to pack. She had expected a vacation in Hawaii with the man she loved to be very romantic. She hadn't counted on a murder to ruin the mood. Now it was time to go home.

Jack came up behind her and put his arms around her. "It's our last night. Let's go down to the beach and see the sunset."

Emily smiled. He was thinking the same thing. At least, they'd have a few minutes of peace in paradise. She held Jack's hand as they walked barefoot along the beach, watching the sky turn shades of red and gold streaked with lavender.

When the sunset was at its most brilliant, Jack stopped and turned to her. "I'd get down on one knee if it wouldn't make my slacks too sandy to pack." He grinned.

Emily's eyes widened in surprise.

Jack took a small velvet box from his pocket. "All during our trip, I've been trying to think of a romantic way to give this to you. I thought of embedding it in an orchid or impaling it on a pineapple spear in your Mai Tai. Finally, I decided to be direct. I love you, Emily, and want you to marry me."

Emily flung her arms around his neck. "Yes, yes, yes."

The End

ABOUT THE AUTHOR

 Like her fictional heroine, Lorrie loves to travel and to learn about the history, art and culture of other cities and countries. She grew up in Wilmette, a suburb of Chicago. She graduated with a BA in English from Wells College in Aurora, New York, where she began to write short stories in a class taught by Mildred Walker, author of *Winter Wheat*. After a year of backpacking through Europe with a friend, she received her MA at the University of Minnesota, specializing in directing for television, and worked at KTCA, the public television station. She has also worked at Dayton's in broadcast advertising and at Walker Art Center in public relations. For many years, she was director of communications for Minnesota Medical Association. It was a fascinating job that allowed her to use her writing skills to support smoking prevention, use of seatbelts and other good causes.

Lorrie lives in Minneapolis with her husband, close to her daughter and son, their spouses, and adorable grandson. In addition to traveling she enjoys Salsa, Bachata, Zumba, aqua aerobics, gardening, and knitting. She also loves to cheer on her grandson in his soccer, hockey, tennis and sailing events.

Homicide in Hawaii: An Emily Swift Travel Mystery is the second novel in the series. Read Emily's first sleuthing adventure in *Murder on Madeline Island*. Learn more at www.lorrieholmgren.com and at: www.facebook.com/lorrieholmgrenauthor.

www.ingramcontent.com/pod-product-compliance
Lightning Source LLC
Chambersburg PA
CBHW020234260626
47156CB00002B/673